Branded
By Beth Williamson

A marriage of convenience shows a determined rancher and a stubborn woman what it means to be branded.

When a clause in his grandfather's will forces Rafe Sinclair to marry or else lose his ranch, he sets his sights on what he thinks is a safe choice—his neighbor Emma Radcliff.

Emma has never wanted anything other than to work her family's horse ranch. But when her father forces her to marry Rafe, she does everything in her power to make the handsome rancher regret his choice of brides.

They say oil and water don't mix, but in Emma's and Rafe's case, it does—and the result is fire. When Emma refuses to consummate the marriage, Rafe sets out to prove that marriage him is the best thing that's ever happened to her.

Warning, this title contains the following: explicit sex and graphic language.

High Noon
By Rebecca Goings

When a full-blooded Comanche risks everything for the honor of the woman he loves, it's a safe bet there'll be a showdown at high noon.

Banning, TX 1872

Alison Williams has loved Talon Holt most of her life, but he broke her heart when he suddenly left town five years ago. Then Alison's father loses a round of poker to the notorious blackguard Garrett Sumrall, and she's shocked to learn he's lost much more than his life savings. He'd bet Alison's hand in marriage!

A full-blooded Comanche raised by a white man, Talon has never fit in to either world. Despite his feelings for his childhood friend, he's sure he did her a favor by leaving so she would be free to marry someone of her own race. But when he hears the news of her father's gambling debt, he returns to rescue Alison from her cruel fate.

A few stolen kisses, and their passion rekindles with fiery intensity. However, Sumrall is not about to give up his winnings without a fight—because he has a much darker reason for making sure Alison makes good on her father's bet.

It's a showdown at high noon, and winner takes all!

Warning: Wild West Justice and Wild West Sex.

The Seduction of Widow McEwan
By Melissa Schroeder

A younger man bent on seduction. An older woman determined to resist. A love that cannot be denied.

Jameson McEwan is widowed, but happy with her lot in life. After suffering through an arranged marriage to an older man, she's had little romance and very little experience with men—other than ordering them around on her ranch.

Seth Conner has harbored a bit of an obsession for Jamie since the tender age of sixteen. Now that she's widowed, he has sensed her reluctance to wed again and has kept his distance. When she says she's marrying another man—strictly as a business arrangement—Seth decides he's waited long enough.

Jamie never expected to find herself in bed shivering with desire, especially not with Seth. One taste of a night filled with passion, and she finds he's as addictive as liquor. But their age difference and her responsibilities hold her back from considering a future with him. Seth refuses to take no for an answer.

As the dance of seduction heats up, trouble brews. Someone is poisoning Jamie's cattle, setting fires on her ranch. Someone is hell-bent on making sure Jamie and Seth never find happiness, someone who will stop at nothing—including murder.

Explicit sex, spanking, seduction by a younger man, a little bit of bondage for fun, and a whole lot of teasing guaranteed to make ya hot under the collar and enough passion to give your spurs a twirl.

Leather & Lace

A Samhain Publishing, Ltd. publication.

Samhain Publishing, Ltd.
577 Mulberry Street, Suite 1520
Macon, GA 31201
www.samhainpublishing.com

Leather and Lace
Print ISBN: 978-1-59998-961-7
Branded Copyright © 2008 by Beth Williamson
High Noon Copyright © 2008 by Rebecca Goings
The Seduction of Widow McEwan Copyright © 2008 by Melissa Schroeder

Editing by Sasha Knight
Cover by Scott Carpenter

This book is a work of fiction. The names, characters, places, and incidents are products of the writer's imagination or have been used fictitiously and are not to be construed as real. Any resemblance to persons, living or dead, actual events, locale or organizations is entirely coincidental.

All Rights Are Reserved. No part of this book may be used or reproduced in any manner whatsoever without written permission, except in the case of brief quotations embodied in critical articles and reviews.
Branded, ISBN 1-59998-679-5
First Samhain Publishing, Ltd. electronic publication: November 2007
High Noon, ISBN 1-59998-685-X
First Samhain Publishing, Ltd. electronic publication: November 2007
The Seduction of Widow McEwan, ISBN 1-59998-691-4
First Samhain Publishing, Ltd. electronic publication: November 2007
First Samhain Publishing, Ltd. print publication: September 2008

Contents

Branded
Beth Williamson
~9~

High Noon
Rebecca Goings
~87~

The Seduction of Widow McEwan
Melissa Schroeder
~163~

Branded

Beth Williamson

Dedication

To my anthology partners, Rebecca Goings and Melissa Schroeder, may the wind be at your back, the grass under your feet and the luck always be yours. Thanks for being my partners!

Chapter One

Eastern Texas, May 1870

Georgette Petrie came sashaying into the kitchen with a big grin on her round face. "Did you hear the news? Rafe Sinclair's gotta get hitched."

Emma Radcliff frowned at the biscuit in her hand. "So what? I don't give a dog's fart what Rafe does."

Emma hadn't fantasized about her neighbor in years. The tall, dark and stupid cowboy had proven himself to be nothing but a huge pain in the ass with a big space between his ears. She'd steered clear of him for more reasons than one. Her childish dreams about him had made her the butt of jokes on her father's ranch after she'd announced to everyone, at the ripe old age of five, that she was going to marry Rafe Sinclair.

Nobody, it seemed, ever let her forget it, especially her stepsister Georgette. The prissy girl had come for her annual summer visit that seemed to stretch out longer and longer each year. What started as two weeks in July now spanned nearly four months from May through August. The rest of the year she lived with her grandfather in Houston. The spoiled little prissy girl annoyed Emma with her constant chatter and her damn dimples.

Emma wolfed down the biscuit as Georgette rambled on about how she could catch the most eligible man in the county. The blonde seemed to have an endless supply of nonsense stored inside her.

"You have to introduce me again." Georgette smiled prettily.

Emma harrumphed. "I don't have to do anything but get my ass out on my horse and go to work."

Georgette's mouth opened in a small "O". "You cussed."

Without bothering to answer her naïve seventeen-year-old stepsister, Emma pushed her chair back and shoved the rest of the biscuit in her mouth. As she tied the chaps to her thighs, Georgette tsked at her.

"Anyone would think you are a man, Emma Radcliff. Wearing britches and working horses ain't no way to get a husband." Georgette sounded like an expert, however Emma knew she'd never even had one proposal of marriage, not that the girl's granddaddy hadn't tried his damnedest to buy her one.

"I'm never getting married, Georgette, so it doesn't matter. I love horses and I'll work with them until I'm old and gray." After snatching another biscuit from the plate on the table, Emma headed for the door. She plopped her hat on her head and stepped out into the May sunshine.

The sounds of the ranch soothed her annoyance with her stepsister. God knows why Pa married Georgette's mother all those years ago because Emma certainly never saw anything likeable about the woman. Then she up and died a year after the wedding leaving the precocious, annoying child in her father's care. Fortunately, Emma didn't have to put up with Georgette all year long anymore since her granddaddy stepped in to see to her care during the winter. Sometimes Emma had to count her blessings.

Emma spent most days from dawn to dusk working with the quarter horses her father had carefully bred over the last twenty years. Ranchers from surrounding counties bought her father's stock consistently and for good reason. The Triple R horses were the best.

"Mornin', Em," Rowdy, the ranch's oldest resident, called from his perch on the front porch.

Emma nodded. "Mornin', Rowdy. Have you seen Pa?" She needed to talk to her father about one of the foals that had her concerned.

"Nope, haven't seen him." Rowdy took a puff from his cigar, the smoke snaking its way through his bushy silver beard. He'd taken a nasty fall off a horse two years ago and hadn't had much luck getting back to normal ranching work like riding the fence line and breaking the horses to ride. Her father kept

Rowdy on to help with the breeding and care of the dams and foals, a much less strenuous job.

"I'm worried about Mariposa's foal. He's not nursing enough." She bracketed her hips with her hands. "We need to keep an eye on him."

"Yep, I noticed that too. Not putting on weight like he should either. He's almost three weeks old, should be bigger." Rowdy rose from the rocking chair with a creak of his bones. "Let's go take a look at the little feller."

Emma spent the morning taking care of the steeldust foal. Steel Dust had been a large blood bay that had stood more than fifteen hands high, a legend in Texas, and fortunately the Sinclair horses were directly related to him. The foal was going to be a beautiful animal when he got bigger, no doubt a new stud for the farm, something they'd need in a few more years.

At dinnertime, she finally took a break and went back to the house for chow. That was when she found her father and her world tilted sideways.

※

"Excuse me?" Emma's entire body heated with anger, disbelief and a healthy dose of outrage. "Did you just say you sold me like a goddamn brood mare to Rafe Sinclair? Tell me you're not serious, Pa."

She leaned over the desk, her hands fisted on the scarred wooden top. Her mind could not grasp the words coming from her father's mouth. It just could not be true.

Her father rubbed a hand along his graying beard, his brown eyes unreadable. "Hell yes, I'm serious. You're too old to be traipsing around a ranch working horses. By the time your ma was your age, she was married and had you cooking in the oven. You're twenty years old, Emma. It's high time you got married."

Emma's throat closed up so tightly she thought she'd choke on her own spit. Fury surged through her fast and hard, and she was afraid she'd try to hit her father. Instead she turned away and punched the bookcase in his office which held books and accounting records.

"Dammit, Pa! I don't want to marry Rafe. He and I don't suit, and besides, I sure as hell don't want to be picked because he's backed into a corner. What kind of marriage is that?" To her dismay, tears of anger and hurt pricked her eyes. Emma simply never cried and this travesty brought them on.

"One that many folks have started off in. You'll get along just fine. Besides, you've known him all your life. Wasn't there a time you wanted to marry him?" Her father stood, his six-foot lanky frame almost dwarfing her five foot four inches.

"Jesus Christ, can you ever forget that? It was fifteen years ago, Pa. I don't want to marry him and I will *not* marry him." She folded her arms across her chest. "I won't spend the rest of my life with a horny cowboy who'll be sniffing after everything in skirts when I turn my back."

"That's enough!" her father thundered. "It was either you or Georgette and I don't think that girl has enough common sense to get out of her own way. She couldn't make it as a rancher's wife no matter what her granddaddy might think."

Emma grasped for something to say that would convince her father to call off the wedding. She couldn't stomach the thought of being forced into a marriage bed for the next fifty years. The very thought made her shudder.

"I won't do it."

"Oh yes you will." Her father took hold of her arm and marched her out of his office. "I already signed the papers. You're not of legal age until you're twenty-one, young lady. You will do what I tell you to do or you will get your ass off my property."

As they walked through the kitchen, several curious pairs of eyes watched their progress, but no one spoke. Emma kept her mouth shut, biting her lip to the point of pain. She could maintain her dignity so she wouldn't embarrass herself in front of the hands.

When they made it to the front porch, her father let her arm loose and put his hands on his hips.

"I've allowed you a lot of free rein around here because you're good with the horses. That doesn't mean you're a man or

Branded

that you can do what you want. If you don't do as I tell you, you can find a new place to live."

Emma couldn't stop the gasp from escaping. "You would do that to me?"

Her father ignored the question. "Rafe is expecting you in an hour to talk over the arrangements. You can either ride over there on your own, or I'll tie you to the saddle and bring you over." He pointed at her, his eyes blazing. "Don't disappoint me, Emma Louise Radcliff. This is an important marriage to all of us. You're a lucky girl to land the most eligible bachelor in the county."

Her father slammed back into the house, leaving Emma standing on the porch, shaking with a million different emotions. Her stomach had twisted into a knot she didn't think would ever unwind.

Sweet Mary.

CR

Rafe Sinclair needed a woman. Not just any woman, but a wife. Any wife. He took his grandfather's will out of his back pocket and read it for the hundredth time that week, but it still said the same thing. Rafe had to be married by June first, his thirtieth birthday, or lose the Circle S Ranch.

"Son of a bitch. That old coot got me by the balls." He kicked at the corral post, spooking the bay nosing in his direction.

He had loved his granddaddy like a father, but this final stab in the back was too much. The older man had always lamented the fact Rafe hadn't settled down. However, he never expected the twist that could cost him the ranch that was a part of his soul. No way in hell he'd let the Circle S slip through his fingers.

Rafe would just have to bite the bullet and get married.

Dammit.

He had less than a month to get hitched and fortunately he'd found a quick solution with his neighbor, Elijah Radcliff.

Rafe would marry his daughter Emma, a girl he'd known all her life. Not a great solution, but it'd do.

As he waited for her to ride over to the ranch, he wondered what mood she'd be in after finding out what her father had done. Hopefully she'd accept the fact that Rafe would be her husband. Now all he needed was to accept that he *had* to have a wife. One woman forever and ever.

Not an easy spoonful to swallow, especially considering the woman in question. A britches-wearing, cussing woman who acted more like a man than half his ranch hands. The only upside Rafe saw was that Emma knew horses better than anyone else in the county. The woman lived and breathed equine.

Hell, she was probably a virgin. The shiver that worked its way through his body had nothing to do with the temperature outside. Truth was, Rafe had no idea what to do with a virgin, much less one who was more male than female.

The thought of their wedding night—

"Yoohoo!" A feminine trill sounded from near the house.

Rafe stopped and frowned. He didn't recognize the voice. Maybe his housekeeper, Frieda, had company.

"Mr. Sinclair," came a second female voice.

"I think I saw him near the barn," chimed in a third.

Rafe stood stock-still, a deer caught in hunter's sights. A virtual army of petticoats started toward him. There had to be at least twelve of them in varying heights, shapes and sizes, including redheads, brunettes and blondes. Even their ages ranged from fresh-faced girls to long-in-the-tooth spinsters.

The only thing they had in common was the look of determination on their faces.

Holy hell.

Rafe's heart raced and his mouth turned dry as a cotton field. No doubt that idiot lawyer Foster had spilled the beans about Rafe's wifely predicament. Now a herd of available women stampeded toward him. He couldn't possibly meet Emma at the ranch with all these husband-hungry hens chasing him around.

He wasn't proud of it, but Rafe turned tail and ran.

He threw himself on top of his buckskin and rode hell-bent-for-leather toward the creek that separated his property from the Radcliffs. He reminded himself to let Foster know about his impending nuptials so the lawyer could somehow keep the women off his ranch. The last thing he needed was more females around.

As he cantered up to the creek, he noticed a beautiful quarter horse tied to a small cottonwood tree. One of the Radcliff's if he wasn't mistaken. They were beautiful animals, one and all.

Then he heard singing—a beautiful haunting melody about a lost lover sung by a woman who could rival an angel with her pipes. He sat on his horse with his eyes closed, savoring the song, wondering who had been blessed with such a voice.

When the music trailed away, he dismounted and went in search of his quarry. He found her, bent at the waist near the water, with the most delectable ass he'd seen in a dog's age poking up in the air. Long, dark brown tresses hung down toward the water as her hands finger-combed the locks. He shifted in his drawers, an erection pushing at his buttons for the mystery lady.

She stood and flipped her hair back, braiding it with the speed of a lightning strike, her plump, full breasts pushing at the blue chambray shirt she wore. That's when Rafe realized he could see her ass so well because she wore britches, and she had pistols riding her hips. He felt a moment of utter disbelief. He was looking at Emma Radcliff, his intended bride, and she didn't look anywhere near as manly as he remembered.

Holy shit.

Chapter Two

Emma turned around to find Rafe Sinclair watching her. Her heart sped up at his handsome chiseled face, his steel gray eyes and raven's wing hair. The man could probably make any woman swoon without trying. Too bad Emma wasn't like other women. His good looks and lean, hard body didn't make her want to marry him, nor did his money. Nothing in the world could do that.

He looked odd, as if someone had pinched him and ran. When he didn't say anything after a few moments, she snorted and walked toward her horse. She'd been right about the space between his ears.

"Wait. Emma, please wait." He stepped toward her, his hat in hand. "I'm sorry. I didn't mean to spy on you. I, uh, had no idea you could sing."

"There's a lot of things you don't know about me, Rafe. I guess that doesn't matter though, does it? My pa is forcing me to marry you or leave the ranch. Not much of a choice, is it?" She couldn't help the anger or resentment in her voice.

"I didn't know Elijah would force you, Emma. I know we haven't been around each other much the last five years, but I think we'll do"—he swallowed—"okay."

Emma's eyebrows shot up. "We'll do okay?" She rolled her eyes. "Let's get this planning over with so I can go back to work."

She started toward his ranch, her gut churning. When she looked back, he was still standing there.

"You have something else you need to do?"

"Well, no, but there's a whole passel of women at the ranch looking for me." He glanced toward the creek. "Do you mind if we talk here?"

Emma thought about what folks would say when they found out she and Rafe had been alone, unchaperoned. She guessed it didn't matter if they were engaged to be married. Still, it didn't sit well with her, aside from the fact that he was hiding from potential brides. That might actually work in her favor.

"Yes, I do mind. Let's get back to your ranch and I'll get rid of those biddies for you. I'll even fire a few warning shots if I need to." She gestured to his horse. "Let's go, cowboy. I'll rescue you."

He frowned as he stepped toward the buckskin. "I don't need rescuing."

"That's not how I see it. I've got chores to do today so let's get this done." Emma hoped like hell one of the women skulking around his ranch would catch Rafe's eye and get her off the hook.

A girl could dream to save herself from a nightmare.

Rafe's mind could not grasp the fact that the woman beside him was Emma Radcliff. She didn't bear even the slightest resemblance to herself at fifteen. Okay, well the face was the same only slimmer, but that ass and those tits...well, they didn't used to look like that. Perhaps being married to her wouldn't be too bad.

It would help if she didn't carry guns though. He didn't know one other woman who wore Colts on her hips. Most, if any, carried a little derringer in their reticule or pulled out a shotgun for protection if necessary.

His bride-to-be wore two six-shooters like she was a man. She was a conundrum of mismatched pieces.

They rode in silence back to the Circle S. The closer they got, the more he worried about all the women waiting for him. Strange thing was, he was glad Emma had come back with him. It didn't make him feel safe, just better. He never thought he'd be hiding from any woman, much less a herd of them, but damned if they hadn't all looked hungry enough to eat him alive. Normally having two or three women inviting him to play might excite him, however this situation wasn't normal, and neither were the sheer number of females.

He glanced around the yard from their vantage point on the hill, noting the white figures that were either large stray sheep or women poking around the ranch.

"They're still here." He sighed. "Nosing around like a pack of coyotes."

Emma glanced at him sideways. "No need for name-calling, Rafe. You can't blame them for trying. Way I hear it, gals have been trying to land you for years." She shook her head. "Can't say as I understand it."

Rafe frowned. "I'm not all that bad, Emma. Once upon a time, you didn't think I was."

She huffed out an impatient-sounding breath. "Well I guess I grew up and got smart. Let's get this over with." Emma spurred her horse down the hill, leaving Rafe behind.

He caught up with her just as she reached the barn and dismounted in a smooth movement that made his eyebrows shoot up. Emma wasn't fooling when she said she knew horses well. Not many men could move like that, much less a woman.

Emma cupped her hands around her mouth. "Ladies, this is Emma Radcliff. I'm here with Rafe Sinclair. Come on out."

A tiny bit of trepidation wiggled around in Rafe's stomach. She made it sound like he was up for auction, for Pete's sake. As he dismounted, the herd of ladies appeared like hungry hands called for chow. With a weak smile, he stepped up next to Emma. He was *not* hiding behind her.

Emma addressed them. "I'm sure you've all heard that Rafe needs to get hitched. I'm here to tell you that's true."

She glanced up at Rafe, and he saw her plan laid out like a map in her eyes right before she opened her mouth. Nothing doing. He wasn't about to let the coyotes loose on him regardless of Emma's reasons for wanting that to happen.

Rafe clamped his hand over her mouth and yanked her under his arm. "I'm officially engaged to Emma here so y'all can go home."

Emma took the opportunity to bite his hand. Instead of looking like a fool in front of the crestfallen ladies, he did what he did best—he kissed his intended bride.

It started as a lesson to her to behave as well as a show for the prospective brides buzzing around. Emma's breasts pushed up against his chest nicely while her stiff lips barely moved beneath his. He thought she even might be growling at him.

Rafe's kiss softened by degrees until he was barely touching her, just a gentle swipe of his lips against hers. Their essences mingled as they swallowed each other's breaths. Before he knew it, Rafe forgot who he was kissing, where he was or what the hell he had intended on doing.

Kissing Emma consumed him.

She was firm yet curvy with a tremendous amount of strength in her body. Her hand crept up and tangled in his hair, knocking his hat off. The haze of arousal thrummed through him as his body reacted to the sensuous woman in his arms. Until she yanked his hair so hard his eyes crossed.

Rafe let her go so fast she almost fell on her ass. He grabbed her hand at the last second and pulled her back to her feet. As he rubbed the back of his head, he noticed how red and plump her lips were, that they were wet from his kisses, and she had a hint of whisker burn on her chin.

He'd not only kissed Emma Radcliff, he'd *enjoyed* it. More than enjoyed it by the reaction of his dick.

Hot damn.

He should have expected the fist, but damn, it hurt like hell when she walloped him with a right hook. When Rafe uncrossed his eyes, he was pleased to discover the other women had disappeared. He didn't know how long he'd been kissing Emma, but it was long enough that they were alone.

"Don't ever take anything from me again," she hissed. "I might marry you, Rafe Sinclair, but I ain't willing to do more than that."

Rafe had to physically force himself not to stare at her chest. Those round, soft tits of hers heaved with each outraged breath she took. He felt topsy-turvy as if his entire world had just shifted under his feet.

Emma pushed at his chest. "Do you understand me?"

He nodded, swallowing at the tightness in his throat. Rafe had no idea what just happened, but he expected it was the beginning of something else, something bigger between them. It should have scared the hell out of him, which in turn would make him do all he could to stop it. However, he had no choice but to forge ahead with the marriage to Emma, come hell or high water.

"Let's get this over with then." Emma tied her horse off at the hitching post and stomped toward the house, little puffs of dirt following her progress with each boot print.

After a long, deep sigh, Rafe followed.

"I want every word written down and signed by both of us." Emma kept her voice steady. "Before I agree to anything."

Rafe steepled his fingers together beneath his chin, leaning his elbows on his knees. "So you're telling me that you want a condition of our marriage to be me signing away any husbandly rights? Forever?"

"That's about it." She knew it sounded crazy, but it was the only way she could swallow being married to Rafe. "I know it ain't normal—"

He chuckled without humor. "It's past that, Em. Way past that."

She squirmed on the hard leather chair and glanced around his living room. The furnishings hadn't changed since his granddaddy died. The settee, animal trophies, and the rag rug were all the same. The man sitting in the wingback chair next to the fire, however, had changed.

Rafe knew he ruled the ranch. It showed in his posture, his actions, even in his voice. Emma was afraid if she didn't lay down the law with him before the wedding, she'd never get the chance. The last thing she wanted was to live under another man's thumb.

"Well, that's my condition to get hitched." She folded her arms across her chest and looked as stern as she could manage. Her dang knees still shook from the force of his kiss. It had taken every smidge of self-control she had to pull away from him, from those lips. Her body tingled in the aftermath of her first heart-pounding kiss from a man. She'd allowed stolen

Branded

kisses here and there, but nothing like what she'd just experienced.

"If I agree to this, and that's a big if, there has to be a clause that you can cancel it at any time." He licked his lips and Emma squeezed her legs around the chair legs to stop herself from jumping like a damn frog. What in God's name was wrong with her? Could she stop thinking about his mouth for two minutes?

With an inner slap to focus, she was able to respond in a normal tone of voice. "What does that mean?"

"It means the future Mrs. Sinclair can decide to have relations with Mr. Sinclair if she changes her mind about her, ah, condition." Rafe smiled a slow, lazy grin she knew had worked on countless women.

She sure as heck wasn't immune to it if her pounding pulse was any indication.

"So you'll agree only if I say that it's not permanent? That I can change my mind?" She wasn't sure putting that clause in to cancel the agreement was a good idea.

"That's my condition to get hitched." He leaned back in the chair and pointed at her. "You choose. Either no clause or a clause with both our conditions."

Emma's mind ran through a million reasons why she should say no. Then a million reasons why she should say yes. Her father had signed a legal contract with Rafe already, this clause probably meant nothing to him. It meant everything to her.

"I want to work with the horses every day at the Triple R."

"I expected no less. Your pa wouldn't know what to do without your skills with those quarter horses." Rafe's eyes were unreadable, and she wished she had more time to think about his proposal to amend her amendment. Dang it.

"When do we need to do this?" She rubbed her hands on her jeans, the desire to run away battling with the curiosity to kiss him again.

"Two weeks. Let's say May seventeenth. I don't want anything to interfere with me taking over this ranch. My birthday is coming up fast and I want to be good and married by then." He raised one eyebrow. "No one can know about the clause but you and me. Not even your pa."

"Agreed." Emma didn't need the world knowing she refused to bed her husband, even if he was unwanted. Folks would point the finger at her, wondering what was wrong with her.

"Did you just say yes?" He leaned forward with his eyebrows knit together, looking very serious.

Emma opened her mouth, but nothing came out.

"Do I need to kiss you again?"

"Yes. I mean no." She muttered a curse. "Yes to the marriage, no to the kiss."

Rafe smiled and stood, holding out his hand to her. Emma stared at his calloused palm, wondering if agreeing to the marriage would be the biggest mistake of her life.

"Thank you."

She grunted and stood, ignoring his hand. "You won't thank me come our honeymoon night, but leastways you get to keep the Circle S. I've got to get back to work. Pa will expect me."

Rafe dropped his hand with a frown. "You know this will go easier if we both accept the fact that the marriage is gonna happen."

"Then it won't go easier." Emma walked toward the door. "I'll have Consuela help me with the wedding stuff. See you on May seventeenth at Triple R. Be there at four o'clock."

With that Emma stepped out into the May sunshine, battling quaking legs and a churning gut.

She was getting married.

Chapter Three

"But why Emma? She's so, so...not like a girl." Georgette pouted in the dining room three days before the wedding.

"We've talked about this." Elijah took a big chunk of bread. "She's fit to be a rancher's wife. You need to marry a doctor or something. Your granddaddy will find you the right man."

Emma barely controlled the urge to roll her eyes. She regretted every second of the last week and a half, waiting for her wedding like a woman condemned to the gallows. Consuela, the housekeeper who'd been on the Triple R since before Emma was born, handled all the arrangements, even the butchering of the steer for the after-party.

It was a good thing too because Emma outwardly pretended like nothing was about to happen. She took care of the horses, the foals and her everyday chores. Three days before she was to be married and she hadn't even started to pack. Not that there was much to pack, just shirts, jeans, chaps and a few personal items like the miniature of her ma.

Everything else stayed put since she needed it to keep working with the horses each day.

"She doesn't even want to get married."

Emma glared at her stepsister. "It ain't about what I want, Georgette. It's about what's best for the ranches. Stop being such a baby. He's not that handsome."

A big fat lie, of course. Emma could lie to others but not to herself. Rafe was beyond handsome, he crossed the line into perfect. Perhaps that was part of the problem. Emma knew she wasn't a raving beauty, and she knew her marriage was a business arrangement. There was no way Rafe wouldn't stray from his vows, and she refused to set herself up for heartache. She'd seen her mother waste away for a year while her father romanced Eloise Stanton, then eventually married her after Emma's mother passed away, a shadow of herself.

Every time she looked at Georgette, Emma was reminded of what the young girl's mother took from her. Emma had promised herself when she was thirteen years old that she'd *never* let a man control her heart, or allow her to lose herself. Emma was strong, smart and knew exactly what she wanted, very different from her mother. She intended on keeping it that way, no matter what Rafe thought.

"You're too ugly to have him," Georgette shouted as she pushed back from the table. She threw her napkin to the floor with a sob. "He was mine and you took him. I hate you, Emma Radcliff!"

With a scream to rival a mountain lion, the blonde ran from the room and up the stairs, followed by a slam that rattled the windows.

"You'd best get all your gear together tomorrow. There's stuff scattered all over the barn that you'll need." Her father slathered butter on his bread.

Emma's eyes narrowed even as her throat went dry with dread at what she figured was coming. "What do you mean, get my gear together? I'm still working at the Triple R, Pa."

"Oh no you're not. Your place is next to your husband, not riding back and forth an hour a day each way." He chewed slowly, giving her a look that brooked no argument.

"You're not serious, Pa. I can't leave the horses." Her heart thundered with the thought of not being around the animals she loved. Her little steeldust foal would be a beauty—she couldn't bear the idea of not seeing him grow. He couldn't take away that which she loved more than anything in the world. Not the horses, anything but them.

"Don't be ridiculous. You'll be close by for visits, Emma." He wiped his mouth.

"Pa, that's not the same and you know it. What will I do at the Circle S? They raise cattle, not horses. I don't know anything about cattle." She sounded shrill even to her own ears, but at that point, Emma didn't care. Her life's work, her passion, was being taken away, something she hadn't even considered when she agreed to marry Rafe.

"You will stay home and be a wife, then a mother. That's what God intended for you, Emma." Her father rose, knocking his chair backwards. "I won't hear another word about it. Tomorrow you start packing your gear."

Emma stared at the gravy as it congealed on her plate. The urge to cry almost overwhelmed her, but she held it back. There was no way she'd let her father see her weakness. She had to be strong, stronger than she'd had to be in a long time.

"If I go, I take Mariposa, her foal, Blackjack and Cinnamon with me." She stood, facing her father down with the will of every woman who'd been forced to marry against her wishes, with her heart in her throat and tears stinging her damn eyes again. "That's not negotiable."

Elijah scowled. "You want two mares, a stallion and a foal? That's a lot of money going with you, girl."

"As you pointed out, Pa, this marriage is good for both of us. I'll need a dowry." She couldn't be separated from all of them, it would break her heart.

"I suppose you're right. Okay, you can have them, along with some tack. Your new husband's already agreed to give us a dozen steer a year for meat."

Emma growled under her breath, feeling more and more like this marriage was a trade of goods, and she was the stock.

"Fine, then I'll take the horses with me on Saturday, along with Rowdy." She walked out of the dining room with her spine straight and her disposition miserable. How could life possibly get any worse?

"It's not so bad, *hija*." Consuela stood in the kitchen doorway, beckoning her inside.

The round, middle-aged Mexican housekeeper had been more like a mother to Emma than anyone in her life. With a choked sob, she stepped into the kitchen and Consuela's warm embrace. As Emma let the frustration and fear pour forth, she babbled into the housekeeper's shoulder. After a few minutes of embarrassing tears, Emma stepped back and wiped her face.

Consuela peered at Emma with all-knowing eyes. "You always wanted to marry Rafael. And before you say a word, don't forget who you tell your secrets to."

Emma didn't bother denying it.

"But he doesn't want to marry me. He wants to keep his precious ranch." She couldn't help the bitterness in her voice. The first fifteen years of her life were spent adoring Rafe Sinclair, and he turned her dreams into a nasty reality.

"Ah, *hija mia*, he will see you for who you are. A woman with a heart of an eagle and the courage of a lion." Consuela cupped Emma's jaw. "Don't worry, Emma, you will be married with love and make beautiful babies for me to spoil."

A small snort popped out of Emma. "What am I going to do, Consuela?"

"You will do what you must." Consuela handed her a churro, a cinnamon-covered treat. "Life is just beginning, *hija*, ride the winds, don't fight them."

Emma didn't pretend to understand what Consuela meant, but she appreciated the comfort. Life as she knew it had just ended, but the path ahead was mighty rocky. Emma was afraid.

ෆ

The day of the wedding dawned gray and bleak with a misty rain. Emma almost refused to put on the dress Consuela had made. In the end, she did as requested and married Rafe.

Pity she didn't feel married.

Folks walked through the house whispering to each other behind their hands and pointing at her. The men kept slapping Rafe on the back and teasing him about "riding that filly 'till she broke". The very idea made Emma's fists clench.

They were treating her like a damn brood mare instead of a person. She sat in the corner, plunking the piano keys as the guests milled around her. No one made the effort to talk to her. Most of them were Rafe's and her father's friends. It wasn't unusual—townsfolk didn't understand Emma and made no effort to do so, and neither did she.

Branded

Aside from Consuela and the ranch hands, Emma had no friends.

She sat up straight and pinched herself in the arm. No need to get all maudlin and self-pitying. What's done was done. She would just live on Rafe's ranch and start her own horse-breeding program. She was walking away with all she needed and then some.

Emma was leaving with a husband.

"Why are you stuck over here in the corner by yourself?"

Emma looked up at her father and made a face. "Nobody wants to talk to me anyway. They all came to see Rafe make a fool of himself marrying the least likely bride in the county." She pinned him with a glare. "I even heard there was some wagering going on in the barn earlier."

Her father grinned. "Emma, you shouldn't be listening to other folks' gossip. No one came to stare at you or make wagers on your wedding. They came to wish you well." He touched her shoulder. "I think Rafe's wanting to leave in just a bit so he's going to say a few words."

Emma glanced over at her husband.

Husband.

That was going to take some work to get straight in her head, much less say.

Rafe was talking to the minister and his wife, grinning like a fool. She wondered what Reverend McAllister would think of a celibate marriage. Probably tell her she was going against God's will and all that nonsense. He had no idea how strong Emma's will was.

"Come on now, join your husband, Emma." Her father pulled her to her feet and led her over to Rafe.

Rafe's eyes darkened as she approached. In the space of a breath, Emma remembered that heart-pounding, soul-stealing kiss from two weeks earlier. She shrugged it away, uncomfortable with the direction of her thoughts. It would be a marriage in name only. Period.

"Emma, I'm glad you're here. I was about to say a few words to everyone." He tucked her arm into his and turned to the room. "Everyone, can I have your attention please."

The room quieted quickly, every eye turned to the newlyweds. Emma cursed her agreement to put her hair up and wear a dang dress—she felt like a gussied up sow's ear. It just didn't feel right.

"I know Emma and I got married quick, but I made the right choice for my bride. She's everything a woman can be plus more." He held up his cup of punch. "Here's to my new wife and partner, Emma Sinclair."

Emma Sinclair.

Damn, she'd forgotten about the name-changing thing. What a silly tradition that was. It would be a wonder if she remembered to turn when someone called her Mrs. Sinclair.

"Here, here!" The guests raised their cups with Rafe and toasted the newlyweds.

Emma didn't even have a cup to raise. She considered whether she'd have toasted along with him or not.

"Now we're going to be heading on back to the Circle S in a few minutes. There's plenty of beef, potatoes and cake, so eat up. Emma and I would like to thank y'all for coming." He squeezed her against him, the hard wall of his chest pinning her in place.

She considered kicking him in the shin to get free, but decided against it. It would be a bad beginning to an already difficult marriage. Instead she smiled, or at least it was a semblance of a smile, at the guests as they filed past, wishing the marriage well.

After they were finished, she looked up at Rafe. "Can you let me go now? I can't feel my left arm anymore."

He looked shocked, then broke out in a wide grin. "I always did love your sass. Let's get going then, Mrs. Sinclair."

Finally free of his arm, she walked outside, heading for the barn and the horses. Rowdy had Cinnamon saddled with lead ropes on Blackjack, Mariposa and the foal. He smiled his nearly toothless grin when he caught sight of her.

"Why you remind me something fierce of your mama, Em. Right beautiful." He whistled. "I cain't hardly believe it's you."

She'd forgotten about being gussied up. Rowdy's compliment actually made her blush. She expected nothing but the truth from any of the hands.

Branded

"Humph. Feel like a dang fool in this getup. I'm gonna go back upstairs and change. Be back in two minutes." She turned and slammed right into Rafe.

His hands steadied her as his rum-laced breath washed over her face. "Easy there, Em."

The moment stretched out as her gaze focused on his full lips, on the memory of how they felt on hers. Her blood thrummed low and thick through her, making every small hair on her skin stand up. Rafe lowered his head just a smidge before she broke free and stumbled backwards.

"I need to change out of these fancy duds." She hurried away before he could say a word. Rafe was dangerous to her well-being.

Emma would do well to remember to stay away from her new husband, or else end up in his bed, throwing her agreement out the window.

Rafe watched her march away and wondered just what the hell he'd agreed to. She was in his thoughts almost constantly. He shook his head to dislodge the memory of the way the dress hugged her incredible breasts.

Then he remembered she'd probably be back in her britches so he could then focus on her ass.

He was in trouble.

For the first time in his life, Rafe didn't know what to do with a woman. He could try to seduce her, but something told him it wouldn't work very well on Emma. He could also treat her like one of the ranch hands, but that didn't feel right either.

He had no plan, just a ball of confusion in his chest. He took a big gulp of air. The misty rain coated his face, clearing away some of his unease. He nodded to old Rowdy, who was standing with the quarter horses that were coming back to the Circle S.

They were all beautiful animals. The little colt had the look of a steeldust, already showing signs of long legs and a full chest. That one might be a runner if he gained some weight. While Rafe saddled his own horse, questions circled around in his brain about his marriage, his wife and their future. She'd obviously come into the marriage because her pa laid down the law. Rafe wondered if she'd ever accept him as her husband—not likely judging by the contract she made him sign to stay out of her bed. That particular promise would be difficult to keep. Just being close to her for a few minutes left him tangled up inside, wanting her. By the time Emma came out of the house in her britches, Rafe still had no answers.

They waved goodbye to the guests and started for the Circle S, riding in silence with the rain falling steadily for more than half an hour. Water dripped down his slicker, pooling on the brim of his hat, making him more uncomfortable than he already was. He had no doubt Emma suffered as much discomfort as him, but he didn't know how to ask. She'd likely think he was trying to get in her good graces. The silence stretched out until Rowdy finally spoke, bless the old man.

"Y'all don't act like newlyweds."

Rafe chuckled. "How are we supposed to act?"

"Ya know, lovey-dovey." He grunted. "I'd think you were hands headed out to work the herd or something."

Rafe thought he heard Emma snort under her breath, but he wasn't sure. "We didn't have a traditional courtship, Rowdy, but we are married and we'll do the best we can."

He said it more for Emma than the crotchety old man. If she continued to treat him like the enemy instead of her husband, he'd have to resort to more drastic measures. A little charm might work, and if it didn't, well, then he'd have to find something else.

The rain came down harder shortly after the brief conversation. They rode as fast as they could, or at least as fast as the foal could. The little horse didn't seem to be bothered by the downpour, although his mistress could've cut rocks with her scowl.

When they arrived at the ranch, Emma headed straight for the barn.

"Hope you've got stalls ready for them," she called over her shoulder.

The first words she'd uttered in an hour and they weren't particularly friendly. Rafe didn't even get a chance to answer before she disappeared into the barn.

Happy wedding day.

Rafe frowned and followed her. She'd obviously found the stalls he'd readied for her horses. The stallion was by himself in the back where he couldn't get to any other horse, proving once again Emma knew what she was doing. He knew they were important to her, and possibly to the future of the Circle S. Radcliff horses were well respected and garnered high prices. With Emma as his wife, she could continue the horse breeding and perhaps teach him a thing or two.

That thought stopped him in his tracks.

Emma would teach him? The very idea seemed flip-flopped from usual. When did a woman ever teach him anything—aside from the whore in Mexico who did amazing things with her mouth? He sighed and led Diamond to his stall. The gelding pulled at the reins, shying away from the newcomers in the barn.

"Easy, boy. They're not going to hurt you." He petted the buckskin's nose. "How about some oats?"

"You surprise me, Rafe."

He glanced up to find her watching him, a rag in her hands and a perplexed look on her face. Her dark tresses hung wet against her equally wet shirt.

"What do you mean?"

"I expected you to treat your horse like every other rancher. He's just a piece of property, but you treat him like a friend." She shrugged. "It surprised me, that's all."

Rafe didn't know whether to be insulted or amused. She had some preconceived notions about men, that was for certain. No man on a ranch treated horses like a piece of property. They were too valuable.

"You've been around the wrong kind of men then." He led his horse into the stall, forestalling any argument with his new wife. It was important to him that they at least get through their wedding day on good terms. After all, they had the next fifty years to fight.

Rafe finished with Diamond in ten minutes and stepped out of the stall. He heard a low murmur coming from the mare's stall. Drawn to the soothing sounds, he stepped as quietly as he could toward her.

Emma was on her knees, brushing the little foal with an expression of pure joy on her face. She murmured softly to the horse in a sweet, low voice that reminded him of the bedroom. Rafe was struck by how beautiful she looked at that moment, how pure and natural she seemed with the horse. His heart thumped hard at the thought he was seeing the true woman he'd married, not the curmudgeon he'd come to expect.

Without alerting her to his presence, Rafe left the barn and headed for the house. Maybe a warm bath might help with her mood.

Emma sighed and pressed her forehead against Mariposa's withers. Exhaustion crept through her like a thief, stealing her energy and her will. It had been an incredibly long day and it was bound to be an even longer night.

She'd sleep in her new husband's house tonight. The thought of being in close proximity to Rafe in just her nightgown gave her the chills. She dared not think about whether the chills were excitement or dread. After making sure all her horses had food and water, she finally left the barn.

Rafe had disappeared at least half an hour earlier. She'd expected him to hover and try to take over her chores. Instead, he'd left her alone, exactly what she needed. Rowdy knew better than to bother her. He'd headed straight for the bunkhouse and a whiskey.

Her new husband was turning out to be a different man than she thought he was, either that or he was really good at pretending to be someone else. It didn't matter one way or the other. Until she was good and ready, if ever, Emma wouldn't trust any man, much less Rafe.

She trudged to the house with a heavy heart and a dose of homesickness. Emma had spent her entire life on her family's ranch. In fact, she'd never slept anywhere else or woken up anywhere else. Everything about this whole marriage thing was turning every aspect of her life sideways.

By the time she reached the house, Emma had built up a head of steam laced with resentment. She opened the kitchen door, ready to give Rafe a piece of her mind. The room was empty of people, but holy hell, he'd been there for sure.

A huge wooden bathtub sat in front of a cheery, crackling fire. Steamy wisps rose from the water. A pitcher of water, a mug and a plate with biscuits and cheese sat on the table. She closed the door behind her with a thump.

What was he up to? Did he think to seduce her already? It hadn't even been twelve hours and he was breaking their contract. Emma wasn't about to let that happen. She tossed her hat on one of the chairs and headed for the living room.

Rafe sat in the chair, an empty glass clutched in his hand. In the firelight, his face was a study in angles and shadows, his eyes hidden. For a moment it was as if she was looking at a different man, one she didn't know. The floor felt unsteady under her feet.

"I, uh, what's going on in the kitchen?"

He peered at the fire through the glass. "I thought you might want a bath and something to eat."

She frowned. "So you weren't trying to seduce me then?"

Rafe sighed. "I'm tired, Emma. Do we have to argue tonight? I wanted to get through our wedding day without fighting." He stood and stretched.

Emma watched his shirt strain from the effect of his muscles tightening and loosening. Her mouth went cotton dry and be damned if her heart didn't kick up a notch. It appeared her body hadn't gotten over her childhood obsession with Rafe.

"I'm headed upstairs. Just leave the bathwater when you're done. One of the men will empty the tub in the morning." Rafe walked over to her, as if he sensed how much she'd reacted to his body. Her hands fisted as the urge to touch him almost overcame her. "Good night, Mrs. Sinclair."

He touched her chin, tilting her head up to meet his gaze. The silvery orbs glittered in the half-light. She'd give him credit, he gave her the option to pull away but she didn't, she couldn't. Instead, she waited for what was coming next.

A kiss.

His lips barely brushed hers, the delicate touch of a butterfly on a flower. When she opened her eyes, she was alone in the room, as if he'd never been there. Emma shook her head to clear it.

Mrs. Sinclair.

"Humph." With one last scowl for her predicament, Emma headed back to the kitchen for a bath and a meal. She'd definitely need food to get through her first night as a wife.

Rafe stepped into the kitchen, not knowing what to expect from his new bride. It was their wedding night and he knew for certain there'd be some consummating going on if he hadn't signed that stupid agreement. He'd been fantasizing about getting his curvy woman under him for days on end. Too bad they'd stay fantasies forever if Emma had her way.

When she hadn't come upstairs after an hour, he decided to investigate. He didn't expect to find her asleep at the table, fork still clutched in her hand. Her long dark hair fell over her face and into the food on the plate. The tub sat empty beside the fireplace. She'd apparently hauled the damn thing outside by herself to dump it. Fool woman.

No doubt she'd had about as much sleep as he had over the last week, more than likely why she fell asleep over her mashed potatoes. With a shake of his head, he took her hair out of the food and wiped it clean on his handkerchief. He slid the plate and utensils out of the way, then gently and ever-so-slowly picked her up.

She murmured something he couldn't quite understand, and snuggled her head under his chin. Her breath puffed out on his skin like a caress. He had to stop himself from kissing her awake as his arousal howled to be fed.

Rafe didn't know what possessed him, but without a second thought he carried her up to the bedroom, took off her boots and laid her on the bed. He contemplated undressing her, but figured he wanted to be able to father children one day and decided to leave her clothes on.

That didn't mean he had to leave his on though. With a wicked grin, Rafe got ready for bed.

ೂ

Emma rolled over and snuggled against the pillow. She didn't want to wake up just yet and the room was dark enough that it couldn't be dawn already. Funny, she didn't remember her bed being so dang comfortable.

Realization hit her like a horse kick and she sat up in bed with a shout.

"What? What's the matter?" Rafe jumped out of bed wearing absolutely nothing. In the gloom she couldn't see much beyond vague shapes, fortunately or not.

Emma didn't know which was worse, knowing that he must have carried her upstairs unconscious or that she'd been sleeping next to a naked man.

It didn't matter which was worse, she wasn't staying in that bedroom.

"Goddammit, Rafe, what the hell are you doing?" she gasped.

"I was sleeping until you started screaming." He ran his hand down his face.

"Not funny. You know our agreement and this wasn't part of it." She scrambled out of bed, realizing she was fully dressed, at least that was a blessing. He hadn't seen her naked, she hoped.

"You knew we'd be sharing a house and a bedroom, Emma. Would you like me to shout from the rooftops that we're not truly husband and wife?" He threw both hands in the air. "I didn't do anything to you but make sure you were comfortable in bed."

Emma's heart pounded so loud, she thought she heard a rib crack. "Is that why you're naked? To make me comfortable?"

He glanced down and pasted an innocent expression on his face. "Oh, sorry about that. I, uh, didn't even think. I always sleep like this."

Emma didn't miss the roguish twinkle in his eye—she didn't believe him for a moment. After grabbing something from the chair beside the bed, he yanked on what appeared to be drawers.

"I can't sleep here, Rafe." She hadn't counted on sharing a bed with him.

"Do you want the entire ranch to know about our agreement then? We are married, Emma, and we're expected to sleep in the same room." He climbed back into the bed and leaned against the pillows with a huff.

"I can't."

"Suit yourself. There's an extra quilt in the chest at the end of the bed. You can sleep on the chair or the floor." He rolled over and gave her his wide back. "Good night, Em."

Emma stared at him, sure he'd been sent by the devil himself to make her crazy. How could Rafe possibly think she could sleep in the bed with him, no matter what everyone else thought? She understood his point about the marriage, but he had to understand that she wasn't kidding about not being intimate with him.

With enough noise to wake the rest of the ranch, Emma yanked the quilt from the chest and the pillow from the bed. She'd slept on hard ground plenty of times, bedding down in Rafe Sinclair's bedroom would be another cold, sleepless night.

Chapter Four

Emma slept fitfully, waking every hour or two plagued by hazy dreams about Rafe. She woke before the sun. The gray light of dawn made the room a play of shadows. She peeked up at the bed and breathed a sigh of relief that Rafe was already gone.

Then again, he'd had the opportunity to observe her as she slept. Of course, he'd also brought her to the damn room while she was asleep. Neither fact pleased her.

The water in the pitcher was cold, but she used it anyway, grateful for the brisk wake-up. She dressed quickly, tucking the agreement in her trouser pocket. The crinkle of the paper reassured her that their agreement would stand, or she'd walk from the house. Rafe had no idea how stubborn Emma could be.

As she made her way downstairs, she rubbed her eyes with the heels of her hands. Her eyes stung from lack of sleep and her mood couldn't get much worse.

"Good morning, Em."

She was wrong. A sweet-talking Rafe could knock her day even more off kilter.

"There's fresh coffee, bacon and biscuits on the stove." He sat at the table, looking as devastating as he always did. His still damp hair and freshly shaven chin shone in the sunshine coming through the window.

With a grunt in his direction, she poured herself coffee and headed out the door before he could throw any more brightness at her. It was time to work and that didn't involve her new husband.

Several of the ranch hands stopped what they were doing and watched as she walked toward the barn. She heard a few whispers and snickers, and wondered if she'd ever feel comfortable as Rafe's wife. Right about then she felt like a brood mare on display. More than likely the men hadn't seen a woman in britches too often. She didn't care what they thought since these clothes were the most practical she owned. They'd just have to get used to the new Mrs. Sinclair.

Emma nodded at a few of them and continued on to the barn and her horses. The least she could do was work herself into exhaustion so she didn't have to look at her husband when she slept in his bedroom, in the bed she'd never truly share with him.

Her silly heart hiccupped at the thought.

Rafe stared at the closed door after Emma left. When he'd originally set out to marry Emma, he never expected that he'd actually want to be married to her. He still wasn't sure if he did or not, but something about her made him want to find out. She was definitely as stubborn as he was.

That could be a problem.

Rafe wasn't about to spend the rest of his life fighting his wife to be civil. Most women were usually not only civil to him, they were downright sweet as honey. Too much lemon was going to sour everything. He wasn't the type of man who'd go into town to visit a working gal rather than his wife. Wincing at the thought of not having sex for a very long time, Rafe pinched the bridge of his nose and focused on what to do.

He needed to seduce Emma. It meant he'd be breaking their agreement, but if it worked, things would be much easier all around. The whole no-sex clause wasn't really legal anyway. She was probably just nervous about being intimate, as many virgins were. It was perfectly natural, but she couldn't know Rafe had more experience than she imagined. What he could give her in pleasure would make up for breaking his word.

Rafe finished his coffee in one gulp, then stood, ready to begin the seduction of his wife. Emma had no idea what she was in for.

He found her in the barn, down on the floor examining the foal's hooves. She'd stuffed her hair up in her hat but a few dark wisps had escaped and trailed on her shoulders. The sharp smell of new hay and horse surrounded him, along with a fresh scent that could only be Emma.

"He's a beaut." Rafe leaned against the stall door.

Without glancing up, she answered. "He's a steeldust foal. I can trace him all the way back to the original."

Rafe wondered if she was kidding, but swallowed back the chuckle. There was a small possibility that this tiny foal was descended from the famous Steel Dust. He'd been dead some years now and had sired quite a few colts, but given the lean nature of this little one, it was unlikely he was a pure steeldust. "What's his name?"

"I haven't given him one yet. I was waiting to see." She stood, wiping her hands on her pants.

"Waiting for what?" He'd never understood why women made such a big deal about names anyway.

She glanced at him. "Waiting to see what he's going to be like. I can't give him a proper name until I see him run. He'll be a champion though."

Rafe kept his mouth shut, unwilling to provoke her more. The foal was small for his age and a bit scrawny. Now that he'd had a chance to really look at him, Rafe figured Emma might be betting on the wrong horse. "With a trainer like you, he's going to be even better."

"I need to get a shovel." She stepped out of the stall, pushed Rafe out of the way, then latched the door behind her.

"For what?" He tried his damnedest not to be insulted by her treatment.

"For you. Your arms must be getting tired handing out shit all day." She picked up a wooden bucket and walked away.

Rafe resisted the urge to spank her, although it was a close call. She was deliberately pushing him away to keep him at a distance. He wasn't stupid, he understood what she was doing. Getting angry wouldn't help his goal of making her his real wife. Obviously sweet-talking was not going to work on this filly.

He'd just have to think of something else and quickly or the entire ranch would know just how un-married-like they were.

She moved onto the other mare, the chestnut-colored one, and started grooming her. Rafe kept watching until Emma threw up her hands.

"What are you doing?" she snapped.

"Just getting to know you. You're a fascinating woman, Em." Strangely enough, Rafe believed what he said. Emma was fascinating.

She rolled her eyes. "And you are the governor of Texas, right? Go peddle your wares someplace else."

"How about we go for a ride and I show you the ranch?" He wasn't giving up that easily. It was the rest of his life at stake, happily ever after or not.

"I'm busy." As she moved past him to get the curry brush, he was again struck by her fresh scent.

"Not too busy to get a look at your new home. I don't think you ever saw the whole thing before." He tugged at her arm. "Please, Em. I want us to go back to being friends."

It was important that they begin anew, to start over again. Neither one of them had truly wanted the marriage, but they were good and wed. A lifetime was a long time without a true partner for a mate. Granted, Emma had a lot more hostility toward him than he had counted on, but some gentle wooing and good old-fashioned hospitality might remedy that situation.

"We haven't been friends in years, Rafe. Not since you decided I was a snot-nosed brat who wouldn't stop following you around. If you'll excuse me, I need to work Cinnamon." She left the barn, leading the mare behind her into the corral, leaving Rafe alone with his thoughts.

Had he really said that to her? He didn't remember, but obviously she did. Years ago when she was five or six, she'd told everyone she was going to marry Rafe. He was a teenager at the time and mighty embarrassed by all the teasing. Perhaps he'd pushed her away even then, but she'd hung on another five years.

Until Rafe discovered the pleasures of a woman's body, and there was no place for a skinny ten-year-old girl with her heart in her eyes.

Holy shit.

She had been in love with him. Granted, it was a young girl's infatuation, but perhaps he could fan the flames of those dead embers again. They'd been close once. He'd even been the one to show her how to use a slingshot and climb a tree. Emma had been his friend. Rafe would make her that again, and more.

☙

Emma spent the first few days of her married life avoiding her husband. She asserted over and over that she was not *hiding*, she was simply choosing not to be in his company. Something in his eyes told her he wanted more from her than Emma was prepared to give.

Every hour or so, she felt his gaze on her, skimming over her trouser-clad form, making those damn goose bumps march up and down her skin. If only he hadn't shown her what it meant to be thoroughly kissed. Her lips tingled from the memory, betraying just how good it had been.

Dammit.

She attacked her saddle with frustration although she was supposed to be oiling the leather. Rafe needed to get out of her head for good. When she agreed to marry him, it wasn't supposed to be like this. Emma didn't want to be thinking about him constantly.

"You're scarce today."

Rafe's voice made her jump a foot. She dropped the oiling cloth and nearly fell on her head. He grabbed her arm, stopping her fall and compounding her embarrassment.

"No need to scare me half to death." She sounded breathless. "I, uh, didn't hear you come in."

Rafe let go of her arm and leaned against the wall beside him. "I didn't sneak if that's what you're thinking. I just wanted to see you."

Emma's gaze snapped to his, and she searched his face for the truth. Unable to read anything from his smile, she frowned at him. "Why?"

"You're my wife, Emma. I like to be with you."

Of all the answers he could've given, that was the last one she expected. He could have said something stupid or mushy, but instead he chose the direct route, deflating her annoyance like a pin in a bubble. Her impractical heart fluttered, and she scrambled for a response that wouldn't make her seem like a silly girl.

"Well, um, thanks. I really need to finish this." She picked up the rag from the floor and tried to focus on brushing off the bits of hay and dirt clinging to it.

He took the rag from her hands and set it on the saddle. Her heart thudded in earnest when he turned her to face him. Rafe removed her hat while his thumb tipped her chin up. His silver gaze searched hers until he apparently found what he was looking for.

As his mouth descended toward her, Emma was frozen in place, unable to run, unable to push away, unable to meet him halfway. His lips were gentle, exploring, giving her all the time in the world to protest.

She didn't.

He deepened the kiss until she couldn't tell where he ended and she began. It was like diving into a shady pond on a hot summer's day. Kissing Rafe enveloped all her senses, surrounded her and turned her into a quivering mess. Her mind whirled while the rest of her pulsed with need. A deep throb began inside her, a slow beat that gained momentum with each pull of his lips and each swipe of his rough tongue against hers.

Emma didn't end the kiss, he did. When he pulled away, she mewled and chased his mouth, eager for more. He kissed her lightly then set her away from him. She was in a fog, almost drunk from the kissing. With a roguish grin, he tipped his hat and walked away.

She had no idea how long she stood there, her nipples rock hard, her drawers wet with need and her lips buzzing. Reality splashed over her when two ranch hands walked into the barn talking. Their gravelly voices reminded her that she stood there like an idiot, likely grinning, while the world went on as if *nothing* had happened.

To Emma, something had happened, something momentous. Rafe had kissed her again, and she'd not only allowed it, she'd wanted more. Even ten minutes after he'd left, she could still feel the rasp of his whiskers against her face and the sweet taste of peppermint on his tongue. This wasn't at all what she wanted.

Emma was falling in love with her husband. Again.

It took almost half an hour for the raging erection in his trousers to go away. Rafe had to resist the urge to adjust himself for the twentieth time and just let the damn thing alone. He hadn't expected to almost fuck Emma on the barn floor, but damned if that wasn't exactly what he wanted to do. She was so sweet, hot and responsive to his kisses. A dream come true for any man, and she was his wife.

Kissing Emma had been the first step in his plan of seduction and it had worked, on both of them. He'd nearly forgotten his plan was to be friends before being lovers. Just touching Emma made every thought in his head disappear. He ran his hand down his face and blew out a breath.

Patience was going to win this race. Too bad he was going to have a hard time convincing the stallion in his britches.

ଔ

After a week of thinking up countless ways to avoid Rafe for self-preservation, including missing meals, Emma was starving. When she peeked her head around the corner, dinner was waiting for her. No one was in the kitchen, thank God, but a plate piled with biscuits and ham sat on the thick-planked tabletop. She waited a moment or two, and no one appeared. Her stomach rumbled like an old hound dog and she couldn't wait any longer.

"That's not for you."

Emma whirled around, clutching her heart and wearing a scowl. "Jesus Christ, Rafe. Stop scaring me!"

His gaze dropped to her shirt where her hand nestled between what she considered too-large breasts. Her traitorous nipples popped like corks.

"I'm sorry, honey. I wanted to invite you to a picnic lunch with me." The slow smile that spread across his face did wild things to her equilibrium.

"A picnic? Don't you have work to do? I know I do." A trickle of sweat snaked down her spine as she held herself rigid. No need for him to know any more about her condition, since he could clearly see she was affected by him already. "I don't have time for a picnic."

"Too bad because I have a surprise for you." He waggled his eyebrows, and a chuckle erupted from her throat.

"Don't try to charm your way into my heart or my britches, Rafe Sinclair. I won't stand for it." She snatched the biscuit off the plate and told her feet to move. They didn't listen and neither did her heart. It did a funny flip when a flash of hurt lit up his eyes.

"I just wanted to spend time with you, Em. It's been years since we did." He put his hat back on, pulling the brim low. "I'll leave you to your dinner then."

When Rafe turned to go, Emma took leave of her senses completely. "Wait. I'm sorry, Rafe, this whole marriage thing is new. I-I don't know how to do this."

That admission left a pink blaze across her cheeks.

Rafe held out his hand. "Neither do I but I do know how to have a picnic."

Pushing aside her instincts currently screaming inside her head, Emma stepped forward and took her husband's hand.

They rode out together, talking about happenings around the ranch, and the time passed more quickly than Emma anticipated.

The picnic was perfect. The clear blue skies, the fun, witty company, and the food all combined to bring back the easy familiarity Rafe and Emma had enjoyed as children. She forgot how funny he was until she laughed so hard her side hurt.

As she gazed up at him, she couldn't remember the last time she felt so relaxed. "What about my surprise?"

"Hmm? Oh, there is no surprise, I just wanted to get you to come with me." He put his hands behind his head and leaned against the oak tree. "You've been avoiding me, Em."

She stood, angry and humiliated at his treatment. Rafe *was* trying to manipulate her, and Emma couldn't let that happen.

"I'm not a young'un you can trick into doing what you want." She shook with the feelings rushing through her, most of which was embarrassment. Emma had allowed herself to start falling in love with him again, and he'd proven himself unworthy of that love. "You're a bastard, Rafe."

She marched toward her horse, a good head of steam building that would take a while to blow. Although angry with him, she didn't want to say something she'd regret later.

"Where are you going?" His boots scrambled for footing as he rose to chase her.

"Home and you're not invited." She untied Cinnamon's reins from the tree and put her foot in the stirrup.

Before she could haul herself up, he plucked her from the ground. Squawking, she hung onto his shoulders, trying to kick her way free. After she came dangerously close to his manly parts, he tsked at her.

"Oh no you don't, Mrs. Sinclair. You won't get me that way." Rafe threw her over his shoulder.

The breath whooshed from her body and all she could do was hang on until she got her wind back, so to speak. Rafe was in trouble when that happened.

Rafe held the squirming woman in place with both arms. Emma was stronger than he realized. He almost dumped her on her head more than once on the way back to the picnic spot.

"Dammit, Rafe, put me down," she puffed out.

"No, I won't." Rafe was determined she'd understand what he was doing. They'd been married less than two weeks, and he already knew it had been the right thing to do, regardless of the Circle S ranch. Emma might not accept it, but she was going to be married to Rafe for the rest of her life. If he was honest with himself, there wasn't another woman who could have fit so nicely in his life.

He set her down gently and lay on top of her before she could scramble away. After pinning her arms above her head and making sure she couldn't kick him, his body sighed with pleasure as her softness pressed against his hardness. A groan crept up his throat and he swallowed it back with difficulty.

Her eyes blazed with a mix of emotions. "Get off me."

"Not until you hear what I have to say."

She bucked beneath him, forcing his burgeoning erection into the hot cleft between her legs. He sucked in a breath as a zip of arousal ran through him from top to bottom. Emma must've realized what she was doing because she froze and her eyes grew wide as saucers.

"I know you can feel that." He moved his hips in a small circle, earning a gasp from his wife. "It's obvious to all and sundry that we fit together. I'm tired of fighting, Em. So tired."

She licked her lips and Rafe's dick jumped. Her gaze slid down between them then back up to his. "Get off me." Her whisper was barely audible.

"You don't mean that. Believe it or not, I like being married to you."

"Liar. You need me to keep this ranch. I won't warm your bed." A sheen of tears appeared in her eyes. "I will keep my dignity."

Rafe thought maybe he understood what was driving Emma's anger. "Ah, honey, I don't want to take your dignity. I just want to find that spark we had between us." He nuzzled her neck. "It's there, burning all the time no matter when or where. You can't deny it, Em. It's there."

She tried to bite his cheek but he moved just in time. "All I know is you kidnapped me with a lie and now you're keeping me hostage."

"Now who's lying? I didn't kidnap you." Rafe kissed her cheek, trailing his lips along her soft skin until he reached the pink shell of her ear. "We fit just right."

"No," she protested even as the rigidness of her body grew fainter. By the time he licked her ear, he could feel her heart pounding against his, could smell the sweetness of her arousal.

"Let me be your husband, truly your husband." He nipped her earlobe and blew gently in her ear. "I want you." Rafe let go of her arms and cupped her face. "Please."

This kiss was no peck, it was a fusion of mouths, tongue and teeth, accented by short bursts of breath. Her hands tangled in his hair as he deepened the kiss. Rafe couldn't stop himself from touching her. As his fingers skimmed down her curves, he shook with the force of his hunger for his wife.

God, he needed her. "Please, Em, let me in."

"Mmm, no, I can't." She bit his shoulder. "You're confusing me."

He chuckled as his lips found home again. Slow, deep kisses pulled him down into the depths of an arousal he'd never felt before. Rafe burned so hot, he was afraid he might explode in his trousers like a greenhorn.

"Please, Em, please." Even to his own ears, he sounded desperate and needy.

Then Emma did something so unexpected, Rafe thought even she was surprised.

"Yes."

His eyes flew open and they stared at each other for two beats.

"Are you sure?"

Her mouth opened and closed. "No."

With something akin to pain, Rafe rose onto his elbows. As he trailed his thumb along her jaw, the throb in his body pulsed hard and fast. "I want you so bad my teeth ache." He smiled.

"Why did you stop then?" Her pupils were nearly black with desire.

A slight tremble in her skin spoke of passion. Rafe had known it was there and he was absurdly pleased he'd been the one to bring it out.

"You need to be ready to rip up that paper of yours, then we can do more than sparking."

Emma frowned. "What if I don't want to rip it up?"

Rafe groaned. "Then we're in for a really long fifty years, darlin'."

Chapter Five

Emma rode like the hounds of hell were after her. Cinnamon, bless her heart, kept up the grueling ride for twenty minutes before she started to show signs of fatigue. Her coat glistened with sweat in the heat yet she continued on, giving her heart into the run. Emma slowed her down gradually, finally easing into a trot that brought them to the stream that bordered the Triple R. A yearning to return to the home she'd left behind swept through Emma. It had all happened so fast, she had no chance to even think about what she was losing.

After her picnic with Rafe, her body thrummed with need, her head ached and her heart was doing flips. She'd been about to throw away her control after ten minutes of Rafe's kisses. What was she going to do?

"Are you okay, miss?"

Emma whirled around to find a fancy-dressed gentleman on a beautiful Kentucky walking horse. He had blond hair and blue eyes and wore one of those fancy bowler hats with a pinstriped suit. His smile shone in the sun.

"Who are you?" Her hand crept toward the pistol riding her hip.

"No need to be alarmed. I'm William Sinclair, or Billy if you prefer. I am Raphael Sinclair's cousin." The stranger's smile widened. "Who might you be?"

Emma didn't trust the man, but he was friendly enough and a rapid glance told her he wasn't armed. "I'm Emma Rad— Sinclair, Rafe's wife."

Branded

The shock washed over his face so fast, she thought she'd imagined it, but Billy's expression changed with her pronouncement.

"I hadn't realized Rafe had married. So quickly after Uncle Lee died too." He shook his head. "Shame that happened. He was a sweet old man."

Emma knew right then Billy Sinclair was dangerous. His sickly sweet tone would make a honey bee roll over dead. Nothing in his eyes could be even remotely called grief. He must've been eyeballing the Circle S for his own like a buzzard circling its prey. She realized Rafe had been in danger of losing the ranch and in a strange way, was glad she'd played a part in keeping it from this dandy.

"Yep, that he was. Are you lost, Mr. Sinclair?" Cinnamon shifted beneath her, and she calmed the mare with her knees.

"Oh no. I was on my way to see Raphael when I saw you riding. I thought I'd stop and offer my assistance." Another blinding smile. "I'm guessing you don't need any judging by the way you handle that horse. She's lovely."

His gaze lingered on Emma's breasts a few moments too long and it annoyed her.

"No, I don't need any help. Thanks for the offer though." With a tip of her hat, she cantered back toward the Circle S and Rafe.

Something told her she had to warn him about Billy Sinclair.

Rafe was picking a rock out of his horse's hoof when Emma came riding back in, kicking up dust and dirt. He waved away the cloud, absurdly pleased to see she had ridden straight toward him.

"You know a man named Billy Sinclair?" She hopped down off the mare.

Rafe's gut churned at the mention of his sidewinder cousin. "Unfortunately, I do. Why?"

She glanced in the distance and pointed. "I ran into him at Blue's Creek. If I'm right, he'll be here any minute."

"Shit." Rafe threw the pick into the ground. "He's enough of a weasel to give varmints a bad name. My grandfather's nephew up and married some poker-playing fancy woman from San Francisco and they had Billy. Whole pack of them are like bad pennies."

"I figured he wasn't your favorite cousin. His charm is worse than yours." One eyebrow arched. "And that's saying a lot."

Rafe laughed and snatched her up in a bear hug, kissing her hard and quick before she could object. Her brown eyes widened in surprise, but she didn't pull away. In fact, she kissed him back. A tiny flame of hope surged to life inside him. He went in for a second kiss when the sound of hoofbeats echoed around them.

He stared at Emma and her mouth tightened in a white line.

"We'll finish this later."

She humphed and extracted herself from his arms.

"How sweet. You and your new bride seem to be well matched." Billy's smile resembled a wolf's rather than a human's. "You're both wearing guns and trousers." He laughed and dismounted.

Rafe stepped up to his cousin and barely controlled the urge to mark the pretty man's face. "What do you want, Billy?"

"Truthfully I wanted the Circle S, but it appears I'm too late for that. You saved the ranch by marrying a female." He nodded toward Emma. "I'm sure her identity has been validated by the proper authorities."

When Rafe realized Billy was insinuating Emma wasn't female, he saw the flash of hurt in her eyes and his fists clenched. Her mask of indifference and roughness slammed down and, without a word, she walked Cinnamon into the barn.

"You insult my wife again, Billy, and I'll break you in two." Rafe crowded the blond man, cursing the fact their heritage made them the same height. In pure bulk, however, Rafe could pound Billy into the dirt.

"I didn't insult her," Billy protested with another one of his smarmy grins. "I only came to have a little visit. I figured you

Branded

would want family around you so soon after your granddaddy's death. You wouldn't turn away family now, would you?"

Son of a bitch. Rafe had forgotten just how sneaky and low-down Billy was. He'd just invited himself to the ranch and used a dead man to do it.

"Where were you six weeks ago when he died? Wasn't he your favorite uncle?" Rafe poked Billy in the chest, pleased to see a mark of dirt left behind on the fancy fabric.

"I was in San Francisco on business." His gaze flickered to the barn where Emma had gone. "The way I heard it, you had less than a week to get hitched. I got here as soon as I could to help since we're family. Looks like I'm too late though."

"There wasn't anything to help with. Em and I have known each other all our lives. It was only natural for us to get hitched. Just happened sooner than expected is all."

"Really? Hmm, the way I heard it, every single woman in the county was hunting you down. Apparently you grabbed the closest thing you could find to keep the ranch." Billy laughed. "Not that I blame you. I'd rather be married to a manly woman than a grasping gold digger."

This time Rafe didn't control the urge. He punched Billy so hard in the jaw, Rafe felt it in his shoulder, and damned if his hand didn't sting like a bitch. Billy went down in the dirt like a bag of bones. Rafe stepped over the inert body, pleased with his handiwork.

Lying on the ground could only improve Billy's position in the world. Rafe went in search of Emma. Their marriage just got much more complicated.

CR

Another week went by and the tension between Emma and Rafe grew to enormous proportions. They slept in the same room, but still separate. Sleep was hard in coming for both of them, judging by the amount of noise he made from the floor tossing and turning. Emma wanted Rafe, but she didn't know how to tell him.

She watched him from the shadows in the barn as he worked his new colt in the corral. His body called to her, the symphony of muscles and sinew playing a song. The music lilted through her, leaving waves of tingles she just couldn't shake. He was a beautiful man, even if he was a pushy fool. She really should step out of the barn and alert him to her presence, but something held her back.

A laugh reminded her of the other man in the corral. Billy had turned into an itch they couldn't scratch, the fish that stank up the house. He sat on the fence and watched as Rafe worked. Emma smiled when she remembered the shiner Rafe had given him. It was the first time she could remember a man standing up for her. She'd been listening from the barn when Billy had insulted her again.

Rafe had laid him out in one punch. Some little girl deep inside her had squealed with feminine delight. She didn't allow it to continue though. The last thing she needed was to fall in love with her husband because he had punched a fool.

"Emma? Where are you?" Georgette's voice floated through the late afternoon air.

Emma groaned and just barely controlled the urge to slap her forehead. Things around the Circle S just kept getting better and better. Emma glanced at Rafe, who looked like he did when the horde of women had invaded his ranch. She stepped out of the barn and told herself not to feel guilty that she'd been watching him. He was, after all, her husband.

"It's my stepsister." She walked toward the corral. "I guess the visiting has started in earnest now."

"Does it have to?" Rafe huffed out a breath and kept the colt going in a circle even as it tugged on the reins.

"I don't think we have a choice." She walked toward the gate, ignoring Billy's smile and hoping like hell he hadn't realized she'd been spying on Rafe. That would be mortifying.

Emma found Georgette standing on the front porch, looking like a confection in her yellow and white lacy dress. Her bonnet was completely impractical for a hot Texas day, but it matched her outfit, which Emma assumed was the point. She wondered how it felt to spend so much time thinking about clothes and appearances.

"What are you doing here, Georgette?" Emma slapped her hat on her thigh, kicking up a small cloud of dust from her work with Blackjack.

"Oh, my, you're so dirty. You're a married woman now. Why aren't you in the house doing wife things?" Georgette's expression was comical, almost horrified by Emma's condition.

"I'm working. That's what I do every day except Sunday." Emma put her hat back on and sighed. "I repeat, what are you doing here?"

"Papa thought I should come see you to make sure you were, ah, doing well." She tittered. "Since you didn't have a woman to talk to about, ah, things." A blush spread across her creamy cheeks.

Emma couldn't help it. She chuckled, which turned into a gut-buster as the hilarity of the situation hit her. She laughed so hard she got a stitch in her side and tears rolled down her cheeks.

"Don't laugh at me." Georgette sounded so put out, it made Emma laugh even harder. "Mr. Sinclair, control your wife."

Rafe's feet appeared beside hers. "You okay, Em?" He leaned down and whispered, "What's so funny?"

Emma waved her hand since she didn't want to explain that Georgette had come to give her sex advice. The very idea was ridiculous coming from a seventeen-year-old. Rafe slapped at Emma's back as if she were choking. Emma kicked him in the shin to make him stop. Her humor fled when he cursed and hopped away from her.

"Emma!" Georgette's mouth dropped open. "Did you just kick him?"

Billy stepped up to the young blonde, taking her gloved hand in his and bringing it to his lips. "Ma'am, might I say that you are as lovely as a daffodil in spring."

Before Emma could say a word, Georgette giggled and looked at him from beneath her lashes. If Emma didn't know any better, she'd think her cousin was a trained whore.

"Why, sir, you're being too forward." Georgette did not remove her hand from his, no matter her words.

"I can't help myself." Billy smiled, showing his pearly white teeth. "You inspire me."

Emma pulled Georgette away from him. "Leave her alone, Billy. She's a child."

"I am not a child." Georgette stepped back toward Billy. "I am a woman."

Emma didn't believe that for a second. "If Pa catches you with this man, I guarantee he isn't going to treat you like a woman." She looked at Rafe. "Aren't you going to say anything?"

Rafe shook his head and limped away. "Try to help and get kicked, then she expects me to be some girl's father." He humphed and kept on going.

"You best leave Georgette alone. My pa wouldn't take kindly to a smooth-talking man like you taking advantage of her." She poked a finger into the man's chest. "You think Rafe was tough on your face? That was a love tap compared to what my pa will do. Let's go, Georgette."

Although her stepsister clearly didn't want to, she allowed Emma to lead her away. Emma would have to keep an eye on her stepsister and the smooth-talking man. There was trouble brewing there.

Rafe had resisted the urge to spank Emma. His hands shook and itched with the effort to control himself. It had been weeks and she hadn't relented yet. He didn't know what to do. Kicking him in front of company was not only embarrassing, it notched up his temper something fierce.

Obviously his attempts at seduction were failing. They couldn't go on like that any longer, or Rafe might go plumb loco. He'd have to think of some other way to get Emma to change her mind.

Whiskey might help. Well, it'd definitely help him anyway.

He spent the rest of the day keeping his distance from everyone but his horse. Most of his ranch hands knew when to leave him be. The embarrassing thing was, they must've all known what was, or wasn't, going on with him and Emma. It annoyed the hell out of Rafe, almost as much as the clawing need in his gut.

After a long day repairing a busted fence, he came back to the ranch late, after suppertime, with a yowling belly and a still surly disposition. When he stepped into the kitchen, he found

Emma sitting at the table, a cup of coffee in her hand. Her eyes glittered in the lamplight, hiding her thoughts from him.

"Thought maybe some coyotes got to you."

He closed the door behind him and weighed his words carefully. "I don't take kindly to my wife treating me like the village idiot. If you're going to be married to me, you're going to treat me with respect, just as I treat you."

Her fingers tightened on the cup. "What does that mean?"

"It means I don't kick you, you don't kick me." He tossed his gloves on the table. "I want to make this work, Em. Accept that we're married and get on with it."

She stood abruptly, knocking her chair to the floor with a bang. "I don't want to be married to you."

Rafe's blood zipped through him like a hot river of fury. "Too bad because the deed is done. You and me are together for good."

"It is not done." She pointed toward the door. "We can undo this right now."

He shushed her. "Not a chance," he whispered harshly. When he got within an inch of her, the fresh scent of Emma mixed with the heat of anger, a heady combination. "You are my wife and you will remain my wife."

Emma opened her mouth to argue, and Rafe wrapped his arm around her and yanked her flush against him.

"*My. Wife.*"

When his mouth descended on hers, she could have pulled away, could have fought against him, but she didn't. It was hot, hard and Rafe put every bit of his frustration and need into it.

Emma responded by throwing her arms around his neck and grabbing hold of his hair. Rafe's body heat mixed with hers, their clothing a barrier he resented. Her breasts pillowed against his chest, the nipples twin points of arousal. He groaned into her mouth as their tongues twined together.

Up until a month ago, he'd never imagined kissing Emma. Now he couldn't imagine kissing anyone else with the fire that flamed between them. His cock lengthened and hardened, straining at the seam of his trousers and pushing into her softness.

She pulled his hair so hard, he actually saw stars. Rafe stepped back, dazed by the kiss and by the assault. Emma breathed as if she'd run a mile. Her cheeks were flushed and her lips as bright as a strawberry. Rafe wanted nothing more than to see her like that in their bed, beneath him. He'd become obsessed with his own wife.

"I can't do this anymore, Rafe. Y-you're confusing me. We had an agreement." Her voice, raspy and lower than normal, sent a shiver of desire through him.

"No, you told me not to bed you. There's a world of difference, Em." More than a world of difference, but he wasn't going to argue the point.

She sputtered. "I-I meant all of this." Pointing a finger at him, she narrowed her eyes. "The picnic, the niceness, all of it. You're trying to seduce me with kisses and it won't work."

Rafe sucked in a deep breath and organized his thoughts before answering. "Maybe I am, but you're letting me. And before you open your mouth to yell at me again, know this. I can smell you, your arousal. I can tell by looking at you that you enjoyed what we just did, that you're aching with a need to find out what happens next."

Rafe forced himself to walk toward the door, needing fresh air to cool his burning flesh.

"You lie," she shot at his back.

Without turning around, Rafe shook his head. "You're lying to yourself, Em. Things would be a lot easier if you would admit you were wrong."

He blocked out her protests and headed outside, toward the bunkhouse. Hopefully the men were playing poker and had some good hooch on hand so he could find some way to forget about Emma, forget about the way his body wanted her so much his goddamn teeth ached. First he'd have to lose the erection currently pulsing between his legs. The last thing he needed was the men knowing he left the house without satisfying him or Emma.

How did everything get so topsy-turvy?

Emma's pulse pounded through her like a big drum, beating with a rhythm so loud it made her eardrums rattle.

She'd never felt so off-kilter, confused or needy in her entire life. Rafe had been right about one thing, she was aroused, painfully so. Her breasts ached while an intense need thrummed through her pussy.

She went to the sink and pumped some cold water. After splashing it on her heated face, she took deep breaths and tried to talk some sense into her shaking, quaking self.

Rafe was dangerous, even more dangerous than she'd imagined. Emma thought she had put him out of her heart and mind a long time ago, but apparently she'd been mistaken. She'd only shoved him to a dark corner and all it took to yank her love for him out of the shadows was a few kisses.

Dammit.

She hadn't wanted to get married and she sure didn't want to be in love with her husband. Turned out, she was, on both counts.

Chapter Six

"You know he's just horny."

Emma whipped her head around to find Billy staring at her. He'd been trying to start trouble between her and Rafe from the moment he arrived. She knew that sidewinder was up to no good. The last thing she needed was Rafe's cousin making things worse between her and Rafe. He'd never come to bed, or at least to their room, the night before. Emma hadn't slept a wink all night.

"Go find someone else to bother," she snapped.

Billy climbed up and perched on top of the fence. He was wearing another one of his fancy suits and that ridiculous bowler hat. She wondered if he'd spent all his money on clothes, which might be why he was hanging around the ranch—his money had been spent already. No doubt he wanted the Circle S to be his and with it, all the ranch's funds at his disposal. He reminded her of a bloodsucking leech.

"I'm not trying to bother you, Emma. I see how he treats you, like one of his conquests." Billy shook his head. "You're far too valuable for the likes of Raphael."

"Just because you keep using his full name doesn't make what you say any more interesting." She glanced at the sun and figured it was a good time to eat breakfast, a great escape from this blundering fool.

As she walked the mare in a circle to cool her down, Billy continued as if Emma hadn't already told him she wasn't interested.

Branded

"It's a shame he went into town last night. All the ranch hands knew about it too. Why do you think they're snickering behind your back?" Billy hopped down from the fence and walked toward her, the perpetual grin on his handsome face. "I know you don't know me very well, Emma, but I'd like to think we could be friends."

Emma scowled at him, trying to maintain her cool while wondering if Rafe really had gone into town. Had he gone to see a whore?

"Look, Billy, I'm not interested in being charmed by you, and I am done listening to your lies, so go peddle your wares to someone else." With her head held high and her heart heavy, Emma went into the cool interior of the barn to escape. She ran into Horace, one of the older ranch hands, as he was leaving. His gaze darted every way but to hers and he skedaddled out of the building like his tail was on fire.

Holy God, maybe Billy was right. It was mortifying enough to be married against her will. If her husband was visiting whores two hours after having his tongue in her mouth, Emma would kill him.

Not that she was jealous, of course.

A big fat lie was only a lie if someone else knew about it. Emma only lied to herself, so it wasn't a lie. It was self-preservation.

Rafe put his hand to the small of his back and stretched. He'd spent the night in the stall with his horse, rather than let anyone know he'd avoided his own bed. He scratched at his whiskers and figured enough time had passed that Emma wasn't in the house anymore.

When Rafe stepped into the house, he knew it was empty. Thank God. He wasn't ready to face Emma just yet.

After making himself a couple of fried eggs, Rafe poured himself a mug of coffee and sat at the table. He winced as the hot brew burned down his throat, bringing tears to his eyes. The door slammed open and Emma filled the doorway.

Her face promised retribution to whatever, or whomever, had angered her. Rafe had a feeling he'd find out quick enough who it was.

"Mornin', Em." He dug into his eggs, ignoring the fire-breathing woman staring holes in him.

"Did you sleep in the bunkhouse last night?" She kept her voice low, but it shook with whatever bee was in her bonnet.

"No, I didn't." That was at least the truth.

"Did you sleep in the house?"

"No." He forked some eggs into his mouth and kept his gaze level.

Without another word, she stormed past him and headed upstairs. As he listened to the thumps and bumps coming from his bedroom, he wondered if he ought to find out what was going on.

Crash.

Nope, too dangerous. He finished his breakfast in record time and hurried out the door before she could come back with a weapon to finish him off. The last thing he needed was another confrontation with Emma. He'd wait until she cooled off before he talked to her. She was a hothead, that was for certain.

And she wasn't even a redhead.

Emma packed her things as fast as she could. She knocked over the pitcher in her haste and left the mess on the floor for Rafe to clean up. Served him right if he slipped and fell, stupid bastard.

How dare he flaunt his philandering right in front of her? Had he no shame? She'd thought it was a bad idea to marry Rafe, now she knew it. Emma couldn't go home to her father because he'd send her right back. Too many bridges had been burned between them.

She'd take a train into Houston and visit with Aunt Harriet for a while. The retired schoolteacher would be only too happy to have her niece there. They'd corresponded regularly for years, no reason why Emma had to have an invitation.

Her mind made up, Emma slung her saddlebags over her shoulder and headed back downstairs. Nobody stopped her, nobody even spoke to her. She felt like a fish flopping on a boat with no air. The Circle S was a nice ranch but it wasn't home. It wasn't right for her, she'd never fit in, especially as Rafe's wife.

It wasn't just her heart that hurt as she saddled Cinnamon. It was her pride. She'd fought all her life to prove her worth as a person, not as a woman. Now as a wife, she had made mistake after mistake with Rafe. She should have listened to her heart or her body, instead of her head. Emma didn't know if she was doing the right thing, but she couldn't stay on the Circle S anymore.

As she rode toward town, she considered whether to turn back and tell Rafe where she was going. In the end, she kept riding, leaving behind the miserable marriage she never wanted, and heading into the future that yawned like an empty canyon.

"Where's my sister?" Georgette appeared, poking her head into the stall Rafe was working in.

He frowned. "I haven't seen her in a couple of hours. She must be around here somewhere." Rafe wasn't about to admit he had started to find his wife several times, but talked himself out of it. He didn't want to look as if he was giving in.

Emma was mad at him for some reason, and he'd be damned if he'd let her control his actions because of her moods. Georgette pouted prettily, no doubt a practiced move.

"She was supposed to come over for dinner today but she didn't." The young woman sighed. "I had to ride over here in the heat to find out why. Did you, um, wear her out last night?"

"Jesus Christ!" Rafe stood, staring at Georgette in horror. "What the hell are you talking about?" He'd never really spent time with the girl, but sure as shit, she should not be talking about sex with her brother-in-law.

"Well, you are newlyweds and you're both young and healthy." Georgette's eyes widened as she backed away from him.

"Somebody ought to take a switch to your backside, little girl. Real ladies don't talk to men about their bed business." Rafe couldn't believe the girl's audacity. "Does your pa know you're over here talking like this?"

"Sort of." She bit her lip. "He thinks she didn't want to visit him, and he's been mad as a wet hen because of it. I came over to make sure she was okay."

"I'll bring Georgette home." Billy appeared beside her. "I've got nothing but time on my hands. I'd love to meet the neighbors."

"They're not your neighbors." Rafe shoved past Billy. "You have no business going over there."

"They will be soon. Without a wife, you'll lose the ranch in a week, cousin." Billy grinned and took Georgette's arm. "May I escort you home?"

"Excuse me?" Rafe stepped into Billy's face, coming nose-to-nose with his cousin. "What do you mean, without a wife?"

"Didn't you know? Why, the new Mrs. Sinclair is gone, left this morning. I expect she's halfway to someplace else by now." Billy's grin grew wider, more feral.

Rafe's heart slammed against his rib cage. Emma had left the ranch? He didn't think things were that bad. For God's sake, they were just having a newlywed spat, not enough to break up the marriage. Unless someone else was meddling where he didn't belong.

"What did you say to her?" Rafe grabbed Billy by the shirt and yanked him up a good six inches off the ground.

"You're wrinkling my shirt." Billy wiggled but couldn't break Rafe's hold.

"What did you do?" Rafe snarled, shaking his cousin. "Did you hurt her?" Billy wouldn't be walking out of there if he had.

"No, I believe you did. Something about not spending the night in your bed and treating your wife like a ranch hand."

Georgette gasped, and Rafe lowered Billy to his feet. Rafe scowled at his cousin, fiercely denying he'd done anything wrong.

"I never treated her—" he began.

"Oh yes you did. You took her from her home and everything she knew." Georgette's face flushed. "She didn't want to get married, but Pa threatened to kick her off the ranch if she didn't. You treated her like a-a horse to be sold to the highest bidder. Emma never had a choice. You and Pa made it for her."

"Of course she had a choice," Rafe protested, but in his heart he recognized the girl was telling the truth. Emma hadn't had a choice in the matter. A young woman did as her father

Branded

bade even if she didn't want to. Rafe had never intended to harm Emma or make her life miserable. Truth was, he thought she'd jump at the chance seeing as how nobody else had offered for her hand.

That was, of course, just an excuse to ease his conscience.

Rafe hadn't considered the fact that Emma truly didn't want to marry him. He was smart, young, passably good-looking and he owned a thriving ranch.

Apparently, he was also a horse's ass.

He had to find her, to tell her...something. Although he wasn't exactly sure what he'd say, Rafe knew he couldn't let Emma leave, not without seeing her. He'd known her most of his life, respected her and owed her more than what she'd been given.

He pointed a finger at Billy. "You're going to stay away from me and mine from now on. I'll have Horace escort Georgette home."

Georgette frowned. "Who's Horace?"

Rafe kissed her cheek. "Thank you for coming by, Georgette. If you were five years older, I might have had to choose between you two."

"Oh, Rafe." She giggled and blushed. "I'm older than I look."

Before Rafe got himself in trouble with another Radcliff, he headed for his saddle. Time to find his wife and grovel at her feet and hope he wasn't too late to save their marriage.

Emma left her horse at the livery with a promise from Byron that Cinnamon would be returned to the Circle S later that day. She felt bad leaving her behind, but the afternoon train didn't have room for a last minute equine passenger. Emma could have waited until morning to leave when there was room for Cinnamon, but her anger might fade if she didn't leave right away. She didn't want that to happen.

Already she regretted not telling Rafe exactly what she felt. Pages of things she wanted to say flipped through her head. She stood on the train platform clenching and unclenching her fists, trying to remind herself that she was worthy of love.

Just not her husband's.

65

Emma had gone into the marriage believing it was doomed. Perhaps that was the wrong way to go about it but what's done was done. She'd been proved right anyway. Now she just had to figure out how the heck to get an annulment and get unmarried to Rafe.

The thought made her stomach hurt, dang it to hell.

She sat heavily on the bench and put her head in her hands. The truth was, while she'd expected the marriage to fail, some small part of her had hoped it wouldn't. She loved him, had always loved him. Being married to him had been a lifelong dream, even if she had tried to block it out. The oppressive feeling of hopelessness lifted a smidge. It wasn't that she was running from what she had. She was running from what she wanted but didn't have.

"Going somewhere?"

Emma's head snapped up to find Rafe standing over her, a confused expression on his handsome face. Her heart did a somersault like the traitorous organ it was.

"I can't be married to you anymore," she blurted.

Rafe frowned. "Why not? Em, I know things aren't perfect but I think we should stay married. You felt what I did, don't deny it. We fit."

Self-righteousness reared its ugly head. "So you can keep your ranch, right? You don't want that snake Billy to get his greasy hands on the Circle S so you'll do anything to keep it." She waved her hand in dismissal, hurt making her voice catch. "Not good enough."

Rafe got down on one knee beside her. "Please don't leave."

Emma wavered between angry and hopeful. She steeled herself to resist him. "If you're going to disrespect me enough to go off and see a whore three weeks after we got married, then I just can't stay."

"What? I didn't go see any whore, and I'm a little surprised you'd even suggest that. I haven't been with a woman since you agreed to marry me." He took off his hat and his black hair beckoned her fingers. "I reckoned I owed you at least that. I know I owe you a lot more."

Shock and disbelief coursed through her. "Then where did you spend last night?"

Branded

He pursed his lips and looked down at the wood planking beneath him. "In a stall. I didn't want to stay in the house or the bunkhouse so I saved face and hid. I'm not proud of any of it and I'm damn sure tired of pretending all the time."

Emma's eyes pricked with relief. He looked too earnest and was enough of a straight shooter to not lie to her. Thank God he hadn't been unfaithful.

"Please, Emma, come home with me." Rafe's normally shuttered eyes were brimming with honesty and regret.

Was that enough for her? Did she want a man who didn't love her but wanted her as a wife? It was typical of most marriages, so why did Emma insist on anything different, especially considering why they got married? Rafe had been the only man she'd ever loved or wanted to marry. Now that she had him, she was throwing him away.

Emma stood and picked up her valise. "Okay, let's go."

Rafe let loose a whoop and grabbed her in a bear hug, swinging her around until her stomach almost rebelled. She dropped her bag and hung on for dear life. When he stopped spinning, she noticed the huge grin on his face and felt better about her decision.

"You'll be faithful to me, t-to us, until I, umm, adjust to being married?" She had to ask even if the answer wasn't truthful.

He kissed her hard and quick. "Always."

"Let me down then before I decorate your shirt."

He laughed and set her on her feet. "Let's go get your horse. She at the livery?"

"Yep, that fool Byron told me he'd make sure she got back to the Circle S." Emma was surprised when Rafe picked up her saddlebags and tucked her arm into his. She shouldn't be too shocked, after all Rafe was the only man who treated her as a woman. With these small gestures, he'd made her feel like a lady and that made her throat tighten.

"Then let's go rescue her."

They walked toward the livery in comfortable silence, nodding and greeting folks, with Rafe's horse trailing behind them. It felt almost normal when one man called her Mrs.

67

Sinclair. By the time they arrived at the livery, Emma's smile was genuine.

Until she found Cinnamon's stall empty.

"Where's the horse, Byron?" Emma's voice was laced with worry and anger.

Byron's gaze darted back and forth between Emma and Rafe. He scratched his whiskers and flipped back his greasy black hair. "Umm, that feller from your ranch came by. Kinda fancy-looking."

"Billy was here?" Rafe growled. "He's supposed to be at the ranch. What the hell was he doing in town?"

"Well, he said he was a Sinclair and was headed back to the ranch." Byron wiped his brow with a dirty cloth. "So I, uh, let him take the mare."

Emma's fist flew before Rafe could stop her. Byron fell back into the wall, blood streaming from his mouth. Damn, his new wife had a hell of a right hook.

"Jesus, why the hell did you hit me?" Byron gingerly felt his mouth. "I think you knocked out a tooth."

"Good. Next time don't give away my mare. Billy Sinclair is a thief and a liar." Emma visibly shook as she stood over Byron.

"Give us another horse and maybe we can catch him." Rafe started looking in the other stalls.

"They's all gone, Mr. Sinclair." Byron's voice trembled.

Rafe took a deep breath and blew it out. "Do you have a buggy we can use then?" The gelding couldn't carry both of them all the way back to the ranch. At least with a buggy they could make good time. He knew Emma wouldn't stay behind and a buggy was a solution.

"Just that old one in the back. Lotsa folks are visiting today." Byron scuttled sideways, away from Emma.

"So you thought with all the horses gone, you could go drinking or sleeping, right?" She kicked at his feet. "Mike should fire you."

Mike was the owner of the livery, away at his sister's for a month. He'd missed Rafe and Emma's wedding and apparently his business was in trouble with this moron in charge.

"Let's go see if we can hook the buggy up to Diamond. He's pulled a wagon before."

Rafe took Emma's arm and tried to move her. It appeared his wife wasn't through with Byron yet.

"If anything happens to Cinnamon, you owe me about five hundred dollars." She pointed at him. "For her and all the foals she'd birth. You've given away a purebred mare."

Byron shook his head. "I ain't got five hunnert dollars!"

"Then you'd better hope we find her safe and sound." She finally loosened up enough for Rafe to pull her away.

"We'll find her. I'm sure Billy's headed back there to settle in as owner of the Circle S." Rafe's anger at his cousin was running a close second to his relief at convincing Emma to stay. The blond man had no idea how much trouble he'd brought on himself.

It took all three of them, but they got the harness on Diamond and pulled the buggy from the tall grass. The seat was cracked and had dead leaves on it, but it appeared serviceable. Emma didn't seem to care. She climbed in and picked up the reins.

"Let's go, Sinclair." She glared at Byron one last time. "We'll be back to deal with you."

Byron nodded jerkily and ran back into the livery.

"I think you scared him." Rafe joined his wife in the buggy.

"I wanted to kick his ass," she groused as she spurred Diamond into motion.

"I think you did that too." He patted her knee. "Any chance I could take the reins?"

Emma snorted. "Not likely. I have a feeling with this old thing, it's going to be a bumpy ride."

Rafe took her advice and held on as his wife drove back to the ranch. She worked the reins like a professional muleskinner, keeping the buggy's wheels on the ground and maneuvering the old bucket. It was one more surprise that just added another layer to Emma, a piece of the puzzle that was his new wife.

When she lost control of the buggy, he didn't know who was more shocked. One minute they were moving along past

Blackfoot Canyon, the next thing he knew the buggy left the trail and tumbled down the incline. He heard Diamond whinny and the crack of the wood as the buggy splintered on the rocks. Rafe slammed into the ground hard enough to steal his breath as he landed at the bottom of the canyon. A sharp crack echoed through his left leg and then pain roared through him.

Chapter Seven

Emma spat out a mouthful of leaves and groaned. Her head pounded, her wrist shouted and about a hundred spots on her body complained. It took a minute to catch her breath enough to remember what happened.

"Rafe?" she called as she got to her knees. A wave of nausea gripped her as blood rushed to her head. She swallowed back the bile then tried to stand. "Rafe?"

When he didn't answer, panic clawed at her. Had he survived the fall? Damn old buggy and reins, probably snapped from the strain. Yet she'd been driving, so if anything happened to Rafe, it was her fault. She didn't know what she'd do if he'd been killed. Her heart rebelled at the thought.

It gave her the impetus to stand and focus her gaze. She swayed a bit, but kept upright, which was a good sign. Glancing around the canyon, she saw pieces of the buggy everywhere. It almost looked as though the damn thing had exploded. Diamond was nowhere to be seen, more than likely he'd headed for home. She also didn't see a sign of her husband.

"Rafe?"

She stepped carefully around the debris, looking for a sign of the blue shirt he'd been wearing. Her wrist throbbed a bit so she took her neckerchief and tied it tightly using her right hand and teeth. After ten minutes of searching the bottom of the canyon without finding him, she widened her search.

Five minutes later, she found him, lying on a rock at the bottom of the canyon like a hunter's prize. Her heart stopped beating for a moment when she saw the blood on his head and the awkward angle of his leg. Emma ran to him repeating his name under her breath until she felt his warm skin.

"Oh thank God." She ran a shaky hand down her face, then wiped the blood on her pants. Her injuries were minor compared to his.

The wound on his head was bleeding as they usually do, but fortunately it wasn't deep. She used a bit of moss from the rock to staunch the blood. When she felt his leg, he woke up with a scream, startling both of them.

"Shit!" He tried to sit up but fell back against the rock.

"Rafe, it's Emma." She cupped his cheek. "I think your leg is broken."

He looked up with pain-filled eyes. "I'm sorry."

Emma shook her head. "What are you sorry for? I was driving the stupid buggy that nearly killed you." Tears clogged her throat. "I almost killed both of us, Rafe."

He nuzzled her hand. "It would've happened if I'd been driving, Em. We're both alive and that's what's important." He hissed in a breath as he tried to shift positions. "I don't think I can move."

Emma could and would help him. She'd save both of them or die trying.

"I'm going to make a splint for your leg. Stay here."

He sighed. "I can't move, so I doubt I'll be going anywhere."

Emma was a woman on a mission. She gathered up pieces of wood from the buggy to make a splint for his leg, then picked up what was left of the reins. The old leather was completely worn through. The ragged edge proved to her that strain had caused the accident.

Strain that had been caused by her driving.

Shaking her head to tuck the guilt away, she went back to Rafe and set the supplies down. His eyes were closed but he was breathing. Unsure if he was awake or asleep, she starting laying the wood on either side of the wound, using her foot to snap six inches off one to fit his leg. She used her knife to cut strips of the reins and bind the wood to his leg.

Rafe didn't make a sound, which knocked Emma's worries to nearly frantic. After making sure the splint was secure, she sat next to his head and touched his cheek.

"Rafe?"

He didn't respond and she worried even more. Granted, he was warm, breathing, but his head was bleeding and he apparently was unable to wake up.

Rafe needed a doctor and fast.

Emma had to build a travois for him using the rest of the buggy. She worked like a madwoman ripping apart the leather from the seat and the canopy to make the sling for his body. Sweat streamed down her face, making her cuts and eyes sting, but she ignored it. Time was too short to worry about small inconveniences.

She fashioned a harness of sorts from the longest part of the reins to wrap around her shoulders so she could pull him. The hardest part would be getting him on the travois—he was not a small man.

After unsuccessfully trying to wake him again, Emma positioned the travois on his left side, then pushed him up enough to slide it under halfway. Her arms screamed as she moved him inch by inch onto the sling. His broken leg stuck on the wooden frame, so she had to move it, eliciting a long moan of pain from Rafe.

He didn't wake up, thank God.

She harnessed herself to the travois and brought him down from the rocks as gently as she could. When she reached the bottom, the grass made it easier to pull him, but it was still hard. She dug her feet into the ground as she walked, step by step, to the shallowest part of the canyon. From there, she could get him to the top and then go for help. There was no way she'd leave him at the bottom to fall prey to a rain deluge or worse, critters of the night.

By the time she'd gone half the distance, Emma could've cried from the pain in her shoulders and arms. She kept pushing the pain aside, remembering that Rafe was hurt because of her. She'd run away from him, and she'd been driving when the accident occurred. It didn't matter if the buggy was old. If she hadn't left home, none of it would've happened.

Besides all that, Emma loved him. She'd known it from the minute she'd laid eyes on him so many years ago, but had hidden it from her heart and him. If she and Rafe survived the ordeal, she'd tell him exactly how she felt, and hope he'd love her back someday.

Thinking about Rafe helped her forget the pain somewhat. By the time she reached the lower edge of the canyon, she'd gotten her third wind. With a mighty heave, she traversed the incline inch by inch, moving her precious cargo to safety.

"Emma?" Rafe woke up just as she reached the top.

"Hang on," she gasped out. Grasping a pine tree, she wrapped the reins around the base and used the strength of the wood to haul him the rest of the way.

When he was safely away from the edge, Emma collapsed onto the ground, breathing like she'd run from one end of the state to the other.

"Emma, where are we? Are you okay?" Rafe rustled in the travois. "Why the hell am I tied down?"

She crawled over to him and laid her head next to his on the grass. "We're down at the shallow end of the canyon. I had to tie you down or you'd fall out of the travois." Each word was punctuated with a breath. "Give me ten minutes and I'll start a fire and find water."

"Jesus, Emma, you pulled me a mile down the canyon then up the embankment?" He sounded flabbergasted. "Are you kidding me?"

Emma smiled through the agony of muscle cramps. For once in her life, she'd impressed Rafe Sinclair. "Yep, sure did. Didn't want you drowning or supper for some mountain lion."

She rolled to her knees and faced him. His face was starting to bruise against the pale, clamminess of his skin. His forehead wasn't hot, but it was warmer than she was comfortable with. Emma hoped like hell he didn't get an infection in his leg.

"I had to save us, Rafe."

He closed his eyes and pursed his lips tightly. "I'm sorry I wasn't man enough to do that."

Emma chuckled rustily. "If we're going to be married, you're going to have to be my partner, not my overlord."

Those gray eyes opened and pinned her with a serious gaze. "Thank you, Emma."

Her heart nearly burst with pride. "You're welcome. Now let me get the fire going."

Rafe leaned against the pine tree and watched the flames flicker in the dying sunlight. Emma had been gone for hours and he was worried, not about himself, but for her. His leg throbbed with a pain he'd never felt before, but for the most part, he tried to ignore it.

Emma had to walk at least ten miles back to town and it would be dark in less than an hour. He hoped she'd made it safely, not that he was any help in that regard. No, he had to lay there helpless as a baby while she rescued his sorry ass.

God, he still couldn't believe what she'd done. Emma had more heart, courage and guts than any man he'd ever met. She was more than just his wife, she was his partner and hopefully his forever. Watching her walk away with only her wits to protect her made his heart pinch something awful.

It was then he realized he loved her. He loved Emma Radcliff Sinclair with every fiber of his heart. She was a treasure he almost lost because of his own stupid notions of what marriage was. He'd liked her as a child, now he was in love with her as a woman.

As he stared into the flames, he remembered all the wonderful times they'd spent together as children and the tumultuous days of their marriage. It was a sobering lesson that Rafe needed to learn—Emma was worth much more than the deed to the Circle S.

A sound in the approaching darkness made Rafe pick up the log she'd left behind for him, along with his knife. A horse and wagon appeared in the gloom with Emma at the reins, the doctor riding beside her, and the sheriff and his deputy riding behind.

Rafe's eyes pricked with tears at the sight of her scraped, dirty face. After setting the brake on the wagon, she jumped down and ran to him, relief evident in her eyes.

"Thank God you're okay." She kneeled beside him and touched his cheek. "Is the pain bad?"

He smiled and touched her wrist. When she hissed, he realized her neckerchief was wrapped around it.

"Don't tell me you did all this with a broken wrist?" he demanded.

"It's just bruised, maybe sprained. Definitely not broken though. Don't worry." She glanced back at the doctor, the brown-haired man making his way a bit slower to his patient. "Doc will fix me up after you."

"Emma." He cupped her face. "I already said thank you but there's something else I need to say." Rafe swallowed hard as he made the leap from unwilling husband to loving mate. "I love you."

Emma's eyes widened and she opened her mouth to speak.

"Rafe Sinclair, how did you get yourself in such a fix?" The sheriff's voice boomed through the twilight air, cutting off anything Emma was going to say.

Rafe almost cursed at the sheriff, but held his tongue. "Just lucky I guess."

"That's bad luck, that's what that is." The sheriff chatted with Rafe about the accident as the doctor examined Rafe's leg.

Although he protested, Rafe drank the laudanum for the pain and drifted off looking at Emma's worried face. His wife, his love.

Emma was in shock from her head to her feet, which were currently tingling. Rafe had told her he loved her. He loved *her*, Emma Sinclair.

Holy cow.

She could hardly believe it. Unfortunately she didn't have a chance to ask him to repeat it because of the dang chatty sheriff. Then Rafe got knocked out by the pain medicine. After they loaded him into the wagon, Emma finally allowed the doctor to check her over. He confirmed her diagnosis of a sprained wrist, minor cuts and bruises, and sent her and her husband home.

Her husband. Jesus, now he sorta even felt like a husband. Emma drove the wagon home with the deputy escorting her all the way to the Circle S. She'd filed a complaint against Billy Sinclair for horse thieving, and she aimed to make it stick.

By the time they reached the ranch, it was full dark. Emma ran into the barn and found Rowdy taking care of Cinnamon. Diamond stood in his stall, happily munching oats.

"Rowdy, thank God. Are they both okay?" She ran her good hand up and down the mare's flanks, looking for anything out of the ordinary.

Rowdy rubbed his whiskered chin. "Diamond's okay, a bit shook up, but he's calmed down. Cinnamon here was rode hard, but I took care of her after that fancy fella brought her in."

Emma cursed. "That bastard. I'm gonna put his sorry ass in jail."

As she stepped out of the barn, Rowdy yelled, "Welcome back, Mrs. Sinclair."

Emma kept walking, a small smile on her face, secretly glad to hear the new name she sported. This time, it fit like a glove. She stormed into the house and found Billy on top of Georgette on the sofa. At least they were both still clothed.

"You son of a bitch!" She yanked him by the collar and he fell hard onto the floor.

When he got to his knees with a snarl, she punched him so hard, she felt it all the way to next week. His nose popped like a geyser and he fell back onto the floor unconscious, his eyes rolling back into his head.

Emma felt a sweet rush of victory for besting the man. He was a lowdown snake who deserved more than a punch from her. Georgette sobbed quietly from the couch as the deputy stepped through the doorway.

"Get that idiot out of here, Dwight." She kicked at Billy's leg. "You can now arrest him for attacking Georgette too. I'll be there in two minutes to help you get Rafe inside, then you can put Billy in the wagon and bring him to jail."

"Will do, Emma." Dwight took Billy by the arms and pulled him out of the room.

"If you need rope, just ask Rowdy in the barn," Emma called as the two men disappeared through the doorway.

Emma sat next to her stepsister and pulled the young girl close. Georgette turned and sobbed in Emma's arms. Emma comforted her with nonsense words, all the while realizing her stepsister was really just a frightened girl who'd dabbled with fire only to be burned.

"It's okay, Georgie. He's going to jail and you don't ever have to worry about him again." Emma rubbed the girl's back.

"You punched him," came Georgette's nasally voice. "I've never seen a girl do that before."

Emma smiled without humor. "He deserved it, rotten snake."

"You protected me." Georgette pulled back, showing her tear-stained, red-cheeked face.

"That's what sisters are for." Emma gave into her impulse and kissed the girl on the forehead. "Now go clean yourself up. I'm going to need help with Rafe."

With a few of the ranch hands assisting, they got Rafe into bed. Emma shooed everyone out of the room and settled in for a long night keeping watch. After washing the dirt off both of them, she pulled the sheets and blanket over him, then crawled up into bed beside him.

For the first time in her marriage, Emma gladly slept beside her husband, grateful they'd both survived the fall, and hugging the thought that he told her he loved her to her heart.

ଔ

Two weeks had passed since the accident, and Rafe spent his days staring at the walls and cursing the fact that he was trapped in his bedroom. He was still annoyed that he wasn't able to kick Billy's sorry ass off the ranch himself. After the sheriff had made sure he left town on the train, Billy hadn't been seen again.

Truth was, Rafe was grumpy about staying in bed and not being able to see Emma as much as he wanted too. She was taking care of the day-to-day running of the ranch while he was unable to. It rankled that a woman was doing this job, seemingly without effort. His foreman even reported that everything was running smoothly.

Dammit.

He knew he was acting like a petulant child but couldn't seem to help it. No matter who came to see him, he snarled and snapped. Little Georgette refused to even come into the room when she was helping Emma. It was pathetic.

Rafe missed Emma and wanted her near him. More than that, he wanted to hear her say she loved him too. He'd thrown his heart to her, and she hadn't even acknowledged it. The thought that she might not love him back wasn't allowed to enter his mind.

It was a Monday morning and the sun had just risen. Through the window, Rafe watched the horizon turn pink, then orange, hoping like hell the next six weeks would go by in an instant so he could walk like a man again.

Emma walked into the room with a tray full of breakfast food. "You look like you're in your normal happy mood."

The smell of coffee and biscuits made his stomach rumble, which made Rafe's control finally snap. When she approached the bed, he lashed out and knocked the tray from her hands. The surprised look on her face gave him grim satisfaction. Now he had her attention and maybe she'd stop treating him like a goddamn piece of glass.

"What the hell did you do that for?" She looked at the mess on the floor. "Who do you think has to clean this up?"

"I don't care." He snatched her arm and pulled her on top of him. "I want to kiss my wife."

Her gaze locked with his.

"I love you, Emma, and I don't care if you don't love me back. I'm tired of waiting for you to say anything, and I'm tired of being in this damn bed." He didn't wait for a response, instead he just kissed her.

It was the kiss of a thousand years, of a passion so great his heart was full to bursting with it. She moved against his lips, opening her lovely mouth to his questing tongue. Sweet, slow kisses that fired his blood and made his dick so hard he could hammer a nail with it.

Emma seemed to understand what to do because she ground her pelvis into his, pushing his pulsing arousal into the cleft of her pussy. He groaned into her mouth, eager to be naked with her.

"Please, Emma, undress and make love with me." He cupped her behind and thrust slightly.

Her eyes fluttered open with passion in their depths. "Yes."

Rafe could've shouted from the rooftops as she scrambled off him to undress. Pain in his leg forgotten, he waited patiently for her, enjoying the display of alabaster skin beneath the plaid shirt and denims. Emma was like one of the thoroughbred mares she'd raised, sleek, muscular and beautiful. She looked at him shyly from beneath her eyelashes.

"My God, you're exquisite." He drank in the sight, the most gorgeous woman he'd ever seen. His heart thundered at the thought that she was his for the rest of his life.

He struggled to take off his shirt, but couldn't quite get the drawers off. With a saucy grin, she peeled them down his legs, mindful of the splint, not that he'd feel any pain at that point with his body pulsing with need.

Her gaze fell on his erection and one eyebrow rose. "Nicely done, Mr. Sinclair."

Rafe laughed and opened his arms. "It's all for you, Mrs. Sinclair. Now come here."

As she lay on him, the exquisite sensation of skin to skin made his entire body sigh. A shudder raced down his spine from the contact. She was so silky smooth, so incredible to touch. His hands roamed her body, relishing in the feel of her softness.

He reached between them and found her clit, already plump and pulsing. As he massaged her pleasure button, she moaned into his mouth and opened her legs wider.

"God, yes, open for me, sweetheart." Rafe maneuvered two fingers up inside her as his thumb continued to pleasure her clit.

Emma's nipples were like diamond points on his chest. His mouth watered to taste them, touch them, bite them. He needed to be one with her, to make her his wife in truth.

"Sit up and ride me, Em."

She lifted up and stared at him. "Ride you?"

"Yep, all you need to do is open your legs and hop on, just like you do a saddle, only this will bring you more pleasure than a piece of leather ever will." He slid a third finger into place and plunged deeper inside her.

Her eyes closed briefly as she pulsed around his fingers. She was so tight, so hot, Rafe was afraid he'd finish before she got started.

As Emma sat up, Rafe captured a breast in his mouth, latching on and sucking. She yipped in surprise, but didn't pull from his reach. Somehow, without moving her breast away from him, she was able to open her legs and position herself over him. Rafe nudged her nether lips and slid the head of his cock in just an inch.

"Do you feel me?"

She nodded jerkily, her face a mask of pleasure. He bit her nipple just as he pulled her down fully on him. Sheathed deep inside, he throbbed with feelings he'd yet to find in his lifetime. It appeared as though Emma's long years on the saddle had readied her for a man, or she wasn't a virgin. It didn't matter, all that mattered was that she was finally his.

"Wow." She gasped. "You're...filling me."

"Yes, sweetheart, yes." He raised her up and down just a smidge to show her how it was done. "Now ride me."

She glanced down at him, her pupils dilated with desire, a sheen of sweat on her face and the blush of arousal on her cheeks. "As long as you keep doing what you're doing to me. I like it."

Rafe grinned and kissed the distended nipple in front of his lips. "My pleasure."

Emma rode him as if she'd been born to be his, and perhaps she had been. She got her rhythm quickly, and he thrust up as much as he could, meeting her in the garden of bliss. He licked and nibbled one nipple as his hand tweaked the other. Emma's moans of delight sent shafts of longing through him.

He didn't think he'd last long and hung on with every scrap of willpower. His body was screaming for release, but he wanted their first time to be about both of them, not just about him. It was so important that she found the ultimate pleasure their first time together. She mattered more to him than anyone ever had.

Emma clenched around him and sucked in a breath. Rafe could feel the waves of her orgasm as they rolled through her muscles. He closed his eyes and bit harder on her nipple as his own pleasure began somewhere near his toes. They rode the sensations together, cresting at the pinnacle of ecstasy.

Rafe gripped her hips, burying himself so deeply inside her, he touched her soul. Entwined in life, in love and in body, they became one.

Epilogue

Emma watched Miracle as Rafe worked him in the corral. The year-old colt had proved to be as resilient as his mistress, and just as strong. Life was good on the Circle S, nearly perfect. She couldn't have asked for a better life. She'd even bred Blackjack to Cinnamon and expected another foal this time next year.

Rafe saw her from the corral and smiled, waggling his eyebrows. Emma rolled her eyes, although she was thankful she and Rafe shared such a bond, physical and emotional.

Funny how life turned out exactly how she didn't plan it. A year ago, she didn't even want to see Rafe Sinclair, much less be carrying his child. Yet here she was, fat, happy and expecting the newest member of the family.

Yep, Emma was happy, her heart branded with Rafe's name for the rest of her life.

About the Author

You can't say cowboys without thinking of Beth Williamson. She likes 'em hard, tall and packing. Read her work and discover for yourself how hot and dangerous a cowboy can be.

Beth lives in North Carolina, with her husband and two sons. Born and raised in New York, she holds a B.F.A. in writing from New York University. She spends her days as a technical writer, and her nights immersed in writing hot romances for her readers.

To learn more about Beth Williamson, please visit www.bethwilliamson.com. Send an email to Beth at beth@bethwilliamson.com join her Yahoo! Group, http://groups.yahoo.com/group/cowboylovers, or sign up for Beth's monthly newsletter, Sexy Spurs, www.janusportal.com/lists/?p=subscribe&id=3.

Look for these titles by Beth Williamson

Now Available:

The Malloy Family Series
The Bounty
The Prize
The Reward
The Treasure
The Gift
The Tribute
The Legacy

Devils on Horseback: Nate
Devils on Horseback: Jake

Hell for Leather
Marielle's Marshal
(Print anthology Sand, Sun and Sex)

Coming Soon:

Devils on Horseback: Zeke

High Noon

Rebecca Goings

Dedication

For Beth and Melissa, who agreed to go on this western adventure with me. Thank you, ladies, for giving me the opportunity to write with you in the Leather & Lace anthology. Talon sends you his utmost gratitude—if you know what I mean. *wink*

Prologue

Banning, TX 1867

"Talon, please don't leave me!"

Alison Williams clutched onto the appaloosa's reins with a vengeance, pleading with the man sitting on the animal's back. She didn't care how pathetic she was being, or the fact Talon Holt was seven years her senior—not to mention a full-blooded Comanche Indian.

He was her best friend, the one she told all her secrets to, and the man she was madly in love with. But he was leaving Banning, leaving his life, leaving *her*.

"Allie, I have to go," he said, his dark, expressive eyes glittering in the noonday sun. "You cannot be allowed to care for me as much as you do."

"Talon, please."

"No. Listen to me. You are both a child and a white woman. You shouldn't spend all your time with an Indian."

"I'm fifteen years old. Almost sixteen. I'm not a child."

"Yes, you are," Talon said in his soft, yet firm voice. "But I am a man full grown. You need to be with other girls your own age. Not me. Even the people in town disapprove."

Tears filled her eyes as Alison gazed up at him on the back of his horse. His short-cropped black hair caught the light breeze and her breath hitched in her chest. Talon was the most handsome man she'd ever laid eyes upon.

He'd been found as a toddler by John Holt, shrieking over the body of a slain Indian woman. It had appeared as if his entire Comanche village had been decimated in a massacre.

Talon had been the only survivor. John Holt, being the kind-hearted man he'd always been, had taken the boy in, giving him the white name of Andrew Holt. However, John only ever called him Talon, due to the fact the boy had fought his new white father with his sharp fingernails on more than one occasion.

"Truth is," Talon said, breaking into her thoughts, "I should have left Banning years ago." His words pierced her heart.

"If I promise to leave you alone, will you stay?" Alison's tears spilled down her cheeks.

Talon's gaze softened. "No."

His one single word seemed to hang in the air.

Alison shuddered and broke his eye contact. With a deep sigh, she finally accepted that nothing could talk him out of leaving. She turned from the horse and walked away, suddenly feeling a cold numbness overtake her. With Talon determined to leave, she had no one left in the world. Her mother had died ten years ago due to an illness she couldn't shake, and her father had taken to drinking and gambling soon after. Talon had been her friend and the only one who'd actually cared what happened to her.

But ever since Alison confessed her deeper feelings for him a few days ago, he'd been withdrawn—until today—when he'd told her he was leaving.

"Allie. Alison!"

Talon's voice carried on the breeze behind her, but she didn't stop. She couldn't watch him leave her. She wouldn't be able to survive another day if she had to witness him ride out of her life forever. Accepting his rejection with quiet determination, Alison chose instead to make Talon watch *her* leave *him.*

She marched up the dirt rise toward town, lamenting the fact that now, when she came to visit the creek, she'd be doing it alone.

"Damn it, Allie, where are you going?" Talon trotted up behind her only to circle in front of her, stopping her retreat with his horse. She didn't look at him.

"Allie," he said in a gentler voice, sliding from the saddle. "I have to go. I can't stay here anymore. These thoughts I'm having—they're no longer appropriate."

"I don't care that you're Comanche," she whispered, staring at his feet. "I've never cared."

"I know. But our friendship changed the day you told me you had feelings for me. I...I can't let you fall in love with me."

Alison found the courage to look into his beautiful brown eyes. Her chin trembled. Was this the last time she'd ever look at him?

"Will I...will I ever see you again?" Her voice wavered.

"I don't know." He lifted his hands to cup her face and wiped her tears away with the pads of his thumbs.

"Please don't touch me, Talon," she begged. "Whenever you touch me, all I want to do is fall into your arms and—"

Talon silenced her with his mouth, moving his gentle lips on hers. The contact shocked her, but she wasn't about to pull away. Alison had dreamt of kissing Talon for far too long. The reality turned her to butter in his arms.

His lips were warm, demanding nothing, and so soft, Alison knew she could kiss him all day and never tire of it. She had to stand on her tiptoes to circle her arms around his neck. He groaned and pulled her closer. Without warning, the silken touch of his tongue dampened her lips. She gasped as butterflies flew wildly in her stomach. Just as she was about to open her mouth to do the same to him, Talon jerked away.

"I'm sorry, Allie," he said, his hands shaking. "I shouldn't have done that."

Without another word, he swung onto his saddle and turned his horse toward the road.

"Talon, wait!"

"You'll make a man a fine wife some day, Alison Williams." His voice was gruff. "Take care of yourself."

He kicked his horse and galloped away in a cloud of dust. Alison crumpled in the dirt, sobbing fitfully as her heart shattered into tiny pieces all around her. She ended up watching Talon Holt leave her after all.

There was no greater pain in all the world.

Chapter One

Devil's Fork, TX 1872

Talon scowled at his glass of whiskey. He'd been sitting in Goldy's Saloon for the past two hours. *What am I doing?* He really should be moving on. He didn't need to be here listening and hoping for news from Banning. It would only torture him, like it had for the past few years.

Goldy's Saloon was in Devil's Fork, the next town over from Banning. Talon had visited Devil's Fork twice a year for five years running, desperate to hear something—anything about Alison.

In the days following his departure, he'd missed her something fierce. He hadn't realized how much he enjoyed her company until he no longer had it.

Making his way in the real world had been hard—harder than he'd first thought. It was impossible to hide the fact he was an Indian, and more than once, he'd been on the receiving end of a hateful attack. It didn't take long before he spent his days practicing with the guns he now wore on his hips. There had even been a few occasions when his practice had come in handy—like the time he'd fought off two drunken white men from beating him senseless in a town up north. Talon had spent a month in jail because of it, but it had been worth it just to see the looks on their faces when he shot their guns right out of their hands.

He grabbed his glass off the bar, downed its contents and made a face. The burning in his belly almost matched the burning in his heart. Even after all these years, he missed Allie.

High Noon

She would be a woman now. He often wondered what she looked like all grown up.

Talon squeezed his eyes shut. Imagining her as a woman was exactly why he'd left Banning in the first place. The day Alison had confessed her feelings for him, he knew he was lost.

Because he'd been feeling the very same thing.

There had been no way he could marry her, not when she was still so young. He knew he wouldn't be able to keep his hands off her if he stayed. Even though she'd said she didn't care he was a Comanche, had she truly meant it? Alison had no idea the life she had in store for her accepting an Indian for a husband, even if he *was* raised as a white man.

That's why Talon left, but not without kissing her into oblivion. That one little taste of Alison had fired his blood. He had to leave or risk doing something he'd regret for the rest of his life.

Goldy, the bartender and owner of the saloon, wiped the countertop near Talon's glass. His golden hair was riddled with gray. The years were catching up to him. He gave Talon a knowing grin.

"When you gonna ask me about Banning, Injun?"

Talon raised his brow, but smiled. "When you stop calling me 'Injun', old man."

Goldy chuckled. "Thought you mighta heard the news by now."

"What news?" Talon pushed his glass away.

"Old Jed Williams has gotten himself into a hell of a mess."

Jed Williams? That was Alison's father.

"What do you mean?" Talon said, almost too afraid to ask. Jed had taken to drinking shortly after his wife's death. Talon's biggest regret was leaving poor Alison behind to fend for herself. He'd always been the one to take care of her—make sure she was all right.

"Lost his life savings to some gambler."

"What?" Talon's blood ran cold. What the hell was Allie going to do now?

"That's not all," Goldy said, lowering his voice and leaning on the bar.

"Tell me."

"Seems the old codger played a hand of poker he couldn't afford. Thought he could win his money back or some such. Ended up betting his ranch."

Talon's gut twisted as if he'd just been punched hard in the stomach. He took a deep breath to calm his raging heart. "Please tell me he didn't lose it."

Goldy nodded. "Yup. That he did. Lost his place. Lost his daughter too."

"Jesus, Alison's *dead*?" Talon stood so fast, the other patrons at the bar glanced at him with curious eyes.

"No, no, no," Goldy said, waving his hand in front of his face, as if shooing a pesky fly. "He bet his daughter's hand in *marriage*. Lost her to... Damn. I can't remember the man's name now."

"Garrett Sumrall," another man in the saloon called out. "Ol' Jed lost her to Sumrall fair and square. Weddin's next week."

Talon's mouth hung open in shock. Garrett Sumrall? Christ, that was one of the drunken men he'd gone to jail for shooting at a few years back. The world couldn't possibly be *that* small.

Could it?

Setting his jaw, Talon grabbed his hat off the stool next to him and strode toward the saloon's swinging doors.

"You gonna pay for your whiskey, Injun?" Goldy called out.

Talon stopped and turned around, digging into his pocket for a few coins. Once he found them, he tossed them onto the bar without counting them.

"The name's Talon," he growled, jamming his hat onto his head.

"What have you got a mind to do, boy?" Goldy asked with wide eyes.

"Ain't no way I'm gonna let Alison become some gambler's wife through her father's own stupidity. No way in hell."

Without another word, he barged through the swinging doors of the saloon and yanked his horse's reins from the

High Noon

hitching post. In one smooth motion, he leapt up onto his horse and kicked him into a gallop. He'd be in Banning by sundown.

He hadn't seen Alison for five years, but Talon didn't care. Right now, she needed him, and he would make damn sure she didn't have to live with her father's ridiculous mistakes.

Chapter Two

Alison sat by the edge of the creek and tossed small stones into the water. She never thought her father would be fool enough to bet away her life in a hand of poker. He'd said his mind had been clouded with booze and he hadn't been thinking straight.

That much was obvious.

Despite pleading with him, it appeared his gambling debt to a man named Garrett Sumrall was legitimate, which meant by this time next week, Alison would be a married woman.

At twenty years old, Alison had stood by and watched her friends marry, some of them even moving away with their new families. Despite turning a few heads on the boardwalk in town, Alison had never had any suitors, and she knew it was due to her notorious gambling father—the laughingstock of Banning, Texas. No man in their right mind would want to marry into such a family.

Often she thought of Talon and where he might have gone. Had he married? Found a woman he could love and settled down? The thought twisted her heart. If he had, she hoped he was happy. Talon deserved happiness, even after leaving her behind like an unwanted piece of...

Allie, stop.

So the man hadn't felt anything for her. That wasn't his fault. Rather than sticking around and watching her fall for him, he'd opted to leave. His absence had left a hole in her heart as wide as the Texas sky. She was no longer confident around men, no longer sure of their feelings toward her. The only way to guard her heart was to withdraw, become detached, and hope no one would ever reject her again.

First Talon. Now her father. What was to become of her?

At least now she wouldn't have to worry about who she was going to marry. Her father had taken care of that. Garrett Sumrall was a fat hulk of a man who stank to high heaven. Alison had no idea the last time he'd had a bath, but she'd be more than happy to dump a bucket of water on his head to get him started. She almost chuckled.

Her imagination began running wild, and things any well-bred lady should never think of ran through her head.

Her wedding night. Sharing Sumrall's bed. Bearing his children. It was enough to make her gag. She couldn't do it. She just couldn't do it.

She'd run away if she could, take a horse and never look back. But Garrett had threatened to kill her father outright if Alison didn't comply with their bet. She wasn't that heartless.

Even though her father didn't do her any favors, she couldn't let a man kill him. He was still family.

Once again, her thoughts drifted to Talon. He'd be older now. She wondered what he looked like. Did he grow his hair or was it still cropped short? Where had he been the past few years?

A quiet sob escaped her at the hopelessness of her life. The man she loved had never loved her. Now she was beginning to wonder if her father ever loved her either. Another sob bubbled to the surface. She was going to enter into a loveless marriage with a man she was terrified of. If he threatened to kill her father unless she complied, then what would her life be like after she'd married him? Sumrall looked like a man who was used to getting his way. God help her if she ever defied him.

Alison rubbed her eyes. What was wrong with her? Why couldn't any man love her? Was she so repulsive that no man in his right mind would want her?

Glancing at her reflection in the creek, she saw her blue eyes and dark brown hair. Her face wasn't overly pretty, but she didn't think she was ugly, either. In fact, her eyes seemed to twinkle when she smiled. But what did she know? Men married women like her best friend Meredith Jackson, with her flowing, raven-colored hair and expressive brown eyes. Mery was a beautiful woman, no doubt about it. But she'd moved away to Montana, to live on the ranch of her well-to-do husband. She'd promised to write, but Alison never received a letter from her, despite writing five letters in as many months.

Her fate was sealed. There would be no getting out of this. Closing her eyes, Alison retreated within herself, to a place where she saw Talon again, but this time, he threw himself at her feet, begging her forgiveness.

After five long years, how could the pain of his rejection still hurt so very much?

CR

The gambling hall of Banning, Texas was inside the Bloody Bull Saloon on Main Street. Loud, raucous laughter could be heard a few blocks away, and it wasn't unheard for the bawdy behavior to last well into the night.

The sun had set by the time Talon rode into town, but he didn't care. He was too pissed off to do much more than jump off his horse and make a half-hearted attempt at tying it to the hitching post before striding into the saloon. A few people glanced at him, but didn't pay him any mind as he scanned the room for Jed Williams' familiar face.

Smoke was thick and Talon had to squint when it stung his eyes. Lots of men smoked pipes or cigars, but he'd never gotten into the habit himself. Whiskey was his vice. Mostly because it numbed his guilt over leaving a starry-eyed girl in the dust.

When Talon didn't immediately see Jed, he made his way to the bar.

"What can I get ye?" The bartender was a burly man, older, with wispy hair on his balding head. Talon recognized him, but couldn't think of his name. "Well I'll be. You're that Indian who used to live 'round these parts, ain't ye?"

Talon sighed and ignored the question. "Know where I can find Jed Williams?"

"God only knows. Might want to look out back. He's taken to pukin' in the alley since his recent loss to Garrett Sumrall.

You heard that one, right? You shoulda been here. Every man in the house was crowded 'round their table wondering if Williams would actually lose his daughter's hand in marriage, and sure enough..."

Without waiting for the man to say more, Talon gave him a scowl and walked toward the back door of the hall. It was wide open to allow fresh air into the place, but once Talon stepped into the alley, all he could smell was the putrid scent of sour booze, piss and vomit.

A man sat on a crate, slumped against the rear wall of the saloon, looking like he was sleeping. Talon recognized him as Jed, although the years had aged him. Deep wrinkles marred his face and his hair was now completely gray. His skin was pale and leathery, as if he hadn't eaten a decent meal in a long while. That probably wasn't too far from the truth.

"Jed?"

The man jerked awake and glanced around the alley with wide, dilated eyes. His body was tense, as if he were going to flee into the shadows.

Once Jed's eyes rested on him, he rubbed them and stared again. "Do I know you?"

Talon nodded. "That you do, and you're going to explain nice and slow-like why the hell you thought it best to gamble away Allie's life, along with your pathetic excuse for a ranch."

Jed's eyes filled with tears. "My God. *Talon*? Is that you?"

"In the flesh. What were you thinking? I have half a mind to beat the living shit out of you."

"I...I wasn't thinking. I had a full house—aces high. I didn't think he could beat me. I'd been on a winning streak all night long. I thought I knew his poker face. But...but when he revealed his royal, I knew I'd lost more than I could afford."

"His royal?"

Jed nodded. "Royal flush. Hearts. Don't know how the bastard did it."

"Who the hell cares how he did it, Williams. You bet your daughter's *life*."

"You think I don't know that?" Jed jumped off the crate and stood before Talon. "You want to take a shot at me? Go right ahead. Please. I would, if I were you."

Talon balled his fist, sorely tempted to do just that. Only the thought of Alison's pretty face in tears stopped him. No matter how angry he was with her father for what he'd done, he couldn't hurt him. The longer he stood there in silence, the more Jed's body trembled.

Without warning, the older man fell to his knees and wept pathetically. "Please. Please, Talon, kill me. I'm such a failure. I've made a colossal mess of things."

"I'm not going to kill you, old man. Stand up." Talon bent over and hauled him to his feet, turning away from the rancid smell of Jed's breath.

"Allie hates me."

"I don't blame her."

"Do you hate me?"

"Damn close." With a sigh of resignation, Talon draped Jed's arm around his shoulders. Alison's father could barely stand on his own two legs. "Let's get you home. We'll talk about it in the morning."

"Christ, what have I done?" Jed's pitiful sobbing echoed down the alley as Talon made his way around to the front of the building. "I'm sorry, Talon. I'm so sorry."

"Don't apologize to me, Jed. Allie's the one you need to beg forgiveness from."

"She hates me…"

Talon tried hard to hold on to his anger, but the longer he was in Jed's presence, all he could feel was pity. Jed had become nothing more than a shell of the man he'd once been. The death of his wife had changed him so severely, he'd never be the same again.

Talon damned himself for leaving all those years ago. No doubt Alison had had a hard life since he'd left, caring for a man who didn't care for himself. "Christ," Talon whispered under his breath. Why did he have to feel so guilty? This wasn't his fault.

But the more Talon thought about it, the more he had to wonder if it truly *was* his fault. If he'd stayed in Banning, he had no doubt in his mind Jed would never have made that crazy bet with Sumrall.

Because Alison would have been *his* wife.

Chapter Three

The next morning, Alison stood in the hallway, her hands on her hips. Her father's bed was crumpled and unmade. He hadn't come home last night. Again.

She tried hard not to let anger get the best of her, but she refused to make the bed for a man who didn't sleep in it. On many occasions her father hadn't come home after a night of drinking and carousing. Alison had even gone to fetch him in town a few times, finding him slumped in a chair in the Bloody Bull Saloon.

Since his infamous bet with Garrett Sumrall, she didn't bother any longer. If he was drunk enough to sleep all night at the Bull, then he could damn well get sober enough to walk home. She was through taking care of him. All he did was sap her strength.

Since her father began to drink and gamble so many years ago, he seldom had money to pay any ranch hands to do the work that needed to get done. Many of his hands, even the loyal ones, had left the Circle Q. No one could work for free. The grounds had become overgrown, and only a few head of cattle remained—just barely enough to turn a profit. Whatever profits they had Jed gambled away at the Bull.

Alison was used to hard work, making sure the cows were milked and fed each morning and put to pasture. When her father was sober, he'd round them up and the process would start anew the next day. Alison was tired of it, tired of being the backbone of a dilapidated ranch that would never be hers.

But by the grace of her *fiancé*, Sumrall had allowed them to stay at *his* ranch until his nuptials to Alison the following week. Garrett had made things quite clear that once they were wed, Alison's father was to find another place to live. Strangely enough, that was the one thing Alison looked forward to.

Scowling, she stormed down the hallway, only to be greeted by the scent of coffee. *Coffee?* It had to have been made by her father, but he never made anything. Why would he suddenly get a hankering to make coffee?

Once she strode into the living room, she saw her father sprawled upon the sofa with one of her mother's handmade quilts draped over his chest. He snored softly and Alison raised a brow. If he was asleep, then who'd made the coffee?

Wandering into the kitchen, she found the pot warming on the stove. Out of the corner of her eye, she could see the shape of a man sitting at the kitchen table. Her heart leapt into her throat. One of the men from town must have brought her father home, having pity on ol' Jed Williams. For whatever reason, Alison was afraid to turn and see who it was. For all she knew, it could be Sumrall himself.

"Damn. You sure did grow up, Allie."

Only one man on Earth had ever called her Allie. Every hair on her body stood on end. The sound of Talon's voice had washed over her like water and she was keenly aware of him with every fiber of her being. She couldn't keep her body from trembling. *He's come back.*

"Aren't you going to say anything?"

Alison was rooted to the spot. She couldn't turn to face him because her feet wouldn't listen to her head. Her eyes refused to look at him, as his face would no doubt be burned into her memories for all time.

"What...?" She paused to clear her throat. "What are *you* doing here?" Good. Her voice didn't waver.

"Came to see how you were doing."

Alison sniffled, but she didn't turn. Instead, she balled her fists at her sides. "I'm fine. We're fine. Everything's fine. Now why don't you just leave? You're good at that."

The chair scraped on the wood floor as Talon stood. Alison's body responded and she jumped at the sound. Once he began walking toward her, she did the only thing she could think to do. She bolted.

The rear door of the ranch house was unlocked and she ripped it open, racing down the steps of the porch and into the yard. She could hear Talon in hot pursuit.

"Allie!" His hand caught her arm and spun her around before she could take a breath to squeal. She lost her footing and fell into his arms, finally gazing into the most beautiful dark eyes she ever did see.

"Alison Nicole Williams, where are you going?"

She flinched, unable to look away from Talon's face. He hadn't shaved in awhile, but his dark stubble gave him an exotic look. He'd grown his hair just a bit, and it now fell below his ears, thick black locks that shone in the early morning light. His eyes were so brown they were almost black, piercing hers ruthlessly. The years had aged him, but if anything, they added character to his fierce, handsome visage.

Alison's breath came in short gasps and her knees were buckling. For as long as she could remember, she'd dreamt of being exactly where she was, in Talon's embrace. She hadn't truly believed she'd ever see him again. Gazing into his face now was like a dream in itself.

"*Talon.* Why are you here? Why now?" She wouldn't cry if it killed her.

"I heard about your father's bet. I heard what Jed had done to you." Talon's grip loosened a bit, but he didn't let her go. He held on to her upper arms, supporting her sagging weight.

Alison's heart melted at his gentle tone, and she desperately wanted to run her fingers through his hair. Even after all this time, she was still smitten with him—the only man who'd given her the time of day. But those childish days were long gone.

"My father...gambled me away. I'm getting married next week."

Talon's look darkened. She recognized that scowl. She imagined what he'd be like if he hadn't been found by a white man as a child. Talon would be running with the Comanche Indians, sweeping across the desert and living off the land. That untamed wildness was not dead in him. He'd once told her he still remembered flashes of his life with the Comanche. She saw some of that wildness in him now.

"You are *not* getting married, Allie. Not if I can help it."

A faint ray of hope lit in her heart. "What do you mean? What are you going to do?"

"I'm going to fix your father's mistake, that's what I'm going to do. I'll be damned before I let *you* pay for *his* blunder."

Alison swallowed hard and looked deep into his eyes. Seeing him again after all this time was nearly too painful to bear.

"Why?" she asked.

He seemed shocked. "What do you mean, why?"

Shaking her head, she broke his eye contact and twisted away from his hands. She took a step back before answering him.

"Why do you care?"

"You're my friend, Allie. I owe it to you."

She gave him an incredulous look. "You don't owe me a thing, Talon Holt. I did just fine when you left me. I'll do just fine without you now."

He sighed. "You're mad at me."

"No," she said, regret lacing her voice. "I'm well beyond mad at you. You left Banning. Without even talking to me about your decision. I knew the day I watched you ride away that you didn't care about me. Please don't pretend to care now."

Lifting her skirts, she attempted to walk past him, but he caught her arm in his painful grip.

"You know damn well I care for you, Allie."

"Do I? Because all those nights I cried into my pillow convinced me otherwise."

"I'm sorry, damn it! Is that what you want me to say?"

"I don't want you to say anything, especially words you don't mean."

"I mean every single word I say, you know that."

"No, I don't." Alison pulled out of his grasp once again. "I'm not your responsibility, Talon, I never was."

"You've done a lot of growing up since I last saw you. But so have I. I'm not running anymore, Allie. I'm here in Banning to stay. And I'm not going to stand by and watch you get married to some gambler you don't love."

"You can't stop it." Alison stared at the ground as her hand absently played in the folds of her skirts. "Sumrall threatened to kill my father if I don't comply."

Talon hooked a finger under her chin, forcing her to look at him. Once she saw the tender light in his eyes, tears welled behind her own. "That won't happen. Sumrall will marry you over *my* dead body, not your father's. If I could undo what I did five years ago, I'd do it in a heartbeat, you've got to believe me on that. Allie, I'm so sorry."

Alison raised her hand to cup his cheek. He closed his eyes and sighed, as if relieved to feel her touch on his skin. Talon turned his face slightly, to nuzzle his cheek further into her palm. She couldn't resist swiping the pad of her thumb across his cheekbone.

"Talon," she breathed, trying desperately to hold in her sobs. "*Sorry* isn't good enough."

Without another word, she walked away and climbed the stairs to the porch, disappearing inside the house.

Chapter Four

It didn't take long for Talon to recognize the fat, sweaty man sitting at the poker table as Garrett Sumrall. With purposeful strides, Talon made his way toward him, remembering with clarity when he'd shot the gun right out of Garrett's hand a few years back. He was the bastard who'd made fun of him for being Comanche, who'd almost beat him senseless, the man Talon had spent weeks in jail for shooting.

Now, he was the man who'd staked his claim on the woman Talon cared for. Garrett would never marry Allie, not if Talon had anything to say about it.

The sun had been low on the horizon when he'd finally made his way to the Bloody Bull. After his exchange with Allie that morning, he'd needed to clear his head. She'd been so damn beautiful, she took his breath away. The years had filled out her figure, and made her face more mature and even prettier somehow. But she hadn't forgiven him for leaving. Could he blame her? She'd begged him to stay. Just the memory of Allie's tears made a muscle tick in his jaw. He'd set things straight with her if it was the last thing he ever did.

Now, however, he pulled out a chair from the poker table and sat down, taking off his hat.

"Garrett. It's been a long time."

The man glanced up from his cards and did a double take, his face paling. "*You.*"

Talon nodded, running his fingers through his hair. "How's your right hand? I seem to remember it was injured last time we met."

Garrett's eyes narrowed. "You have one hell of a nerve, *Injun*." He spat the word and Talon had to wipe his face.

"Well now, what a coincidence. That's exactly what I was going to say to you."

Garrett pursed his lips and held his cards with an iron grip. The poker game had come to a stop as all the men at the table watched the exchange warily.

"I don't know what you're talking about."

Talon glared at him. "Yes, you do. The name Alison Williams mean anything to you?"

"Sure does." Garrett puffed out his chest. "She's my fiancée. She's gonna do me, and do me right, if you know what I mean." The men at the table chuckled.

"Uh-uh," Talon said, shaking his head. "You're not getting within fifty feet of her, I'll make sure of that. I think you and me both know I can live up to my word."

"You might be a fancy shooter, but Jed lost his bet fair and square. And that means I get his ranch *and* his daughter."

"That's where you're wrong, Sumrall. I'm sure winning a woman in a poker bet is the only way a man like you could ever get married." More chuckles erupted from the men around them. "But know this. If you try to force Alison's hand, I'll make sure you're no good—to *any* woman."

"I'm not afraid of you. Goddamn savage."

Talon grabbed Garrett's collar in his fist and yanked him close, making the man yelp in surprise. "*You should be.*"

Without another word, Talon stood, jamming his hat back on his head. The room was deathly quiet as he walked out of the saloon. That gambler was going to learn, one way or the other. Talon knew Garrett wouldn't give up so easily. It would probably be best if Talon stayed on the Circle Q until this whole thing blew over. He knew Allie wouldn't like him sleeping in the stables, but he didn't give a damn. She needed him whether she admitted it or not.

Talon mounted his horse and galloped toward Jed's ranch. Allie would just have to deal with the fact that he was back in her life to stay. Damn it.

"You gonna let some high an' mighty Injun talk to you that way, Garrett?"

With a scowl, Garrett stared at Virgil McKay across the poker table. "What do you think?"

Virgil had the nerve to shrug. "Dunno. Seems you're losing your edge."

"Watch your mouth, Virge. I'm not above putting a bullet in you right here and now."

"Oh, I don't doubt it." Virgil chuckled as Garrett's temper fumed.

"If that savage thinks he can waltz right in here and tell me what to do, he's got another think coming. Deal me out." Garrett stood and grabbed his jacket off his chair. Virgil stood as well and they both walked to the door.

"What you gonna do?" Virgil asked.

"I'm not going to do a damn thing. *You're* going to kidnap ol' Jed."

Virgil's eyes went wide. "What?"

"You heard me."

"But...but..."

Garrett clutched the back of Virgil's neck and hissed in his ear. "George's money is buried somewhere on that property, or have you forgotten that? I'm not about to lose the Circle Q to some filthy Indian."

He shoved Virgil away and the man stumbled before regaining his footing. Once they were both outside the saloon, Garrett saw no trace of the man known as Talon.

"Why do I gotta do it?" Virgil whined, rubbing his neck.

"Because I said so. We have to force Jed's daughter into marriage. It's the only way to seal the deal and make sure the ranch is in my name. I'm not losing that money, Virge."

"And what if I don't do it?"

Garrett turned abruptly, growling low in his throat. "You don't want to cross me, McKay. I know where your family lives. And Lynn looks good enough to eat."

"You…you stay away from my daughter, Garrett. She's only twelve."

Garrett smiled. "You kidnap Jed—then we'll talk."

With that, Garrett strode down the boardwalk, making his way toward the brothel.

Chapter Five

Alison lay back on the blanket she'd spread upon the ground, gazing up at the starry night sky. Her father was off doing whatever it was he did in the evenings and she couldn't care less. When he'd awoken some hours ago, she didn't speak to him at all, opting instead to give him the silent treatment as he shambled around the house.

Eventually, he'd had enough strength to saddle his horse and herd their cattle back into the barn for the night. Now he was gone and Alison felt a small burden lift from her shoulders. She resented her father for forcing her into a life she didn't want to lead, even long before he'd lost his famous bet.

Remembering happier days, Alison recalled her mother's beautiful face, and how joyous her father had been back then. When her mother had gotten ill and died, Jed had never been the same. Elizabeth had been the love of his life, and he'd spiraled into a deep despair after her death, finding comfort every night at the bottom of a bottle.

Alison had been left to fend for herself most nights, learning to cook on her own and trying her hardest to keep the house as clean as she could with a man who didn't lift a finger to help.

She heaved a sigh as her thoughts shifted to Talon. He'd returned to Banning from God knows where, determined to be her avenging angel. She scoffed at the thought. What could he possibly do to prevent her fate? And did she even want his help? Talon was the man she'd pined over for five years. She was *still* pining over him. Seeing him in her kitchen that morning had spun her world out of control, and she no longer knew what to expect anymore.

Often she came down to the creek, where she and Talon had spent many days together in their youth. The sound of the babbling water calmed her raging emotions, and she took refuge in the fond memories she had of spending time with the man she adored.

He'd taught her how to skip a rock on the water and how to fish. He'd also been the only one to ever see her without her shoes, daring her to dip her bare feet into the cool water one hot summer's day. She and Talon used to be inseparable. What had happened to them?

"Thought I might find you here."

Alison gasped at the sound of Talon's deep voice a split second before he sat on the blanket next to her. He didn't spare her a glance, but instead gazed at the stars. "Beautiful night."

"How did you...how did you sneak up on me?" She sat up in a huff, desperately trying to straighten her hair, even though it was likely he couldn't see her too well anyhow.

"Didn't do much sneaking, honey, I just walked up and sat down. You must have been lost in thought."

Alison's heart leapt at his casual use of the word "honey". Hearing it from him sounded both foreign and completely wonderful at the same time. He'd never called her that when they were younger.

"I'm surprised to see you're still here," she said.

"Told you I was back in Banning to stay."

"Well forgive me for not exactly believing you."

Talon sighed and turned to her. "I was a fool all those years ago, Allie. I left because...because..."

"What?" she prompted.

"I left because I was afraid. Afraid of my feelings for you. When you told me you felt more for me than friendship, I panicked. The only thing that had been keeping me at arm's length from you was the knowledge that you only looked at me as a friend. But Christ, Allie, you were *fifteen*. I was twenty-two. Quite the age gap, don't you think?"

Her heart raced. Talon had actually cared for her? Alison's head spun. "We're still seven years apart now."

He nodded. "True. But now, you're twenty. I'm twenty-seven. I'm thinking that's a much better stretch."

It was hard for her to take a breath. Something changed in Talon's tone of voice, and Alison's stomach flopped. The night air was cool, but her skin burned, and she desperately wished she wasn't encumbered by her heavy skirts.

"What are you saying, Talon?" Her voice sounded breathless, even to her own ears.

"Remember that kiss I gave you before I left?"

How could she forget? It was seared onto her brain like a brand. "Yes," she said, panting.

He leaned closer to her, planting his fists on either side of her thighs. Rising up on his knees, Talon commanded every ounce of her attention. "I stopped it short. Do you know why?"

Alison shook her head so fast, he chuckled. Ever so slowly, he leaned in just a bit more, his eyes boring into hers.

"I wanted to kiss you like a man kisses a woman, but you were too young. You weren't ready for it then."

Blood rushed in her ears and she could barely hear his words. She resisted the urge to circle his neck with her arms. His body warmed her, and despite her own heated skin, she shivered.

"Talon—"

"Shh." He placed one finger on her lips. "I want to kiss you proper, honey. Will you let me?"

He was so close now, their breath mingled. She didn't know where hers ended and his began. She could smell his clean scent, purely male, like dust and leather. He must have found time to freshen up some. His stubble had been shaved and his hair combed.

As her silence stretched on, Talon's hands roamed up her arms and neck, one palm cupping her cheek while the other held the back of her head. He was urging her slightly closer to him and she couldn't fight him. Her resolve to shield her heart was crumbling. She wanted him to kiss her too badly.

His eyes pleaded with her and Alison knew she couldn't deny him. She nodded right before he closed the gap between them, pressing his lips to hers.

The contact sent tremors throughout her body, and she whimpered loudly. Talon responded with a low growl, leaning her back onto the blanket, following her without breaking the kiss. She knew she should be scandalized that he'd settled on top of her, but his weight felt so good, she wouldn't have moved him for all riches in the world.

He angled her head, giving him better access to her mouth. Without warning, his tongue snaked out, parting her lips almost forcefully. The bold move shocked her, but she'd often wondered what it would be like to kiss him like this. She surrendered without a fight.

In and out his tongue plunged, playing with hers. It was silky soft and so dominating, she could hardly keep up with him. She responded by thrusting her own tongue into his mouth with ardor. He surged against her, fisting his hands in her hair.

Alison broke the kiss just to get a mouthful of air, but that didn't deter Talon. He merely kissed and suckled his way down the skin of her neck, leaving trails of wet fire behind. Every nerve-ending in her body prickled at his touch, and an unfamiliar yearning lit within her.

"Christ, Allie, I missed you so damn much."

His voice sounded tortured as his mouth latched on to the side of her throat. She gasped, but did nothing to stop him, threading her fingers through his long, soft hair. "Not as much as I missed you," she managed to say, her voice barely a whisper.

Before she knew his intent, his mouth was on hers again, tasting deeply, demanding her full and total submission. Talon's hand wandered between them, grazing her breast and tightening her nipple. She moaned into his mouth at the sensation, arching her back to feel it again. He became bolder at her response and caressed her fully, puckering her nipple through the thick layers of her dress.

He panted as he stroked her, a fire alight in his eyes. "I want to kiss you all over, Allie. I want to know what every inch of you tastes like."

Talon's heated words brought a blush to her cheeks. She was thankful he couldn't see it in the darkness.

"We sh-shouldn't," she whispered, her voice trembling. "I'm engaged."

He gave her a few chaste kisses. "No, you're not. You will *not* marry that man. He has no claim on you."

"But the bet?"

Talon pulled back just enough to gaze into her eyes. Alison's fingers still played in his hair. "Doesn't mean a damn thing. You told me five years ago you had feelings for me. Do you still?"

She wasn't expecting him to ask her so bluntly. She was desperately in love with Talon, but did she dare tell him that? He alone held the power to destroy her heart if he so desired.

"Do you, Allie?"

"I wish I didn't," she admitted, biting her lip. "I...I don't think I ever stopped wishing you'd come back some day."

"I'm here now, and I'm not leaving. Do you know what that means?"

"No."

"It means you're mine. You belong to *me*. And I will not see *my* woman married to a man who isn't me."

Her eyes widened at his words. She was speechless. As the silence dragged on, Talon graced her with a sexy grin.

"Shocked you, didn't I?"

She could only stare at him, astonished.

"Get used to it, honey."

Chapter Six

Talon held Alison's hand as he walked her home after their interlude by the creek. Neither one spoke. Alison was too afraid of ruining the moment with words. It wasn't until Talon had brought her to the porch of her house that his voice penetrated the still of the night.

"I should find Jed and rescue him from himself."

"Why?" Alison knew she was being flippant, but she was far beyond caring. "He *wants* to be at the Bull all night long."

"He's your father, Allie."

"I know." She stood on the second step while Talon stood next to her on the dirt. At that height, she was finally looking him square in the eye. "But he's nothing more than a shell of the man he used to be."

"I *remember* how he used to be," Talon said softly, gazing up at the moon. "He's just lost his way. He needs the people he loves now more than anything."

Alison kept quiet. Perhaps Talon was right. Perhaps her father did need to feel loved right now. But so did she. Talon's words about her being *his* woman came back to her in a rush, and her cheeks reddened with embarrassment. He'd been gone a long time. Hearing him talk so casually about her belonging to him confused her. It was what she'd always dreamt he'd say, but was it too good to be true?

As if sensing something was amiss, he glanced at her. "You all right?"

Alison swallowed hard. "Where have you been all these years?"

Her question lingered in the air as the silence stretched on. Talon played with a few pebbles beneath his boot.

"Nowhere special," he said. "Bounced around from place to place. Learned how to shoot and shoot good. But I always made it back to Devil's Fork twice a year."

"Devil's Fork? But that's just a few miles away."

He nodded. "I'd go to Goldy's and just sit and listen. The men there usually gossiped about anything of interest, from all over the place. I would even ask Goldy himself if he'd heard any news."

"News about what?" She shivered when his dark eyes rested on hers.

"News about you. About what you were up to. Had you found yourself a husband? A suitor? I needed to know."

"Why didn't you just come back and ask me?"

Talon ran his fingers through his thick hair. Alison watched him, remembering her own fingers doing the same not too long ago. She yearned to do it again.

"I was a coward, Allie," he whispered. "I'd left all those years ago, and I didn't know how to come back—until I heard Goldy talking about your father's poker bet. It woke me up and slapped some sense into me. I...thought I'd lost you forever. I never want to feel that way again."

"So you came back to Banning intent on wooing me?"

"No." Talon's terse answer disappointed her. However, her depression faded away when she heard his next words. "I came back to save you. But once I saw you standing before me, all grown up, I was lost."

"Talon," she began, placing her hand on his shoulder. "In one day, you've slammed back into my life like a runaway train. And suddenly you expect me to fall into your arms? I've been miserable for five years, dreaming of you out there somewhere, never thinking of me."

"I thought of you *every* damn day." His voice was low, but she could still hear its slight tremor.

"I'm a different person now. I'm not that same little girl you knew back then."

"Mmm, that's obvious, honey." He looked her up and down, making Alison feel as if she didn't have a stitch on. She crossed her arms over her chest.

"That's not what I meant."

He chuckled. "I know. I'm sorry. But you've admitted to thinking about me. That counts for something. Every single day of these past five years, even though we were far apart, we still spent time with each other."

His words touched her heart. "I used to dream you'd come back to me, on your knees, begging my forgiveness. But then thoughts of you happily married would spring up and I'd be miserable for weeks."

Talon took a step closer and wrapped his large arms around her waist. His warmth was delicious and made her lightheaded. "Allie, I've never wanted another woman as badly as I want you, right here and now. If you'd let me, I'd make love to you all night long on these very steps."

She gasped and hid her embarrassment by embracing him. "You shouldn't talk to me so."

"I'm through with pretenses, honey. I've wasted too many years of my life, I don't intend on wasting any more." He knelt in the dirt before her. "Here I am. On my knees. Begging your forgiveness. Allie, please. Forgive me."

Without a word, she sat on the step, framing his face in her hands. His eyes were full of unspoken emotion, as if he were hanging on her next words. "Andrew Talon Holt…I…I don't know what to say."

"Say you forgive me, say you'll look at me again like you used to. Dear God in Heaven, Alison, if I could take back what I did, take back all the hurt I've caused us both, I'd do it in a heartbeat. I was a fool, an ass—"

Alison stopped him with her finger on his lips. "Shh. You talk too much. I forgive you."

A wide, handsome smile spread out upon his face, taking her breath away. Talon hugged her once again, his strong arms trembling something fierce. She couldn't break away from him—but she didn't want to. His arms were where she'd always longed to be. He began kissing her neck with feather-soft pecks, rising higher and higher to trace along the underside of her jaw.

Grazing up her cheeks, he stopped at her ear, lightly taking her earlobe into his mouth. Alison shivered with pleasure as her nipples puckered. This man was determined to drive her insane.

"Don't ever leave me again, Talon," she breathed, clutching onto the back of his head. "Please don't."

"I want to make things right between us, Allie," he said, his nose touching hers. "I want to take care of you. Be there for you. Are you sure you don't care that I'm Comanche?"

"When have I *ever* cared? When we were younger, the kids made fun of us, but I never left you. When we were older, all I saw was the man I wanted to..."

"Wanted to what?"

Alison swallowed hard before she answered him. "The man I wanted to spend my life with."

Talon closed his eyes, his short breaths tickling her cheeks. When he opened them again, his gaze was intense. It overwhelmed her.

"I promise you, Allie, I will never leave you again."

The sting of tears clouded her eyes right before one slipped down her cheek. She couldn't stop the sob that ripped from her throat. Talon didn't say a word, he merely held her in his comforting arms.

Chapter Seven

Virgil McKay hid in the shadows, sweating like a stuck pig. Jed Williams sat before him on a crate outside the Bloody Bull Saloon, where he'd spent many a night. The man rarely went inside to gamble anymore ever since he'd lost his notorious bet, and instead, he chose to sit outside, drinking his cares away with his own private bottle of tequila. Didn't make no never mind to Virgil. In fact, it made his job that much easier.

No one but rats wandered the back alleyway behind the Bull, and Virgil was damned happy about that. Kidnapping a man for Sumrall's gain didn't exactly sit well with him. Sure, he wanted his share of George's money, but God only knew where the bastard buried his stash.

Before he died, George had sent a telegram to Garrett, saying he'd come into a lot of money up in Cactus, fancy words for telling him he'd knocked over a bank. Apparently, George used to be one of Jed Williams' ranch hands back in the day, and he'd buried the money on the Circle Q. The husband of the woman George had been sleeping with hadn't been too keen about sharing his wife and was out for blood, or some such. George had decided to bury the money to keep it safe, letting Garrett know about it, in case something happened to him.

The cruel irony of it all was that George had been shot in the back by that very man right there in the telegram office—before he'd been able to reveal the location of the money. Sumrall had no idea where it was buried, but was desperate to get his hands on it. When Jed had taken a seat at Garrett's poker table, Garrett had swindled the old man out of his ranch *and* his daughter.

Virgil knew Garrett didn't give a damn about Alison Williams. He only wanted to marry her to make sure the ranch fell into his hands. Virgil didn't think Jed was stupid enough to back out of a poker bet with Garrett. But that damned Indian was going to make things complicated. Kidnapping Jed was the only way to get the upper hand and make Alison comply to marrying Garrett, seeing as how Talon Holt had been adamant he wasn't going to get anywhere near her.

"Excuse me, sir, you got a light?" Virgil walked up to Jed, putting an unlit cigarette in his mouth.

"What?" Jed glanced up at him with glazed eyes. "Oh, no. Sorry. I don't smoke."

Without another word, Virgil balled his fist and punched Jed hard, making the man spin off the crate and hit the dirt. A small cloud of dust rose from the impact, and Jed lay there, not moving a muscle. He was out cold.

"Perfect," Virgil whispered.

○₹

Talon rode into Banning, determined to find Jed and bring him home. Once he'd tethered his horse in front of the Bloody Bull, he roamed the alley behind the saloon, but saw no trace of Alison's father. Wandering into the building through the back door, he saw a few people talking amongst themselves, some drinking at the bar, others playing a few friendly games of cards. One of the men puffing on his cigar without a care in the world was Sumrall himself, a wry grin on his face.

Talon scowled darkly. Jed's horse was still hitched out front, yet the man was nowhere to be seen. He knew damn well Jed wouldn't have gone anywhere else but the saloon. Something wasn't right.

"Looking for someone, Injun?" Sumrall's voice drifted over to him. Talon turned to look at him, then made his way to the table without breaking eye contact.

"You got something you want to tell me, Garrett?" Talon's heart raced and he desperately wanted to knock that smug look off the older man's pudgy face.

Sumrall shrugged, arranging the cards in his hand. "Seems odd ol' Jed ain't here tonight, don't it, boys?"

All the men at the poker table nodded and grinned.

Talon placed both his palms on the table and leaned far over it, trying to ignore every instinct he had to beat the shit out of this man. "What did you do to him?"

"Me? I did nothing. Just figured I might give Alison some incentive."

"What the hell does that mean?"

"Come on, Talon. You're a smart man." Garrett shook his head and gave him a look of criticism. "You forced my hand is all. I want the lady for my wife. Her father's merely insurance."

Talon tried his hardest not to make a scene, but the other patrons of the bar seemed eager for a fight. A few of them were even exchanging money, and he had to wonder if they were placing bets.

"You took Alison's father to *make* her marry you?" Talon narrowed his eyes and leaned even farther across the table.

"Let's just say I invited him to spend some time at my place." Garrett chuckled as he puffed on his cigar. He blew the smoke in Talon's direction.

Talon had enough. Grabbing Garrett's collar in both hands, he heaved the man out of his chair and onto the table, making his cards and poker chips fly every which way.

"Oh, you're going to pay for that, you son of a bitch." Talon drew his fist back and let it fly, landing solidly in the middle of Garrett's face. With a cry, Garrett flew off the table into another man's lap. But Talon wasn't through with him.

Rounding the table, Talon once again grabbed Garrett's collar and pulled his arm back as if to strike. "You'll let Jed go or so help me God, I'm going to kill you."

Garrett smiled as he panted, revealing bloody teeth. The sound of a cocking gun made the room go deathly quiet. "Not if you're dead first, *savage*."

Glancing between them, Talon saw the barrel of Garrett's revolver pointed right at his chest.

"Let me go."

Talon did as Garrett said, but couldn't resist the urge to knock his head on the floor in the process. "You think you've won, Sumrall?" He scoffed loudly. "Think again."

Without looking back, Talon stormed out of the saloon, determined to raise a little hell.

Chapter Eight

The banging on the front door of the ranch house woke Alison out of a fitful sleep. Glancing out her window, she could see the sun had already risen, meaning she'd slept in longer than she meant to. Grabbing her robe, she yanked open her bedroom door and raced down the hall, not even bothering to look in her father's room. She knew he wouldn't be there.

The pounding continued, as if the Devil himself were trying to break in.

"Allie! Allie, it's me. Open up."

That was Talon. With her heart in her throat, she pulled the lock, wondering what the heck he'd be so adamant about first thing in the morning.

She yanked the door open wide and her braid flung over the front of her shoulder. "Talon, what is it?"

He stood on the porch, his arm raised as if to continue beating the door, but his eyes were glued to her, roaming the length of her body. Despite the memory of his hand on her breast the night before, Alison shivered and drew the robe tighter around herself. A sudden heat pooled between her legs at the thought of what his hand might feel like without the layers of her dress to hinder him.

"Damn, honey. You're a fine-lookin' woman."

Talon took the step that brought him over the threshold and grasped her waist, tugging her close. Alison knew in that split-second what he was going to do and she turned her face to meet him.

His lips were hard on hers, his kiss almost brutal. But he'd looked haggard when she opened the door. His clothing hung wrinkled and dirty on his lithe frame. Had he even slept?

Alison's thoughts scattered when his tongue forced its entry into her mouth, and she whimpered, raising her hands to frame his face.

He ripped away from her, his eyes on fire. "You have no idea how close I am to throwing you over my shoulder, woman."

Alison's breath came in harsh gasps. "Why...why would you want to do that?"

Talon lifted a brow, his dark eyes glittering with sinful promises. "To take you to bed and have my way with you."

She couldn't hide her blush. "Why are you pounding on my front door like a madman?" she asked, trying desperately to change the subject.

Talon's face darkened and he let her go only to run his fingers through his hair. "Garrett's got your father."

"What do you mean he's got my father?"

"I mean he took him somewhere. Said he's insurance to make sure you'll marry him."

"My God!" Alison covered her mouth with both hands. "He kidnapped my father?"

"It would seem so." Talon raised his hand and caressed her cheek. "I searched high and low all night long, but I couldn't find where that bastard had taken him."

"He has my father. Dear Lord, what am I going to do?" The room spun around her and she stumbled to the sofa. "That hateful man is going to make me marry him."

"Allie, listen to me." Talon sat beside her and took one of her hands in his. "You are not going to marry that man."

"But he—"

Talon stopped her with a finger to her lips. "I know what he's done, honey. He thinks he's going to win both you and this ranch by forcing your hand. But we have an ace up our sleeve he doesn't know about."

"What's that?" Alison looked at him curiously.

"Our history. Think about it, Allie. You and I have known each other for years. We can practically finish each other's sentences."

"I don't understand. What does that have to do with anything?"

Talon licked his lips and cleared his throat before kneeling before her. "You can marry me, Allie. Before that son of a bitch Sumrall gets his claws into you."

Alison's eyes went wide. "Marry *you*?"

He gave her a single nod. "Today."

Gazing deep into his eyes, she knew without a doubt she wanted to be Talon's wife. The thought of sharing his bed and bearing his children made her tingle from head to toe. She'd often dreamt he would ask her, but her dreams were never quite like this.

"I've already claimed you as mine," he said, his voice dropping an octave. "Might as well make it official."

"This is so..."

"Sudden?"

She nodded. "Yes."

"We've both been through hell these past few years, honey. I think it's time we have a taste of heaven, don't you?" His hand cupped her face only to travel down to her chest, wandering lower and lower until it brushed her breast. She shuddered at the contact and closed her eyes, yelping when Talon's rough stubble pricked the skin of her neck. His tongue was hot upon her as he leaned her back, following her into the throw pillows.

"I know I haven't been there for you, honey. I know I'm not the finest choice for a husband. But Christ, Allie, I want you to be my wife. Say yes to me."

Without warning, his hand was inside her robe, puckering her nipple between his thumb and forefinger through the fabric of her nightgown. Alison bucked underneath him, wanting to feel full contact with his body. Her loins were on fire and as if reading her thoughts, he brought his knee between her legs, rubbing against her in a most wicked way. No matter how hard she tried to get her body to listen to her brain and stop, it wouldn't cooperate.

Talon's hand dipped inside her nightgown, kneading her breast fully, skin on skin. When she whimpered, he kissed her, pressing his knee harder against her. She was helpless in his onslaught, thinking of nothing but him, shocking herself by wishing they were in her bed right then and there.

When Talon's mouth left hers, she only had a moment to be confused before he pulled her nightgown low, exposing her breast to his hungry eyes. The second he touched her nipple with the tip of his tongue, she cried out, burying her fingers in his hair. It wasn't until he latched on to her breast with his entire mouth that she shuddered against him, lost in a sea of whirling sensation, rubbing herself on his knee again and again as loud groans escaped her. She was shocked to find he'd moved his knee only to bring his hand between them, cupping and stroking her intimately.

"There's more pleasure where that came from, honey," he said, his voice husky. "Don't make me beg. Say yes." Talon gave her a few chaste kisses on the lips, pressing his hand against her nightgown once again. Alison found herself opening her legs even more. Since when had she become so wanton?

"Will you make love to me if we're married?"

"Without a damn doubt." He gave her a heart-stopping grin.

Alison blushed but grinned back. "Then make me an honest woman, Talon Holt."

Chapter Nine

I don't deserve her.

Staring into Allie's eyes, Talon took a deep breath and held it while she recited her vows to love, honor and cherish him. It had taken less than three hours to obtain a license and talk Pastor Whitaker into performing a hasty service, with his wife and two sons as witnesses. Their family had known Talon and Allie most of their lives, as the two of them used to attend church together. Judging by the wide smile on the pastor's face as he said the final prayers, he seemed more than happy to marry them.

Tears fell down Allie's face when she gazed at Talon. She appeared to be holding in sobs of joy. His heart swelled, relief pouring through him like summer rain. As Pastor Whitaker pronounced them man and wife, Allie was truly his. *Finally.*

"You may kiss your bride." The pastor stood back and held his Bible with a grin, nodding at Talon. "Congratulations, son."

Talon smiled, glancing at Alison, who was trembling like a leaf. He bent down and captured her lips, holding the back of her head to make sure she couldn't pull away. She was beauty and light, filling his soul with such happiness, he thought he'd burst from it.

Allie's arms curled around his neck and she stood on her tiptoes. Without breaking the kiss, Talon lifted her against him and twirled her about the sanctuary. She pulled away from his mouth and gave him a smile that touched his heart. Alison tossed her head back and laughed delightedly, the sound of it echoing off the four walls of the church.

High Noon

"Can't get away from me now." Talon put her down and tapped her nose playfully with his forefinger. "You're stuck with me, honey."

"I'm more than happy to be *stuck* with you."

"Mrs. Alison Holt." He spoke her new name with reverence, bending his head low for another kiss. She shivered in his arms and he longed to make love to her, if only to hear his name on her lips. Allie embraced him, giving him soft kisses on his neck. Talon had no idea how he maintained control of himself in front of the pastor, but peeling out of her arms, he grabbed her hand and began walking down the aisle.

"Let's go home," he said with a wink.

A loud bang sounded from the front of the church as the double doors were thrown open. Garrett Sumrall and his lackey, Virgil McKay, strode into the church, bringing the warm summer breeze with them. Allie gasped and clutched onto Talon's hand almost painfully.

"What the hell did you just do?" Garrett demanded, his eyes on fire.

Talon took a step in front of Allie before he spoke. "Why, I just got married. I would have invited you, but it was a rather hasty affair. Seems word travels fast in Banning."

"Son of a bitch!" Sumrall yanked his hat off his head and sent it flying before he marched up the aisle. His hand hovered above the gun on his hip, and Talon instantly regretted the decision not to wear his weapons at his own wedding.

"Talon!" Alison sounded frantic.

"Stay where you are," he commanded, keeping his body between her and Garrett.

The gambler drew his gun, pointing it directly at Talon's head. "She's mine, savage. I won her fair and square."

"Fair and square don't cut it in my book." Talon narrowed his eyes. "Your poker bet doesn't amount to a hill of beans. Alison's father might have been willing to offer his daughter on the altar, but I sure as hell am *not*. Seen as how ol' Jed isn't here to argue with me, I'm going to make my own rules. Alison is *my* wife now, Sumrall. And the Circle Q is mine, too."

129

"Seems a shame to make this pretty little lady a widow before she gets to enjoy her wedding night." Garrett cocked his revolver, the sound of it resonating around them.

"Now see here." Pastor Whitaker trotted up behind Talon and Allie. "This is the house of God."

"Then this damned Injun better make his peace."

Virgil tugged on Garrett's arm. "Don't do it. You'll hang for murder."

Talon arched a brow, watching the barrel of Garrett's gun bounce up and down. The man was angrier than hell, but he wasn't stupid.

"Cool your head in the horse trough outside, Sumrall," Pastor Whitaker exclaimed. "There will be no bloodshed in here."

With a growl, Garrett lowered the weapon, but as quick as a flash, he balled his fist and hit Talon hard. Talon wasn't ready for the blow and fell into one of the pews with Allie screaming behind him.

"You've dishonored me, *redskin*—" Garrett gritted through his teeth, "—and we're gonna settle this, you got that? Tomorrow. High noon—in front of the Bloody Bull. You don't show to face me, I'll send Alison's father home. *In a box.*" Garrett hocked deep in his throat and spat on Talon before turning his sights on Allie. "Enjoy your husband, darlin'. Tonight's the only night you'll get."

Talon jumped up to shield her from Garrett once again, but the man had already begun walking out of the church with Virgil in tow.

"Are...are you all right, Talon?" She was scared as shit but unharmed. That was all that mattered.

"Yeah, I'm all right, honey. Nothing's bruised but my pride."

"What are we going to do?"

He stared at her long and hard before answering. "Sumrall wants a fight, I'll damn well give him one."

CR

"Holy Christ, Garrett, a gunfight? You challenged that Injun to a gunfight? Don't you remember what he did to you up north a couple years back?"

Garrett rounded on Virgil, his rage apparent in his eyes. He slammed the smaller man into the wall of the general store. "Of course I remember!" Holding up his right hand, he wiggled his scarred fingers. "Bastard damn near severed my fingers shooting that gun out of my hand. He should have hanged for it."

"But he didn't kill you." Virgil felt icy fear creeping up his spine as Garrett's look darkened.

"I am going to kill that son of a bitch, even if I end up killing myself to do it. He's already stolen my ranch and my fiancée. He will *not* steal my money."

"But how can you possibly win against him tomorrow? Ever since he shot you, your draw ain't what it used to be."

"That's where you come in."

Virgil was confused. "What do you mean?"

Reaching behind him, Garrett pulled a wicked-looking knife from the waistband of his jeans. "Before the fight, I want you to stick him with this."

Virgil's heart stopped. "You want me to *murder* him?"

"No, you idiot. I want you to hurt him, put him at a disadvantage. With Talon limping in the middle of the street, I got a chance."

"You brought this on yourself, you…you should be able to get yourself out."

The point of the blade pricked the underside of Virgil's jaw before he even saw it move. A small cry escaped him as his eyes widened.

"You'll help me, *Virge*, if it's the last thing you ever do. Or should I say the last thing Bessie and Lynn ever do?"

"I told you to keep them out of this."

"I will, mark my words. As long as you do what I say."

Virgil set his jaw and scowled. He knew Garrett wouldn't hesitate about taking the life of his wife and daughter. For their sakes, he grabbed the hilt of the knife and wrestled it out of Garrett's grasp.

"Tell me exactly what you want me to do." Virgil tried hard not to show his boiling anger when Garrett grinned from ear to ear.

Chapter Ten

The ranch house was quiet when Talon and Alison returned. She jumped at the sound of the door slamming shut behind her new husband. Every hair on her body stood on end once that thought flitted through her mind. Talon was her husband now. She should have been overjoyed. Instead, her insides turned to jelly.

Sumrall had challenged him to a gunfight. The man had looked mad enough to breathe fire. The possibilities of what could happen played endlessly in her head. Would tonight truly be the only night she'd get with Talon?

He glanced at her and gave her a lopsided grin.

"What's the matter?" Sauntering over to her, Talon wrapped his arms around her, pulling her close.

"I'm terrified."

"Of what?"

She raised a brow. "You know damn well what."

Talon looked shocked for a moment at her use of language, then chuckled annoyingly. "Allie, darlin', you should be more concerned for Garrett."

She swallowed hard. "He drew his gun on you, Talon. In the middle of the church. That man won't stop until you're six feet under."

"I bested him once, I can do it again."

"You've fought him before?"

Talon shook his head. "Not so much fought as merely defended myself. He and his buddy...uh, George, I think, if memory serves, were fixing to beat me bloody a few years back, when I was staying in Cactus." Alison gasped, covering her mouth. He raised his hand to caress her cheek. "Don't you worry none. They didn't hurt me. I shot their guns right out of their hands. You should have seen the look on their faces. Spent a month in jail because of it, but damn, it was worth it."

Alison stood speechless for a long moment. "Is that why he hates you so much?"

"Probably. But knowing Sumrall, I wouldn't be surprised if something else is going on with regards to this bet he made with your father. When I met him, it was no secret the man was shady. He was no longer allowed in the gambling hall in Cactus. There's no doubt in my mind your father's *friendly* little card game was fixed."

"But why? Why would Garrett go through all the trouble?"

"I don't know. He was pretty close to George Carter, but I haven't seen Sumrall's friend around Banning. Seems he has a new pet in Virgil McKay."

Alison's eyes widened. "Did you just say George Carter?"

Talon nodded.

"Oh my goodness."

"What?" His tone turned serious. "Do you recognize the name?"

"Yes. He used to be one of my father's ranch hands. Didn't stay for more than a few months. He came to us after you...well, after you left Banning."

Talon's eyes narrowed. "Seems like more than a coincidence this man George worked on your ranch and then his buddy Sumrall wants the deed to the property, don't you think?"

"What's going on?" Cold dread raced throughout her body and she pressed closer to Talon's warmth.

"I have no idea, honey. But I'm going to find out."

"Do you think they'll hurt my father?" Alison glanced up at him, her heart skipping a beat at the tender light in his eyes.

"They might. But once I win this gunfight tomorrow, he'll be set free. You'll see."

"But if you kill Garrett..." She let the sentence hang.

"I'll make sure Virgil takes me straight to him. If he doesn't, then he's got a date with my gun as well."

"What if Garrett kills you?"

Talon leaned in close, kissing her cheek. "Won't happen."

"But—"

"Allie, trust me. The man has an injured hand that I gave him. There's no way he can be faster than me on the draw. I'll win."

She sniffled, but bit her trembling lip. She wanted to believe him, but her own doubt kept getting in the way.

"I'll win, honey," he repeated. "I'm not going to leave you again."

Without another word, he took her mouth, lightly tracing her lips with his tongue. Alison mewled low in her throat and brought her arms around his neck. Talon bent low, hooking his arms under her knees. The world suddenly tilted and she held on tight, blushing like the new bride she was when he strode confidently down the hallway.

He walked into her room, kicking the door shut behind him. Talon dropped her on the bed none too gently, making Alison squeal in both fear and delight. *He's going to make love to me.* She'd wished for this moment a thousand times before. Now here she was, staring into his flaming eyes, feeling her own fire igniting between her legs. Her nipples puckered for him, and he hadn't even touched her yet.

He undid the buttons on his sleeves before attacking the ones on his shirt. Watching him scrambling out of his clothes made her raise her hands to the buttons on her dress. She hadn't worn anything fancy to their wedding, as her wardrobe was sparse. Just a cream-colored gown that had gone out of style two years prior. But Talon hadn't seemed to mind.

Once his shirt was unfastened, he yanked it out of the waistband of his jeans and let it slide to the floor. The sight of his golden-bronze skin had her mouth watering. He'd said he wanted to know what every inch of her tasted like. She found she wanted to know the very same thing about him.

Sitting on the edge of the bed, Talon helped her when her hands refused to cooperate. He didn't say a word, but his eyes were expressive, seeming to flash with desire. Once her arms were free of the gown, he tugged the rest of the material off her legs, then started unlacing the ties to her petticoats.

Alison watched his dark hands work at her bows, and her breath hitched in her throat. He was so intent on what he was doing, she couldn't resist reaching out to touch him. Talon jumped, startling her.

"I'm sorry," he whispered. "I'm just all wound up, I guess."

"Don't apologize." Was that her voice? It sounded husky, laced with passion. But Alison didn't blush. Instead, she sat up and began pulling at the ties to her corset.

"I'm about a hairsbreadth away from ripping this damn fabric from your body." His eyes caught hers and a spark of yearning ignited her blood.

"Then rip them."

He hesitated for only a moment before he grabbed the petticoats in his strong hands, tearing them to shreds. Once they were gone, he pulled off her drawers, urging her legs open.

"Do you trust me, honey?"

"Yes," she answered breathlessly. She felt a twinge of self-consciousness when he gazed at her, half-naked before him, but the hunger in his eyes tamped it down. She was his wife—he had every right to her body.

Talon climbed fully on the bed, crouching between her knees. "Close your eyes," he commanded. He looked like an Indian brave who'd just conquered his enemy and planned on pillaging his prize. Imagining him with war paint on his face and feathers in his hair had her heart racing, not in panic, but in excitement. Talon was Comanche, and she had a feeling he was about to show her how savage he could be.

Alison complied with his demand, closing her eyes tightly. It didn't take long before she felt the silken caress of his tongue on her, opening her folds with his fingers and plundering even deeper. With a cry, she clutched the pillows.

Talon licked her again, swirling around the one place that burned for his touch. She opened her legs wider and lifted her hips, silently asking for more. The feelings he gave her were unreal. Straining against him, she moaned when he gently entered her with his finger. He began a slow rhythm, driving her wild with need. She remembered the pleasure she felt with him that morning, but this was much more intense.

"Talon," she whispered, threading one of her hands through his hair. "Don't stop."

He didn't. Again and again he tasted her, making love to her with his mouth alone. It didn't take long before Alison fell over the edge, crying out her pleasure, pressing his head even closer to her center.

Once her shudders subsided, he climbed over her, kissing what skin was bare along the way. She hadn't successfully removed her corset, but he took care of the laces with one rip from his powerful hands. Once her corset was tossed aside and her chemise thrown over her head, Talon wasted no time before he pounced on her breasts, feasting.

Alison sighed in pleasure and wrapped her legs around him, completely naked beneath his muscular frame. The rough texture of his jeans grated on the soft skin of her inner thighs. Her hands found their way between them and tugged at his belt.

He knew what she wanted and pulled away just enough to unfasten his pants, making them fly across the room with her corset. She giggled at his haste, but then whimpered at the sight of him naked before her. Talon was perfectly made, his manhood swelling tall and proud.

He must have seen fear in her eyes. "Don't be afraid. I will not hurt you."

"Talon, you're beautiful." Alison could have sworn she saw him blush. He hid it by kissing her neck and settling between her legs once more.

"I've dreamt of this moment." His breath tickled her ear.

"Really?" Her thoughts scattered as a fresh wetness rushed to greet him. He seemed to be slicking himself in her essence.

"Every night, Allie."

She pushed his hair away from his face and smiled. "From this night forward, it will no longer be a dream."

Talon groaned and claimed her mouth. Once again, she wrapped her legs around his hips, inviting him to plunge inside her. He didn't hesitate. Slowly, he advanced, but his entry didn't hurt as much as she thought it would.

"You're so wet," he growled through his kisses.

"You excite me."

"Christ. You're tight too." He pushed a little more, inching forward bit by bit.

"You're the only man who's ever..." She couldn't finish. A look of fierce possessiveness crossed his face.

"You're *all* mine, Allie Holt. Goddamn. I love you, woman."

She couldn't answer him. His mouth cut off the words she wanted to say—that she loved him as well. But suddenly, he thrust forward, burying himself deep. She cried into his mouth, marveling at the sensation of having him inside of her. It was exquisite.

When he began to move, she moaned as he plunged again and again, bringing her closer to another explosive climax. She met him with every stroke, caressing his arms, his chest, his waist—any part of his skin she could reach. He released her mouth only to grab her hips, angling them upward.

Alison couldn't think, couldn't even breathe as unimaginable pleasure rippled through her once again. She screamed this time, pulling Talon back down, kissing him voraciously. He grunted loudly himself, slowing his rhythm, telling her he'd found his pleasure as well.

With tiny thrusts, he intensified the feeling of being rooted within her, smiling wickedly. She blushed but didn't look away.

"I love you too, Talon."

He closed his eyes, quaking above her. Scooping her into his arms, he rolled off her, but still held her close. He hid his face in her neck.

"You don't know how long I've wanted to hear you say that." His voice was muffled, but wavered regardless.

She tried her best to soothe him. "We've both waited a long time."

"Too long." Pulling back, Talon gazed at her with red-rimmed eyes. "Too long, baby."

He kissed her once more, only to roll back on top of her, pinning her with his weight. "Tell me again. Tell me that you love me."

"I love you, Talon. I love y—oh *God.*"

He entered her again, thrusting slow and deep, taking his time and stroking her already-sensitive flesh to another earth-shattering crescendo. Alison knew, in that moment, she'd never love another man for as long as she lived.

Chapter Eleven

Talon stood on the boardwalk in front of the Bloody Bull Saloon and took a deep, calming breath of acrid air. A light breeze kicked up the dust on Main Street and a few tumbleweeds found their way into the middle of the road. It wasn't quite noon, and already the walk on either side of the road was full of spectators. It wasn't every day a gunfight went down in Banning, and the townsfolk were curious to say the least.

The street had been cleared of all wagons and horses, as no one wanted a wayward bullet to damage their goods. Talon had to shake his head at the backwards logic. They were all standing on the sidelines—any one of them could get shot themselves.

A few of the more vocal folk seemed to be on his side, giving him the random pat on the back or shouting at him to "kill the son of a bitch." He wasn't nervous, but he did want this whole silly affair over with. Sumrall was no match for Talon's guns, and the man damn well knew it. He must be up to something.

Alison had stayed by Talon's side all morning, despite the fact that he'd told her to go on home. She wouldn't listen, demanding to be present for this gunfight, to be here for him should he need her. He was confident of his own skill, but anything could happen. He wasn't sure he wanted her to witness him shot down if it came to that. But no matter how hard he pushed her to leave, she dug her heels in even deeper, refusing to be moved.

"Just because you're my husband doesn't mean I'm always going to listen to you, Talon," she said loud enough for everyone around them to hear. "I'm staying, and that's final."

"Allie—"

"No. You're in this fight for me and for my father. I'm not going to let you do it alone."

He had to admire the fire in her spirit. She was more Comanche than she realized. Pouncing on her, Talon captured her lips and kissed her soundly for all to see. A few whistles and hoots filled the air, but he didn't care. It was about time these people knew Alison was now his wife.

"You're determined to be the death of me," he breathed into her ear. She smiled.

At that moment, a few boos drifted to them on the warm Texas wind, and Talon noticed Garrett striding through the crowd. He stopped in front of them, only to glare at Alison.

"Mr. Holt. *Mrs. Holt.* Glad to see you're not a coward, Talon."

He gave Garrett a single nod. "And I'm glad to see you're not afraid to die."

Sumrall threw back his head and laughed heartily. "Cocky to the end, eh, redskin? It's just about noon. What do you say we settle this like men? Winner takes all." With one look at Alison, Talon knew without a doubt what the fat man alluded to. A dark cloud descended upon his heart, and he thrust his wife behind him.

"You'll never have Alison."

Garrett cocked a brow. "We'll just see about that."

The man drifted back into the crowd and out onto the street. Talon turned to Allie and cupped her face. "Say a prayer for me."

"I've already said a thousand. I'll say a thousand more."

He gave her another kiss and turned—only to bump right into Virgil McKay. The man gazed at him as if all the hounds of Hell were on his heels.

"I can't do it," Virgil whispered, his eyes wide. Sweat poured down his face and darkened his shirt at his armpits. Even his hair was wet with sweat.

"Do what?" Talon asked.

Pulling out a long, serrated knife, Virgil shielded it from the crowd so they couldn't see. "Garrett wants me to stick you. With this."

Talon stared at him, suddenly realizing why Garrett seemed so self-assured. He'd wanted him injured, to make it a *fair* fight. *Bastard.*

"Can you kill him?" Virgil's eyes pleaded with him. "If I don't stick you, he'll go after my family. But…but if you kill him, he can't. Will you kill him, Mr. Holt?"

Anger, thick and deep, roiled over Talon. Every drop of his blood boiled, and he couldn't hold back the growl that emanated deep in his throat. "He won't hurt your family. You have my word."

Virgil's body went limp with relief, and he gave Talon the briefest of smiles. "Thank you so much."

"Give me the knife." Talon was through playing games. He was surprised he didn't knock Virgil out cold for pulling the damn thing on him in the first place.

With a trembling hand, Virgil handed him the blade and slinked back into the crowd. Talon tucked it into the waistband of his jeans and sauntered out onto the road himself. The crowd cheered and clapped when the two men stood in front of each other.

He stared hard at Garrett, who looked Talon up and down, presumably to see any bleeding wounds.

"Looking for this?" Talon asked, tossing the knife tip-first into the dirt. Its hilt vibrated back and forth. Garrett's face paled. "That's right. I'm perfectly healthy. And I'm going to fill you full of lead. Better make your peace, Sumrall. You're about to meet your Maker."

Both men walked ten paces from each other and turned. Silence engulfed the crowd and only the wind could be heard moaning through the nearby trees. Even from where he stood, Talon could see Garrett trembling with fear. Good. Let that man ponder his own mortality for a few more moments.

After an eternity, Talon reached for his gun, drawing it from its holster within a split second. Garrett drew at exactly the same time, and both guns went off, the loud report echoing all around them. Talon watched as Garrett crumpled to the ground. Garrett's bullet missed, but Talon felt something whiz by his left ear. He was damned lucky.

No one in the crowd moved an inch, except for Talon, who wandered up the road toward the man he'd just shot. Garrett was gasping for breath, trying in vain to stem the blood pumping from his chest. Talon didn't relish killing a man, and he'd meant to shoot him in the shoulder. But his aim must have been off.

"You've...killed me...bastard savage."

Talon knelt in the dirt and sighed. "Should have backed out of that poker bet."

Garrett chuckled, then coughed blood a second later. "You took everything from me. My ranch, my woman, my money..."

"Money?"

"Seems only fair I take...something from you, don't it?"

What the hell was Garrett talking about?

Before he could react, Sumrall cocked his gun one last time, took aim and fired. But he hadn't shot at Talon. A few women in the crowd screamed and Talon turned to look behind him, standing from the dirt.

"He shot her!" someone yelled.

"*Talon!*" That was Pastor Whitaker's voice. "He's shot Alison!"

Time stopped. Talon didn't even think before he cocked his gun, turning his sights back on Sumrall. But the man's dilated eyes told him all he needed to know. The asshole was already dead.

Without another thought, Talon raced up the road, his heart pounding in his throat.

Please, God. Don't take her from me.

Chapter Twelve

Alison lay on the boardwalk, watching the clouds meander through the sky. They were so beautiful. One even looked like a cute little bunny. People were yelling. Why were they yelling? She tried to clear her head, but an intense pressure in her side jabbed at her painfully. It didn't take long until she realized she couldn't get a full breath.

Then Talon was there, his handsome face above her, his brown eyes ringed with tears. Tears? Why was he crying? Had he been hurt? She turned her head a bit, watching as his mouth moved, but she couldn't understand his words. How odd.

His features blurred for a minute until he grabbed hold of both her cheeks, forcing her gaze to his.

"Can you hear me?" His voice seemed muffled. Alison opened her mouth to answer—nothing came out but a sigh. She merely nodded.

"Oh God, can anyone stop the bleeding?" he yelled.

Reaching up to his forearm, she held on tight, not really understanding what was happening. But she was tired, so very tired, and that gnawing pain in her side just wouldn't go away.

"Are you all right, honey?" Talon sniffled. "I can't lose you. Not now. Don't you dare leave me, Allie."

What was he talking about? The world tilted and her vision blurred once more. No matter how hard she blinked, she couldn't escape the darkness engulfing her.

"Tal...on..." Closing her eyes, Alison fell back into emptiness.

൬

The crowd parted to let a man through. Talon was barely aware of him, feeling nothing but consuming despair. Allie had closed her eyes. No matter how hard he patted her cheeks, she wouldn't awaken.

"She's been gut shot."

Turning his head, Talon finally gazed at the man next to him, on his knees, examining her wound.

"I'm Dr. Krauss. You her husband?"

Talon wiped his eyes. "Yes. Can you help her? Is she going to...?"

"I don't know," the doctor said. "She needs to be operated on, that's for damn sure. Bring her to my office. I'll tell my nurse to get ready for emergency surgery."

A single sob escaped Talon as he stood with Alison in his arms. The people around him gave him a wide berth as he hurried behind Dr. Krauss, who'd begun sprinting down the boardwalk. He entered a wide door with a window that had his name painted on it. *Dr. Victor Krauss.* Talon vaguely remembered walking past this very office many times in his youth, but he'd never met the doctor—until now.

"Susan, get my scalpels ready!" Dr. Krauss yelled at a young woman inside the office. She stood, her face as white as a sheet as the doctor moved past her.

"The gunfight?" she breathed.

The doctor nodded. "Hurry." Turning to Talon, he waved him into a large room with a bed in the middle. Susan scurried around them, collecting scalpels and cloths, knocking over a few trays in the meantime. "Leave them," Dr. Krauss said, not sparing her a glance as he drew the curtain that separated his exam room from the outer office. "We've got to get the bullet out of Mrs...."

"Holt. Alison Holt." Talon laid Allie on the bed and ran his fingers through his hair. He felt as if he were going to be sick. Sumrall shot her. That bastard was going to take the one woman he'd ever loved. And for what? *A goddamned poker bet.* "Christ!"

"Mr. Holt, this might take awhile. You're welcome to wait out in the office, but you might want to get yourself cleaned up while I operate on your wife."

Talon looked down, taking in his soiled shirt and jeans— covered in Allie's blood. "Oh God." He glanced back at the doctor. "Is she...going to be all right?"

"I won't lie to you, son," he answered, ripping the dress from Allie's body. "A gut shot is nothing to turn your nose at. I've got to get this bullet out of her and stop the bleeding. After that, it'll be anyone's guess."

A muscle ticked in Talon's jaw when Allie's creamy flesh was exposed, torn to shreds by Sumrall's bullet. He had half a mind to unload his gun in that man's rotting corpse.

"Take good care of her," Talon said, his voice cracking.

"I'll do my best."

Bending over the bed, Talon pushed a few stray hairs from Allie's face before kissing her forehead. "I'll be back, honey," he whispered in her ear. "Hang in there. I love you."

Turning on his heel, Talon strode through the doctor's office, determined to find Virgil and make the asshole give him some answers.

This Comanche was on the warpath.

છર

Once Talon emerged from Dr. Krauss's office, most of the crowd had dispersed. The undertaker had come for Garrett's body, dumping him in a pine box and loading him onto a wagon bound for the cemetery just outside of town. Talon resisted the urge to shoot the coffin.

The Bloody Bull Saloon was busy, full of people who wanted a drink after watching a man die. Talon scanned the crowd but didn't see Virgil's face. He asked a few men if they knew where he was. They had no idea. On a whim, he walked through the middle of the saloon, ignoring the pats on the back and many cheers in his name. Talon couldn't possibly be happy he'd killed Sumrall. The man deserved to die more than once and he itched to kill him again.

Making his way to the back door, he entered the alleyway behind the Bull and spotted Virgil sitting on the very crate where Jed had once reclined.

"Afternoon, Injun," Virgil said, puffing on his cigarette.

Talon's temper was holding on by a thread. Without a word, he pulled his gun and aimed it at Virgil's head. "Where's Alison's father?"

Virgil took a long drag and blew the smoke into the air, as if he didn't have a pissed off Indian pointing a loaded gun at his head.

"In a shallow grave somewhere in the foothills."

Talon's blood ran cold and he cocked the hammer. "I'm in no mood to play games, McKay. I just killed a man and I'm covered in my wife's blood. I'm not above snuffing out your worthless life as well."

Looking him in the eye, Virgil narrowed his gaze. "I'm telling you the truth. Garrett never intended on bringing Jed back into the picture. Killed him not more than an hour after I..."

"After you what?"

"After I kidnapped him."

The barrel of Talon's gun shook and tears stung the back of his eyes. "You son of a bitch."

"You think I wanted to do it?" Virgil jumped off the crate and walked right up to him, resting his chest against the barrel of the gun. "That bastard made me do it. Promised to have his way with my daughter if I didn't. And my wife. I had to comply. You don't know a damn thing about my motivations."

"You took Jed to his death." Talon was cracking. He knew damn well he wouldn't be able to keep his rage at bay for very much longer.

"I had no idea Garrett was going to shoot Alison's father in the head. If I'd known that, I might have thought twice about it. But when he told me to knife you, I'd had enough. I saw a chance and I took it. We both knew you were the better gunman. Garrett just didn't count on the fact that I'd betray him. But he'd threatened the lives of my family one too many times. So if you want to shoot me, please do. I'm not too pleased with myself either, as if you couldn't tell." Virgil held up a half-empty bottle of whiskey and swirled its contents.

An uneasy silence passed between them as Talon tried hard to get a grip on his raging emotions. Jed was dead. How could he tell Allie? Would he *ever* get a chance to tell her? Sumrall just might have killed her too.

"What about the money?" he asked. "Garrett mentioned that I'd taken his money. What was he talking about?"

Virgil took a swig of his bottle and leaned back against the crate, apparently satisfied Talon wasn't going to shoot him. Yet Talon kept his gun trained on him just the same. "Garrett had a friend a few years back named George."

"George Carter?"

The man nodded. "One and the same. Guess he used to be a ranch hand workin' for ol' Jed. But he was also an outlaw. Maybe he came to Banning to lay low for awhile, who knows. He telegraphed Garrett about some money he'd come into. We both knew it was money from the bank he'd knocked over in Cactus. But he buried it. On the Circle Q. He was in some relationship with a man's wife and the husband didn't take too kindly to another man warming his bed. He shot George dead right there in the telegram office before George had a chance to relay where the money was buried. All Garrett had to go on was the name of the ranch and the man who owned it. The fact that Jed was a poor gambler was a bonus. Garrett was a master at stacking a deck of cards."

With a sigh, Talon uncocked his gun and lowered it. "I know. Ran into Sumrall and George in Cactus myself."

"And Garrett never forgot that. He hated you something fierce for crippling his shootin' hand. But I don't think he ever cared about Alison. He only wanted her to make sure the ranch would fall into his hands. Killing Jed would have made that a reality. Once he'd married the woman, no one could dispute his ownership of the Circle Q. That is, until you came along and spoiled his plans by marrying Alison first."

Talon holstered his gun and took a deep breath. He rubbed his eyes and exhaustion swept over him. "So there's a stash of money buried somewhere on Jed's ranch?"

Virgil nodded. "Good luck finding it. I don't want to have any part of that blood money. I'm washing my hands of the whole mess."

Talon didn't blame him. "Take me to Jed's grave. I want to pay my respects."

Wordlessly, Virgil waved for him to follow as he turned and walked toward Main Street. Alison would be in surgery for a few more hours yet and Talon needed something to do to keep himself sane. Digging haphazardly on Jed's ranch—no, on *his* ranch—for phantom bags of money didn't appeal to him at all. Talon needed closure, and he owed it to Jed to make his peace.

Chapter Thirteen

A small mound of dirt was all that marked Jed Williams' grave. Talon knelt and placed his hand on it. About five miles outside of Banning, Virgil had brought Jed to the rolling foothills where Garrett had been waiting for them. He must have made it back to Banning just in time after shooting Jed, because Talon had gone looking for Alison's father not too long after he'd been killed. Which meant that Sumrall had known damn good and well he was dead when Talon confronted him the second time.

"I buried him," Virgil said in a quiet voice. "Said a few prayers."

Talon took a deep breath and closed his eyes. "I'm sorry, Jed," he whispered. "You didn't deserve the hand life dealt you."

The day was waning as the sun hung low on the horizon, and a light breeze pulled a few stray tendrils of hair across Talon's face. Virgil walked away, apparently to give him some time alone at the grave. He was thankful for that.

"Goddamn, Jed, what the hell am I going to do if Alison dies? The only thing that kept me going these past five years was the thought that she was still here in Banning." A few tears slipped through his firm countenance. "I promise you, I will take care of her. Keep her safe. I love her so much more than I'd ever dreamed. Allie is my world."

After a few more moments of silence, Talon stood, wiping his hands on the backside of his jeans. "I'll be back for you, Jed. I won't leave you out here. You deserve to be buried in Banning's cemetery—next to your wife."

Dabbing his eyes, Talon walked to his horse, then swung into the saddle. Looking at Virgil, who'd mounted his own horse, Talon said, "You'd best keep far away from me, McKay. If I see you coming, you better cross the street to avoid me. The only reason I'm not going to turn you in to the sheriff is because you didn't stick me with Garrett's knife. Now we're even. But if you so much as cross my path again, I won't be so merciful."

Virgil answered him without hesitation. "You have my word."

Nodding toward Banning, Talon said, "Go on home. Spend the evening with your family."

Virgil tipped his hat and kicked his horse into a gallop. Talon followed at a more subdued pace. He was terrified at what he might find back in town. Had Allie died in surgery? He didn't know if he had the strength to face that kind of horror.

But if she was alive, she needed him, and he'd be damned if he wasn't there when she woke up. Not this time.

CR

She was thirsty. Smacking her lips, she found them to be dry and cracked, and her mouth felt as if she'd swallowed the entire Texas desert. Alison tried to sit up, but cried out and laid her head back on a pillow.

"Don't you do that again, woman."

Talon's voice sent a shiver of awareness through her. "Talon?" It was dark and she couldn't see him. Reaching out, she tried to touch him. His strong, warm hand grasped hers.

"I'm right here."

Alison clutched onto him. "Where am I?"

"Our bed."

As memories of their wedding night flooded through her mind, she blushed, but knew he couldn't see it. "What happened?"

"You were shot."

"*Shot?*" Alison tried hard to remember, but she only managed to give herself a headache.

"Sumrall shot you out of spite."

She gasped. "Are...are *you* all right?"

"I'm just fine, honey. Killed that asshole, though. He won't be around to bother us anymore." After a short pause, he asked, "You thirsty?"

"Yes." A moment later, a cool glass was brought to her lips and she opened her mouth, taking a few sips of water. She groaned. "That's wonderful."

"How do you feel?" Talon's hand threaded through her hair again and again, making her close her eyes and sigh with contentment.

"Not that bad, all things considering."

"Dr. Krauss has given you some medication that should help with the pain. But I'm going to play your nursemaid for the next few weeks, so don't even think about getting out of this bed to do anything for yourself, Alison Holt."

She didn't miss the harshness of his tone.

"Wouldn't think of it."

He chuckled and the bed dipped as he sat next to her. "Had to talk the doctor into letting me bring you back to the Circle Q. He wanted to keep you at his office, but I wasn't about to let you stay there all alone."

"I'm glad you brought me home."

"You need anything?" His face was close. She could feel his breath on her cheek. Now that her eyes were adjusted to the dark, she could see his shadowy form above her.

"Just you," she breathed.

Talon gave her a feather-soft kiss. "Aw, baby, you've always had me." He kissed her again, gentle and loving, teasing her with the wetness of his tongue. She opened for him and he slipped inside her mouth, barely playing with her own tongue. His kiss was one of love, not of passion, and Alison let go of his hand to stroke his face.

When he pulled back, she ran her thumb over his lips. "I love you."

He kissed her thumb, then brought her hand to his chest where his heart pounded underneath her fingertips. "I love you too."

Talon spread his long body next to hers, curling around her and laying his head on her shoulder, being sure not to bump her injury. His leg draped over hers intimately.

Alison stared at the ceiling, thinking about everything that had happened. "Talon?"

"Hmm?" he answered, sounding as if he were half-asleep.

"Did you ever find my father?"

His breathing suddenly stopped. Talon leaned up on his elbow, looking down at her. "I found him."

"How is he? Is he well?"

He shook his head. "No, Allie. Sumrall... He...he..."

"What?"

"Sumrall killed him. Jed's gone."

Her eyes went wide a split-second before they filled with tears. "Oh no." Instantly Talon cradled her once more, pressing her into his warmth. Alison didn't fight him as she hid her face in his neck. Her father hadn't been a man she'd respected too highly, but he'd been family. Now, the only person she had left was Talon. But Alison supposed her father's death was a good thing.

"I think I understand now why my father lived like he did," she murmured through her sniffles.

"Oh?" Talon kissed her forehead.

"My mother was the love of his life. His heart was broken when she died. If you died, Talon, I can't say I wouldn't do the same—turn to drinking and gambling."

Talon gave her a gentle squeeze. "I don't plan on dying on you, lady. Better get used to me being around for a very long time."

"Oh, I'm counting on it, Mr. Holt," she said, snuggling deep into his arms. "After our wedding night, there's no way in hell I'm ever letting such a *talented* man go."

Talon's sudden, delighted laughter filled the room, warming her heart. Leaning her back into the pillows, he kissed her once more and the entire world fell away.

Chapter Fourteen

Two Months Later

Alison bent down to pull her fresh-baked bread from the oven. Her wound only gave her a slight twinge nowadays. It was still pink and a little tender, but she was going to have one heck of a scar.

Dr. Krauss had visited them a few times in the weeks past, finally giving Alison permission to get out of bed about a month ago. Talon insisted she not take things too fast, no matter how good she felt. Therefore, she endured his burnt biscuits and thin soup on more than one occasion. But the man took care of her, no doubt about it.

They hadn't made love since the night before the gunfight—Talon didn't want to aggravate her injury any further. And she'd been glad for it, as even rolling over in bed had been excruciating. But now, when her husband wandered in from a long day of digging around the ranch, she couldn't help but notice the way his jeans molded to his hips, and how his shirt clung to his sweaty skin. A triumphant grin split his face and he held a dirty cloth bag.

"Find something?" she asked, arching a brow.

Talon nodded. "Over in the barracks. I never thought to look where the ranch hands slept until just this morning. Been digging all over creation, but all I needed to do was wander about two hundred yards away."

Turning the bag upside down, he dumped its contents onto the dining table. Bundles of neatly stacked bills spilled onto the floor. Alison gasped behind her hand.

"Oh my goodness."

"There's about nine more of these out there," he said, his eyes sparkling. "There must be about one thousand dollars in this bag alone."

She glanced at him with wide eyes. And there were *ten* bags altogether? "Do you think there's *ten thousand dollars* on this ranch?"

Talon nodded. "There's a good chance. But we aren't going to keep this, honey. It belongs to a bank up in Cactus. We should return it. Every last dime."

Alison smiled and wiped her hands on her apron before wandering over to where Talon stood. He pulled her into a loose embrace and sighed. "Seems this saga of the bank money is finally over."

"Thank God." Alison rolled her eyes.

"Maybe now we can concentrate on other things."

"Oh?"

"Yup. Like starting a family."

She stared at him in shock, the weight of his words finally sinking in. Her pulse quickened as she gazed into his dark eyes, his expression leaving no doubt about where his thoughts were headed.

"Don't you want to enjoy our time together for awhile? Alone?"

One side of his mouth rose in an alluring grin. "Why, Mrs. Holt. Are you saying you won't enjoy making babies with me?"

Alison giggled at his look of mock indignation. "I didn't say that. I just meant that we haven't been married long. Thought maybe you might want to take things slow."

With a squeeze, Talon hugged her close. "Why don't we just see what happens?"

Alison stood on her toes, hugging him with contentment. With Talon, she was safe. Protected. He was all she'd ever need. After a brief silence, she whispered, "Take me to bed."

Leaning back, he looked at her, raising both eyebrows as if to ask if she was sure. She nodded and broke eye contact, feeling her belly twist in knots at the anticipation.

"The bed's not the only place we can get cozy," he said, his rough voice sending a wave of shivers through her. "Come with me."

He held out his hand and waited until she took it timidly in her own. He turned on his heel and walked out the door.

"Where are we going?"

"You'll see," he tossed over his shoulder.

After a few minutes of walking, Alison knew exactly where he was taking her. Down by the creek. Where they'd spent many a lazy afternoon in their youth.

"Remember this rock?" he asked, pointing to a large boulder on the bank of the creek, partially hidden by low-hanging trees.

"How could I forget?" It was where he'd challenged her to take off her boots and splash in the cold water one summer. Where he'd taught her how to fish. And where she'd first told him she had feelings for him.

"There's a lot of memories here." He bent down to smooth his hand over its surface. Alison nodded, admiring him. He was older, wiser, but still the same man she fell in love with all those years ago.

The sun was low in the sky but far from setting when he glanced back up at her, a sinful gleam in his eye. "Let's make another memory," he said, pulling her down with him.

Alison smiled and threaded her fingers through his hair. It was as black as pitch, but so very soft. He closed his eyes to the sensation and a muscle ticked in his jaw. That gave her the courage to unbutton his shirt.

"Have I ever told you how handsome you are?" she asked, caressing his shoulders and arms in an effort to slide the shirt off his body.

"I'm handsome?"

"Definitely. Magnificent. One of God's most perfect creations."

He chuckled and tapped her on her nose. "Let's not go makin' stories now, honey."

"I'm not. You're a wonderful man, Talon. On the inside *and* on the outside. I'm a lucky woman."

"I think I got the better end of the deal," he said, working the buttons of her dress as well. "You're one of the most breathtaking women I've ever known. You're caring and loving, and I pray the Good Lord never takes you from me. I'm just a good-for-nothing Comanche pretending to be a white man."

"Don't you dare talk like that," she scolded. "I won't have it."

Talon took a deep breath. "I'm sorry."

"Besides," Alison continued, fumbling with his belt. "I happen to know you *are* good for *something.*"

He gave her a smile that stopped her heart. "Oh, is that why you love me?"

"Could be, Mr. Holt."

With a growl, he pounced, pinning her against the boulder, uncaring for her cry of alarm. She laughed out loud as he playfully bit her neck, but then gasped for breath when he kicked off his jeans, and was finally naked on top of her. She was still wearing her dress, but she'd taken to not wearing her corset and petticoats after she'd been shot.

Talon's warm hands stroked her thighs, hiking her skirt higher on her legs. She bucked beneath him, impatient to feel him inside her. She helped him bunch the fabric, twisting her body this way and that to free herself from her drawers.

"Forgive me, honey?" he panted, kissing her cheeks.

"For what?" she asked, rejoicing when she felt contact with his erection against her moist flesh.

"For not taking the time to undress you."

Alison turned her head and took his mouth, plunging her tongue inside. He groaned loudly and she felt his manhood press even harder against her.

"I don't care. Make love to me."

No sooner had she said her last word than Talon thrust forward, burying himself within her. Her cry echoed all around them as he possessed her, keeping time with her pounding heart.

Planting her feet on the rock, Alison lifted her hips and groaned with ecstasy as he plunged deeper, the tip of him touching a place that excited her even more. She followed him stroke for stroke, and held his head to hers, kissing him voraciously as her orgasm wracked her body. A few moments later, Talon joined her in bliss, holding on to her thighs and pressing into her as far as he could go.

His breaths came in harsh gusts as Talon collapsed onto her chest. A few blessed moments later, he lifted himself and continued to unbutton her dress.

"What are you doing?" Alison asked dreamily.

"Taking off your clothes."

"Why?"

"We're going to wash off in the creek and do this again."

Opening her eyes, she couldn't help but chuckle. "Maybe we can do it in the water this time."

Talon's eyes widened a moment before he grinned from ear to ear. "I knew I married you for something."

She smiled back. "My pound cake?"

Leaning down, he whispered in her ear, "The torrid sex."

"Talon Holt!" She smacked him on the shoulder. "Behave yourself."

"Around you? Never. Now don't make me drag you kicking and screaming into that water."

"I won't kick and scream," she said with a grin. "But I might bite."

"Woman, I hope that's a threat you intend to keep." He grinned as he stood, allowing her to stand and finally shed her dress.

"You'll just have to find out, now won't you?" Alison turned and waded into the cool water. Talon was close on her heels, his arms curling around her like bands of steel. He turned her in his embrace and didn't say a word. He merely studied her face, as if memorizing every line.

Stroking the skin of his chest, she leaned in and kissed the water droplets from his golden skin. "My husband," she breathed. "I love you."

He twisted his hand in her hair and gently urged her head back. "I don't know why you love me. I probably never will. I don't deserve you, Allie. But I love you too. My sweet wife."

High Noon

Lowering his head, he kissed her thoroughly, and nothing else mattered but Talon, making love to her once more.

It was a long time indeed before they emerged from the water. But Alison didn't care in the least. The man she loved more than life itself had come back to her.

She would never let him go again.

About the Author

Rebecca Goings enjoys writing many different genres of romance, from historical to contemporary, and fantasy to paranormal. Her life's goal has been to become an author, and finally she is living her dream. She loves to crochet in her spare time, and watches many different TV series through Netflix with her husband. She also homeschools her children and finds it to be one of the most rewarding things she's ever done.

Rebecca lives in the Pacific Northwest with her husband Jim, and their four children, two cats, and a big, stubborn dog. You can find her online at www.rebeccagoings.com or at her author loop at http://groups.google.com/group/themagicofromance. Rebecca also has a newsletter group at http://groups.google.com/group/rebeccagoingsnewsletter.

Look for these titles by *Rebecca Goings*

Now Available:

The Cursed Heart Series
(also in the print anthology Cursed Hearts)
Hearts Eternal
Hearts Unbound

The Legends of Mynos Series
Wolverine and the Rose
Wolverine and the Jewel
Wolverine and the Flame

The Seduction of Widow McEwan

Melissa Schroeder

Dedication

To Lou Jean Baker for taking my children and caring for them as if they were your own, and Beth Peters for racing me to the ER and even offering me a Nora Roberts book to pass the time. You both proved once again how supportive and special the Air Force family truly is. Thank you both for coming to my aid in my hour of need.

To Dr. Sweicki, his surgical team A, and the nurses, medical techs and staff of Two Ward West of Brooks Army Medical Center who worked from April 2-10, 2007. It took nine long days, but you patched me up and got me back on my feet. Thank you.

And especially to Kally Jo Surbeck, who took on everything in my absence. You know I would not make it without Goose to back me up.

A special thanks to Becka Goings and Beth Williamson. Two wonderfully talented authors who took a chance and included me in the anthology. Thanks, ladies.

Chapter One

Texas, 1883

It was a damn fine day.

Seth Conner watched the first fingers of light dance across the yard as he took a sip of coffee and smiled. Life was pretty wonderful at the moment. It had been a bitch of a night, but they had a brand spanking new filly in their barn now. His muscles ached, his head felt like it was filled with cotton, but he just didn't care. The Double C horse ranch had their very first birth, and it had been successful as all get out.

Jackson Calder, his partner of the last five years and best friend since they were sixteen, stomped down the stairs. He glared at Seth as he headed for the stove. Seth just smiled and settled in one of the kitchen chairs.

"Hey, I sent word to your sister's ranch as soon as I realized Sand Dollar was foaling early. Not my fault it took you forever to get here."

If possible, Jack's frown turned darker as he sipped his coffee. "Jamie and I got in a fight last night."

"What's new? You two are always squabbling."

"Naw. This time it's different. She threw me out of the house."

That gave Seth pause. The siblings did fight constantly, but unlike his own family, Jack and Jamie used it as a way to communicate. Seth's family spoke in measured tones.

"What was the argument about?"

"Tucker Portman." Jack spat out the name as if it were poison. And with good reason. Portman was known for his shady deals and his expensive tastes in women, not to mention his two dead wives. Seth couldn't think of one reason for Jameson McEwan to be dealing with Portman other than business.

"Why?"

This time Jack sighed. "Bastard asked her to marry him."

Seth laughed and choked on the sip of coffee he had just taken. Jamie had turned down every man who had come sniffing around her for the last few years, and she surely wouldn't even consider someone like Portman. Not when he had been Sid McEwan's partner in all his whoring. "Right. And I'm sure she said yes."

Jack's eyebrows drew down as he scowled. "She didn't say no."

Seth's heart stopped for just a moment. "Are you telling me she said yes to that degenerate?"

Jack shook his head, his eyes, so like his sister's, dead serious. "But she's considering it."

Swift anger shifted through Seth. "Why the hell is she even thinking of doing it?"

Jack plopped down in the chair opposite of Seth's and sighed again. "He suggested it would be a good way to combine the ranches. Their properties butt up against each other. That fence comes down, that would be one big ranch. Probably the biggest in South Texas, if not the whole danged state."

"Tell her she can't."

This time Jack snorted. "Yeah, and she's going to listen to me."

Panic quickly replaced the anger speeding through his blood and chilling his body. Jamie had never seriously considered any proposal before now. With the spread that was left to her when Sid died, she was considered one of the most eligible women in the area. For years she had ignored all overtures, not even attempting to hide the fact she was just plain not interested in any man in particular. The idea that she was considering Portman's offer scared the hell out of Seth. To hide his feelings, he set his face with a sneer and decided to try and get under his best friend's skin.

"Jesus, Jack. You're her brother—"

"*Younger* brother. That doesn't mean anything to Jamie. She's been on her own for four years."

"But with your father gone, you're the man of the family." Seth was grasping at straws but the idea of Jamie marrying anyone else was not something he could face like a man.

"Again, I'm her younger brother and she practically raised me." Jack slouched in his chair and anyone who didn't know him would think that he was half-asleep. Being his friend for more than ten years, Seth knew better. "She says she's going to San Antonio without me later this week."

"She can't do that."

"She can, and she will. You know how stubborn my sister is. The only time she didn't dig in her heels was when Pa told her she was marrying Sid."

He ignored that little fact and pushed on. The idea of Jamie riding all the way into San Antonio by herself sent a chill into his gut. He knew she had some business to do there from time to time, but she'd never attempted the trip alone. "Figure out a way to have someone go with her."

"I thought you'd never ask."

"What?"

"I figure if you show up and just say you're doing me a favor, she won't be able to say no. You know how she is with you. You're the one she likes."

"That's because I don't try and tell her what to do." He would sure like to. Jamie was an independent widow, one used to ordering men around. He'd love to see how she'd react to being under his control. But just as Jack said, she saw Seth as a family member. She patted him on the head like he was a sibling when all he could think about was stripping her naked, slipping into her and capturing her cries of completion in his mouth.

Bad direction there, Seth. Clearing his throat and hopefully the image of his fantasy, he said, "That may be, but do you really think she'll fall for it? If she's still mad at you, I'm damn sure she'd not be in the mood to put up with me."

Jack waved Seth's comment away. "She may view you as a sort of adopted brother, but she still talks to you when she's mad at you."

He winced inwardly, knowing there was no way Jack understood why he wouldn't want that type of relationship. He'd never told his best friend about his fascination with Jamie. For good reason. Jack would probably not be that friendly if Seth told him he wanted to take his sister to bed and keep her there until she couldn't see straight.

"I don't want her going by herself, and with Walt laid up after he got hurt from that fall, she's shorthanded. There's been a few problems around her ranch—"

"Problems?"

Jack gave him a strange look. Probably because his voice had been sharp. It was hard not to be a little alarmed. Jamie was talking about marrying, going to San Antonio by herself and now there had been problems at her ranch he didn't know about.

"She had a few cattle go missing and apparently there's been some incidents she didn't tell me about." He shrugged. "Some sabotage, Walt told me. He didn't seem that worried about, says it's regular shit that goes on, but Jamie still shouldn't be out by herself riding to San Antonio."

Sabotage was common, especially on a spread as big as Jamie's, but riding to San Antonio by herself, that was plain stupid. The pleading look in his best friend's eyes told Seth he lost the argument before it even started.

With an aggravated sigh, Seth said, "I'll try, but you know the way she is. There's a good chance I won't convince her to let me tag along."

Jack took a healthy swallow of coffee and smiled. "I have a feeling you'll have no problem."

CR

Jameson McEwan looked out over the cattle grazing in the pasture and drew in a deep breath of fresh air. The lingering scent of hay filled her senses and calmed her guilt. No one got under her skin like her brother and this time he'd gone a step too far. She hadn't meant to lose her temper with Jack three nights earlier, but she could no longer let a man tell her what to do. Especially her *younger* brother.

It wasn't as if she had been serious about marrying Portman. She'd told him no when he asked and she meant it. Sid, her late husband, hadn't trusted Portman, even though they'd spent their childhood together. Lord knew they had spent more than one night whoring, before and after her marriage. In fact, they'd been on one of their whorehouse visits when Sid had suffered his heart seizure four years earlier. But when it came to money, Sid was smart, and he said never to trust Portman.

She shifted in her saddle and turned Sadie toward the house. As they slowly made their way home, she thought about her argument, thought about how to apologize, but a tiny part of her was rejoicing. This was the first time she had told her brother to butt out of her business and stood her ground. With a ranch that spread out over fifty thousand acres, Jamie was comfortable with being in charge, except with the men in her family.

First her father had bullied her for years, and into a marriage that had been far from satisfying. Now her brother, whom she helped raise, had the nerve to tell her what to do with her life...it was too much. She had been a little mean, and completely out of control, but she refused to let Jack tell her what to do. He must still be madder than an angry hornet about it because he had yet to come back to her ranch. It had been three days and she hadn't heard anything from him. After her trip to San Antonio she would have to go see him and smooth things over. It irritated her, but she was the older sibling and Jack had not fully grown up yet. She guessed she was to blame for that, as much as her father. After their mother's death, she did baby Jack a bit, but her father had made it worse with his *boys will be boys* mentality. Jack had never had to live up to anything in his entire life.

She'd been worried over their loss of cattle. With five thousand head, it wasn't much to have fewer than thirty go missing but it still bothered her. Hank had asked around, as had Jack, and no one else seemed to be missing any. With that worry, not to mention the upcoming negotiations with Johnson to buy his cattle, she really didn't need the added pressure she got from Jack. She loved him, but if he told her what to do again, she might just have to shoot his big toe.

As she rode into the barnyard, Jamie smiled at the activity. Even with all his failings, Sid McEwan had built something real, something solid here. It never failed to give her satisfaction to watch the workings of the ranch. Things were winding down for the day, and most of the hands were washing up for their evening meal. She had never intruded in their private time, left them to their own in the evenings. Sid hadn't believed in that. He'd thought he owned the men. Although they had feared Sid, they had more respect for her. Knowing her late husband, he was probably turning over in his grave. That notion made her smile wider.

"Boss!" Hank Goings flagged her down as she dismounted. By the time he reached her, he was wheezing and breathing heavily. A portly man some twenty years her senior, he'd been there when Sid had bought the ranch. His hair had gone white, his skin resembled leather from the years spent in the sun, and she loved him like a father. Making him foreman when Sid died was the smartest thing she'd ever done.

"Take it easy, Hank. What has you in such a rush?"

"You have a visitor."

She cringed and tightened her hold on Sadie's reins, all the while hoping it was her brother and not Portman. One thing she didn't want was to deal with her neighbor. She'd rather have another argument with her brother than have Portman slobber on her.

"Is that a fact?" she asked as she removed the harness.

"Yes'm. Seth Conner rode in a few minutes ago."

She whirled around to face Hank, her heart jumping into her throat. "What for?"

He grimaced. "Beg your pardon. I didn't mean to worry ya none. Seth said something about the trip to San Antonio tomorrow."

Laying her hand against her chest, she took a deep breath and allowed her heart to stop jumping. "Well, thank goodness for that. Can you see to Sadie for me?"

He nodded. "Yes'm."

When she entered the house, she stripped off her hat and tossed it on the hat rack in the foyer. The sounds from the kitchen told her where Seth was. He was pouring himself a cup of coffee, acting as if he owned the place. He'd always been like that. From the first time her brother brought him home, Seth seemed to be part of their family. But not. He came from different stock. With Jack and Jamie, you could see their Spanish ancestry stamped on their faces. No one would mistake Seth, with his sandy blond hair and gray green eyes, as a sibling.

Of course, Seth fit in just about anywhere. Whether he was in the company of rough and tumble cowboys, or spending time with his parents at the capitol, Seth succeeded in easing his way through the crowd and making lasting friendships. Her brother was the same way, although Seth preferred simple folk more than the state legislators his parents frequently socialized with.

She took her time studying him, watching the way his hair curled over his collar and thinking that once again, the boy needed a haircut. Her gaze traveled down his strong back, to his narrow waist, to his rear. Sighing even as her blood heated, she reminded herself that a young man like Seth was just that. *Young.* If she couldn't satisfy an old bastard like Sid, there was no way she'd gain the interest of Seth, who hadn't yet reached the age of thirty.

At that moment, he turned. A wave of guilt and embarrassment flooded her face. From the cocky curve of his lips, she knew he suspected where she had been looking. Seth Conner was accustomed to women falling all over themselves when he was around. He was considered quite the catch thanks to be being a state legislator's son. Add in the fact that he had a body that would make a Greek god jealous, well that was just a cherry on top of all that cream. And wouldn't it be wonderful to lick it off.

Good night! She needed to quit thinking of Seth that way. More than once in the past year she'd drifted off into lustful thoughts about him. She'd also had several rather naughty dreams of the man, his hands coursing over her skin, his mouth on hers. The fantasies were becoming more lewd and more frequent. Just thinking about them had her face heating, her body reacting. Fighting the urge to fidget, she crossed her arms over her chest and leaned against the doorjamb.

"Did Jack come whining to you about our fight?"

"No. Although he was mighty upset to miss the birth of Sand Dollar's foal."

"Oh." Remorse filled her. If Jack had not spent so much time arguing with her, he'd have been home in time. "I'm sorry for that. But you know my brother, he would argue with a fence post."

"I can't say I disagree with his position." His smile slid into a frown. "I can't believe you're thinking of marrying that jackass."

She raised an eyebrow. "And you felt the need to offer this opinion because…"

He took a sip of his coffee, never moving his attention from her face. "I know Portman. He's not a good man."

Jamie swallowed back the aggravated scream threatening to escape. Jack had made the same argument. All the men in her life danced a jig around the real reason they didn't want her to marry Portman. All of them—her brother, Seth and Hank—refused to tell her about Portman's perverted cravings. She was sick of being protected like some idiot with only air in her brain. Before he died, Sid had told her exactly what Portman was like in colorful detail. Jamie assumed that Sid had worried that Portman might have tried this move earlier and wanted to warn her. Instead, the years had passed without an overture from her neighbor. It struck her as decidedly odd that he now paid attention to her. After Sid's funeral Portman had waited over six months before he'd paid a call to the Circle M.

In his sixties, Portman appeared older mainly due to his balding hair and excess weight. She was sure the amount of booze and food he took in had a lot to do with it. Married twice, he had done a lot of hard living, and it added age and meanness to his features. The idea of having him touch her turned her stomach. He might have been handsome some time ago, but his love of liquor and cheap women truly did not help his appearance. She shuddered thinking of just what sharing a bed with him would be like.

The Seduction of Widow McEwan

She shook her head, trying to bring her mind back from that horrendous vision, and asked, "That may be, but don't you think it's for me to decide? It isn't like I don't have a mind of my own."

His features softened at her question. "I'd normally say that you have every right to your decisions. You've done just fine by this ranch since Sid died. You know I've backed almost every one of your decisions."

That much was true, and Seth had been the one man in her life who hadn't tried to tell her what to do. Well, until now. When her father and brother had ganged up on her and told her she couldn't go on the cattle drive, Seth had stood up for her. He'd agreed with her argument that she had to establish herself as the owner of Circle M Ranch.

"So, you disagree with my choice in men?"

Now it was his turn to sigh. "I didn't know you even paid attention to men before Jack told me about this."

"Really? So you see me as the sort of woman who isn't interested in men? Who do you think I'm interested in? Other women?"

For a second, he looked confused. Then the implication of what she meant hit him. His brows drew down over narrowed eyes. "Just what do you mean by that?"

"If I'm not interested in men, then I'd guess I'd have a hankering for women."

Shock rounded his eyes and she laughed. Pushing away from the door, she walked over to help herself to some much-needed coffee. Although she should act more proper, it tickled her to shock Seth.

"How in hell do you know about things like that?"

Before answering, she poured the thick brew into her cup and took a sip. She chuckled at his tone. Seth Conner sounded like an outraged virgin. If that didn't beat all.

"Why do all men assume women don't know about such things?" She shrugged off the irritation—mostly. "Besides, I was a married woman, Seth."

"Sid told you about things like that?"

Unfortunately, he had. He'd accused her several times of preferring women when he couldn't perform in bed. As usual, he'd blamed her for his shortcomings and she'd fallen for it. Not knowing anything about those matters, she'd asked Hank. He'd turned bright red and muttered something about not worrying her pretty little head about it. Then he'd stomped off.

Moving away from memories that should be left buried, she decided to confront the irritated male she had in front of her.

"You hear about things, Seth. But that doesn't matter. What does matter is why in the hell you're here."

Chapter Two

Seth took another sip of coffee and tried to gather his thoughts. From the moment Jamie had walked through the door, his brain had refused to function. The last rays of sunlight sliced through her hair, bringing out the golden highlights within the dark curls. They spilled over her shoulders. Windblown from her ride, she looked wonderfully tangled. Even dressed in her usual work clothes—a plain shirt tucked into a split skirt, a layer of dust coating her boots—she sparked something inside of him. He couldn't help it. She looked so damn delicious he wanted to eat her up in one bite.

When he'd arrived to find Sadie and Jamie both missing, his worst fear had been that she had left a day early. It would be just like Jamie to allow her temper to get the best of her. He could understand her anger. Jack more than likely talked to her as if she was a ninny. That was something she was definitely not.

At a young age, for a man *or* a woman, she'd taken over one of the biggest ranches in the area and made it more profitable. Even with that proof, Jack and their father treated her like a bit of fluff.

Seth waited until she sat down then took the chair opposite her across the table. He watched her drink her coffee and wondered just how long he'd been in love with her.

He knew the exact moment he began lusting for her. It started the day he'd first seen her. He had only been sixteen to her twenty-one. She'd already been married for four years, but that hadn't mattered. Any man with a mind and blood left in his veins would have been attracted to her. Tall, in a willowy kind of way, with long black hair that curled over her shoulders, and the biggest golden brown eyes Seth had ever seen, she'd been a pretty little thing. Being as randy as a stallion scenting a mare, he'd barely been able to talk to her without embarrassing himself. His usual quick tongue seemed to stop working, and when she smiled at him, he'd almost come right there and then.

Over the years, she'd matured, filled out, and his feelings for her had followed the same path. He'd watched her hold on to her dignity against the gossip of her husband's death and took on a ranch most men couldn't handle. Sometime during all of that, he'd realized he was no longer lusting, but was knee-deep in a rising creek. He'd never thought of doing anything about it. It'd been enough to admire her from afar, out of touch, with just his fantasies to keep him warm. The idea another man might have the right to touch her, though, had changed his mind.

"Seth?"

He blinked and tried to remember her last question. Ahh, the trip.

"Jack wanted me to go with you to San Antonio."

She frowned. "I don't need you to go with me, Seth. I'm a grown woman—"

"Who knows better than to ride off by herself. Admit it. You're doing this to get back at Jack."

The fire lighting her eyes was enough to tell him she was ready to argue the point. He'd been through it more than once with Jack. She opened her mouth, but he pressed ahead. "Listen, I understand why you're mad at him. But you can't go off on some half-cocked idea of traveling alone. Not with the reports of rustlers and a few lingering Indian problems."

"I know." She frowned and threaded her fingers through her hair. The familiar action never failed to capture his attention. "I thought by now he'd quit his sulking and come back over."

"And I need to pick up the supplies Jack was going to get when he went with you." He smiled. "Besides, it makes you the lucky one."

"Lucky one?"

"You get the privilege of my company for the trip."

She snorted. "That's a fine way of describing it. As long as you behave yourself, we should be just fine."

"Behave myself?"

"Seems I took both you and Jack into San Antone about three years ago, and there was that incident with a rather...busty working woman."

"Oh." Damn, he'd forgotten about that whore who'd tried to steal Seth's money. Jack had come to his rescue, but the ruckus had landed them and the whore's accomplice in jail for the night. The tips of Seth's ears burned in embarrassment as he remembered having to explain it to Jamie when she showed up for them the next morning. "I promise to act like a proper gentleman."

She smiled. That's all it took for his heart to turn over. One true smile that lit up her face, her joy shining through, easy for anyone to see. "I didn't say you had to be proper. I'm sure that's damn near impossible for you. Just stay away from women who try to steal your money."

She finished off her coffee and left to clean up from her ride. Inwardly he snorted at her last comment. Seth didn't lose sleep over women stealing his money. What kept him tossing and turning all night was the woman who'd stolen his heart.

☙

As Jamie handled the reins, Seth rode beside her on his gelding. The growth of the city amazed her as they made their way down Crockett Street in San Antonio. Since the arrival of the railroad just a few years ago, it seemed the city had doubled in size. Talk of a new line in from the Northeast had been all the buzz a few months earlier, but there was doubt it would be soon. Contracts and negotiations had held up the first train into San Antonio for years, and no one thought this one would be different.

The ride itself had been uneventful. She'd been pretty sure there wouldn't be any trouble, but she had to admit she felt better having Seth along for companionship. It would have been a long, boring ride without him to talk to.

"You have a room at the Menger, right?"

She turned to look at him and tried again to ignore the way her heart fluttered beneath her breast. It was embarrassing to be affected by him this way. Men rarely got a second glance from her and they definitely didn't cause this reaction—or hadn't in a long time. Sid had done his best to stomp out any romantic daydreams she'd had as a young girl. She couldn't understand why she was acting like a debutante out on her first date—with a man she thought of as a brother.

It had started when he'd said good night to her. The way he had looked at her, his gaze slipping down her body and then back up to her face had been intimate. As if he knew what she looked like naked. She'd gotten very little sleep, waking with gritty eyes and in a bad mood. During the trip, it seemed he spent more time touching her, holding her hand, offering to help her up on her horse than he ever had in the past. This was odd behavior for Seth, who rarely came within ten feet of her. With each glance he gave her, each touch, her body throbbed. She felt the need to scratch an itch, and for the first time in years, she thought a man, one in particular to be exact, might be the only thing to satisfy it.

"Yes. I had planned on sharing the room with Jack, so we'll have to get another room."

He shrugged. "Whatever."

There was a good chance Seth could find lodgings with the benefit of a woman. He and Jack usually did that when they came to town without her. A spike of pain hit her in the chest at the thought of his going to another woman. Silly, really, because it hadn't mattered to her before today. It wasn't like she expected anything from him, and she had no right to feel as if he was abandoning her. Jealousy whipped through her with such an amazing force, it stunned her. She yearned to be that woman he would take for the evening. The reaction not only shamed her but it saddened her as well. In all the years Sid had frequented the whorehouses, she'd never felt envy. The only thing she could remember was feeling relieved he was gone.

She cleared her throat. "I was thinking after we got settled we could head on down to Military Plaza for chili."

He glanced over at her and smiled. Not his usual friendly grin, but a sensuous tilting of his lips. Her blood heated. Her breath tangled in her throat. Seth held her gaze for just a moment, then broke away.

"That sounds like a fine idea. We should get there for the first servings from the Chili Queens," he suggested, referring to the Mexican women who gathered in the Plaza every day to offer up a frugal and much-loved treat.

She nodded as she took a deep breath. Sneaking a peek at Seth, she grimaced. There was no reason for her reaction. It made no sense whatsoever. Since Seth and Jack had become friends, Jamie had spent time in his company on a regular basis, and it wasn't as if he was different than one of her hands from the ranch. Every day, she worked side by side with men, spending more time with them than she did with women. Since Sid's death, several of the younger men had tried to get fresh with her. Not once had she been tempted and it hadn't caused any problems with work. With her life dedicated to the ranch, she found comfort in working alongside the men and would never jeopardize those relationships with an affair.

Seth's reputation with women was legendary. True, most of the women he spent time with weren't the socialites his parents kept throwing at him. Even though her obsession with him was new, there had always been something that drew her to him. Where her brother worked well with horses, Seth had shown a gentleness with the creatures you didn't see in most men. All of their stock responded to him immediately, and there hadn't been one he couldn't train yet. Every now and then, she found herself looking at him, wondering how gentle he would be in bed.

They turned onto Alamo Plaza where the Menger was located. Jamie hoped Seth hadn't noticed her odd behavior. He seemed comfortable with her as always, so it had to be her imagination. She brushed away her strange feelings.

As they stopped in front of the hotel, Seth said, "Why don't I get the horses and carriage stabled for the night and you check in. Then we can clean up and get some food in our stomachs."

Pleasantly surprised, she agreed and moved to step down. She didn't make it off the wagon. Seth reached up and grabbed her by the waist. The heat of his palms burned through the fabric of her shirt, warming her flesh. Her pulse tripped like a newborn colt the moment he lifted her to the ground. She looked up, way up, and found Seth smiling at her.

"Gotcha."

His voice seemed deeper, his Texas accent more pronounced. The sound of it shivered down her spine. Her skin tingled where he touched her. She licked her suddenly dry lips, and Seth followed the action with his gaze. Every thought slipped away but for one. Just how good it would feel to have his mouth against hers. The taste of him, the wildness she sensed beneath the surface, was as tempting as a fresh peach pie.

Leaning closer, she considered acting on that desire. The masculine scent of him, leather and man, filled her senses, making her mind whirl. What would it feel like to have him pull her into his arms, feel his breath upon her face the moment before he kissed her?

What in tarnation was she doing? She was five years his senior and standing in the middle of one of the most crowded areas of the city. Her marriage had taught her that some women were not equipped for relations. Knowing she was ready to mortify both of them and possibly cause a scandal, she dragged herself away.

"Thanks." Without looking at him, she asked, "Do you need me to get you a room?"

There was nothing but silence from behind her so she turned on the first step and glanced at him. Jamie couldn't read his expression as he cocked his head to one side and watched her. After several moments passed, he shook his head.

"No. I can take care of that myself."

She knew what that meant. He planned on staying at one of the saloons and getting a tart for the night. Again, the green-eyed monster of jealousy reared its ugly head, and she didn't like that one bit.

"Of course." Her voice had grown cold and ugly. It shamed her but she didn't care. Without another word, she whirled around and walked up the steps and into the lobby of the Menger. It was best to concentrate on her business and not flirtatious rogues who preferred the company of saloon women.

Seth drank the last of his beer and set the glass down on the bar. He'd arrived at the hotel earlier than he'd planned but his anticipation was high. To be this close to fulfilling his fantasy was driving him crazy, his usual patience nonexistent. The woman he'd loved for years was within his reach and Seth was going to make damn sure he didn't miss grabbing her.

The plan to catch her off guard had come to him before they'd both gone to bed the night before at her house. Since then, he had been doing small things to throw her off. Just a touch or a look seemed to fluster her. It surprised him how innocent she appeared, more so than most of the virginal debutantes his mother threw at him. It was as if she wasn't accustomed to men paying attention to her.

It took every ounce of his self-control not to head up the stairs to her room. He knew she was in 205, knew exactly where that room was located, but he refused to ruin her reputation deliberately. He left the bar and headed to the lobby to wait a few moments and gather his resolve.

A few people milled around. He recognized a couple of the businessmen from his dealings in town. A few women eyed him with interest, but he ignored them. All of them faded away when he heard Jamie's voice.

She was beautiful. She'd pulled her hair up into one of those loose arrangements that made a man's fingers itch to muss it and watch it fall. She'd put something on her lips to make them glossy, and for once she was wearing a dress. It wasn't fancy, plain really since she'd forgone the bustle that most women preferred these days. The unfussy design draped her curves and hugged her breasts, and the shade of yellow brought out the golden tone of her skin.

His mouth suddenly went dry. For years he'd been dreaming of this, lusting after Jamie and loving her, thinking that he would never get the honor of touching her. The sweet torture caused by spending time in her presence had been worth it, but now that he was determined to have her, his body was raring to go.

Damn, he was acting like a greenhorn. She'd always been able to do this to him, and the sad thing was the woman had no idea of the affect she had on him. It was worse than before. Now, he would do everything in his power to get her beneath him.

After taking a couple deep breaths and ordering his cock to take a rest, he smiled and moved toward her.

"Why, you cleaned up nicely, Mr. Conner." Her voice had a breathless quality to it that made his cock twitch. It took every bit of his willpower to not throw her over his shoulder, march up those stairs and show her just how he felt about her. That was not exactly the way he had it planned, but at the moment it sounded like a damn good idea. She'd be madder than a hornet, but he could use that passion in another way. He imagined pulling the fabric of her dress away from her golden skin, watching her eyes go blurry as he brushed his fingers over her nipples.

"Seth."

Brought out of his daydream by the sound of her voice, he cleared his throat as he felt the tips of his ears burn in embarrassment.

Damn if that sharp tone didn't turn him on more. He loved feisty women. Jack always went for women who twittered. They drove Seth crazy. He didn't want a woman who couldn't stand on her own.

He smiled. "Sorry."

She rolled her eyes in response. "Just where did you go there?"

He winked and felt a surge of satisfaction when she drew a deep breath in reaction. "Just off gathering wool."

She frowned. "Was today too much for you? It was pretty hot coming in."

He chuckled and offered her his arm. "Naw, I'm fine. Shouldn't have had a beer on an empty stomach."

She hesitated, then slipped her arm through his. The simple touch sent a blaze through his blood that would rival any wildfire. His groin tightened and he felt lightheaded.

"Seth."

He looked down at the woman he loved, the one he knew he always would love.

"I think you need a good long rest in bed," she said.

"I think you might be right."

As he led her through the front doors of the hotel, he ordered himself to be patient. He'd have plenty of time later to show her how wonderful a good long time in bed could be.

Chapter Three

The scent of chili peppers and other spices filled the air in Military Plaza as Jamie scooped up the last of her chili. The activity still hummed even though the sun had almost set. Tables were scattered amongst the wagons and people. A strange combination of patrons milled around the square. Military officers, workers and tourists, along with the occasional cowboy, had gathered to enjoy the nightly offerings from the Chili Queens. The lowliest worker rubbed elbows with some of the wealthiest members of San Antonio society here in the square. It was one of the many reasons Jamie loved this area. It didn't matter who you were, you came for the food and enjoyed the atmosphere.

"Did you need anything else?" Seth asked her, breaking into her thoughts.

She had attempted to ignore the jumble of feelings he'd brought to life, but he had made it dang near impossible. From walking down the street arm in arm, to insisting he buy their dinner, he'd taken control. She suspected he had brushed up against her several times on purpose, but she couldn't be sure.

"Jamie?" He touched her arm, and like a silly woman, her skin tingled. She turned in his direction and tried not to sigh. The setting sun caressed his facial features. Jamie had observed things about him in the last few hours that she hadn't before. Little things she was sure other women had noticed, but she never let herself.

"No, I've had enough to eat. If I keep eating beans and tortillas there's a good chance Sadie won't be able to carry me home."

The Seduction of Widow McEwan

He chuckled. "I doubt that." Finishing off his tortilla, he continued to watch her, his gaze intent on her face. "You definitely aren't as skinny as you used to be."

She smiled, remembering what she'd looked like at fifteen. "That's for sure. You didn't even know me when I was still in school. All the boys called me slim."

"I doubt very much that any of them would call you that today."

She snorted and almost apologized, but apparently Seth had no problem with the rude sound. He laughed. Snorting was one of her worst habits and Sid had constantly chastised her for it.

"How about we take a walk by the river before heading in for the night?" Seth suggested.

She nodded. Once they returned their plates, they strolled to the river. It'd been years since she had taken the time to enjoy San Antonio. The only trips she made here were for business, and that was a shame. Each time she visited, she fell more in love with the city. There was something in the air, romance maybe, that seemed to cast a spell over the visitors. The mix of cultures intrigued and fascinated her.

"What are you looking so serious for?"

She glanced up at him and smiled. "I was just thinking I never do things like this."

He cocked his head and studied her. "That is a right shame. Didn't Sid bring you here after y'all married?"

Shaking her head, she slipped her hand away from his arm and stood at the riverbank. "No. He usually came here with Portman. Sid said San Antonio wasn't truly a place for a gentlewoman."

Seth scoffed, "That's just stupid."

She bent to pick a wildflower and twirled it between her fingers. "I have to agree with you on that. Especially since the railroad got here." Looking out over the river, she watched the fireflies dance above water. "I just haven't had time for pleasure trips."

"You should, Jamie. You're the type of woman who should be pampered." The seriousness of his tone had her turning back to look at him. His somber expression made her skin itch. Seth was rarely serious.

"What do you mean by that?"

"A woman like you should have time for pleasure."

The way he said the word pleasure sent a wave of heat over her flesh. Just that one word, the syllables stretched out in his Southern drawl, sounded so wicked. Her clothing suddenly felt too restrictive. She wanted nothing more than to be rid of them, and the fact that she craved having Seth around for that was a little upsetting. Afraid of the feelings his words had stirred, she backed up a few paces and almost fell into the river. He grabbed her arm and pulled her out of danger, but she wrenched away from him.

"What are you talking about, Seth?"

"You're a gentlewoman; you should have someone to take care of you."

She needed steady ground because she was too close to giving in to him. Anger would be the only thing that saved her, that kept her safely away from begging him to come back to her room with her. His misconception that she was weak provided the catalyst she needed. "Really? So you think the little woman needs someone to take care of her? That I'm too stupid to keep myself out of trouble?"

"That isn't what I meant."

"What did you mean?" Her voice was sharp. She sounded like a harpy but she required some distance between them.

"I meant that you should have a man to make you happy."

She laughed at that but there was no happiness in it. "Make me happy, a man? I had the benefit of being married, and let me assure you, there is no advantage that I could see." He opened his mouth to argue but she was in no mood. Tired and wanting to be alone, away from his unsettling presence, she held up her hand. "I don't want to talk about my marriage or what I need in a man. Men are good to have as employees and that's it."

Although he didn't look happy, he nodded and offered his arm to her again.

She shook her head. "I think it's better that I go back by myself."

The Seduction of Widow McEwan

Without giving him a chance to argue, she turned and walked away, hoping once and for all to rid herself of her strange urges.

൙

Seth stole down the hall to Jamie's room. With his plans not proceeding as quickly as he'd thought they would, he'd had to change course. One night was all he had and he refused to allow it to slip through his hands. He thought for sure, given just another thirty minutes, he would've at least gained the right to escort her back to the hotel. He'd hoped for an invite up to her room. He'd failed at both. The woman wasn't making his plans of seduction easy.

From the moment he met her, he'd misstepped. Hell, the first time in her presence, he'd been so tongue-tied he couldn't do anything but stare at her. It had taken years for him to build the friendship between them. Plenty of times he had taken her side when her brother and father had tried to tell her how to run the ranch. Many people, if they knew his true feelings, might have said he did it because he was in love with her. But it wasn't that. No, if he were honest with himself, it started out that way. But watching her gain her ground and come into her own had astounded him and made him love her even more.

Seth had been ready to admire from a distance, until the ugly thoughts of Portman touching Jamie had entered his mind. From that point on, he had only two things on his mind—seduction, and eventually marriage.

The truth was, after that little talk with her earlier, he had done a lot of thinking. He started off by cursing Sid McEwan for being a jackass. How could a man be married to a woman like Jamie and see the need to frequent whores? There was no doubt the man had treated her badly. Seth knew now that Jamie would be suspicious of any declarations from him. She didn't trust men, and with good reason.

Not that he was giving up. He just had to change his plan a bit. That was the reason he was sneaking down the hall, with a set of instruments he'd borrowed from a friend on the Texas

Rangers, to pick her lock. It was illegal, it was childish, but he didn't give a damn.

Pulling out the long metal object, he set to work on stealing into the room of Jameson McEwan.

☙

Delicious heat crawled through Jamie's body as magical hands swept over her flesh. She moved restlessly against the bed, the linens wrapping around her ankles. Wet kisses, then warm hands skimmed up her legs, drifting over her body, until a lean hard body covered hers.

"Jamie," a familiar voice whispered. "Wake up, sweetheart."

Breath feathered against her skin, followed by another wet, openmouthed kiss. She shivered as she felt the scrape of teeth against her flesh. She didn't want to wake up, ever. Of all her dreams, she had never had one so vivid, so mesmerizing. The temptation to give in, to indulge in her reverie was just too much. Opening her eyes, even acknowledging there was a world outside her dream, would cause it to crash.

She pressed her legs together as the pressure built between her thighs. Sparks of heat flowed through her blood.

"Jamie." Low, seductive, the voice called out to her again. She wanted to respond to the request, to the desire she heard, but she didn't want to leave the delectable fantasy.

Jamie shifted her weight, her body brushing up against something solid, something altogether too real. She paused, first in confusion, then in fear. This was no dream. Afraid of what she would find, she slowly opened her eyes. Her heart stuttered when she found Seth above her.

"What are you doing here?" She meant it as a reprimand, but her voice was husky with desire.

His lips curved into a tempting smile filled with sensual promise. For a second, she couldn't think, couldn't separate the reality from the fantasy, until her mind finally merged the two together. Every bit of moisture dried up in her mouth, while her palms grew damp.

"I thought I'd show what I meant by pleasure."

Again, the way he said the word had her curling her toes. She knew he would be more than knowledgeable about the subject. No matter how much she tried, she couldn't repress the shiver of delight at the thought of having those talented hands—not to mention that mouth—skimming over her body.

Traitorous hope stirred to life in her heart. If there was one man who knew about passion—who could teach her—it had to be Seth. His reputation with women was enough to make a soiled dove blush. For one brief moment, she thought maybe, just maybe, she could find satisfaction with him.

As fast as it came to life the hope slipped away. Sid had no problems with whores, as he as he told her on more than one occasion. Swallowing her regret, her despair, she shook her head.

"It would be a waste of time, Seth."

He frowned. "Now, don't let my age fool ya none. I know more—"

"I'm sure you do, Seth. It has nothing to do with you, and everything to do with me."

He didn't say anything for a second or two, just stared down at her. Her eyes had adjusted to the minimal light, and she could read the expressions darting over his face. Aggravation, then confusion, melted into comprehension and finally determination.

"Jamie." His tone was a strange mixture of irritation and tenderness. He bent his head to brush his mouth over hers once, twice, then pressed his lips to hers. She wanted to tell him to stop, that there was no use in this nonsense because she could find no satisfaction in the marital act. When his tongue traced the seam of her lips, she lost a bit more of her resistance.

Closing her eyes, she opened her mouth for him. He stole inside as he cupped her face. He rubbed his fingers over her cheeks, his calluses rough against her skin. He murmured something she couldn't make out. The words didn't matter. It was the rough tone, the arousal in his voice that spoke to her. Something stirred deep within her soul, something she thought dead, long-ago damaged by her marriage.

The thought of that horrible mistake poured a barrel of cold water on her. She dragged her mouth from his. Both of them were breathing heavily. He heaved himself up, balancing his weight on his hands.

"What's the matter?"

"This isn't going to work." Although she wanted it to, craved it in a way that left her dizzy.

With a sigh filled with irritation, he rolled away and sat up. Leaning over, he lit the gas lamp on the bedside table. She winced at the sudden light, then pulled herself into a sitting position. When Seth's gaze focused on her bosom, she remembered her state of undress and tugged up the covers.

He raised his attention to her face and smiled. There was no hint of the boy she knew in that expression. She needed to quit thinking of him that way. He was a man full grown with desires he had never hidden from the world. When he focused them on her, a rush of goose bumps pebbled her skin.

When he spoke, his voice was calm. "So, explain to me why you can't do this."

"I'd really rather not talk about it."

He frowned. "I'm not leaving until you tell me."

Seth could be like a dog with a bone. If she didn't divert his attention, she would be stuck explaining her married life to him. That was not something she wanted to repeat out loud to anyone. Arguing was the only thing that would stop his questions.

"Speaking of which, just how in the blazes did you get in here?"

He shrugged. "I picked the lock."

"Picked the..." Shock held her tongue, but only for a moment. "Seth Allen Conner, you should be ashamed of yourself. Why, if your mamma knew you were breaking into hotel rooms, I'm sure she'd give you a good tanning."

He gestured impatiently. "Jamie, that isn't going to work. You can come up with all kinds of arguments, but I meant what I said. I'm not leaving until we discuss this. Is it because of the difference in our ages?"

She shook her head. "I told you it wasn't you. Can't we leave it at that?"

His frown developed into a nasty scowl. "No."

"No?"

He popped up from the bed to pace. "I've waited too long. I want some kind of explanation."

The unusual nervous energy he displayed gave her pause. Patience was one thing Seth possessed in great quantity. He didn't hurry unless it was important and his nervousness never showed.

"I don't believe I owe you any kind of explanation."

He stopped his pacing and moved back to the bed. Leaning closer, he braced his hands on the mattress, bringing his face within inches of her. In any other man she would have seen it as intimidation. With Seth, she knew he just wanted her attention.

"There's no way I'm leaving without a reason. I know you want this."

She did. Maybe she'd known all along that she wanted him. In a dark corner of her mind, Jamie understood she was attracted to him and the forbidden pleasures he could give her. She couldn't deny the attraction...the need still simmering within her. From the look on his face, he was ready to argue it to death. What did it matter? She'd learned to live with the humiliation for years. But she would not tell her embarrassing secrets with him hovering over her.

"Back off."

"I'm not leaving—"

"I didn't say leave, I said move away. That's it."

From the way his eyes narrowed, he didn't like it, but he did as she asked. Once he moved, she reached for her wrapper. Sliding off the bed, keeping her back to him, she slipped it on, tying the sash and making sure she was well covered before facing him.

When she did, she found him watching her with an unreadable expression. That was odd. Seth might not be the easiest man to read, but he rarely looked so blank.

"So, why don't you tell me your reasons?" A twinge of sarcasm colored his voice.

Knowing there was no way to get out of it, she drew in a deep breath and said, "I'm a miserable failure at lovemaking, and I refuse to suffer through it ever again."

Chapter Four

Seth didn't say anything, didn't seem to move a muscle or even take a breath. Jamie chewed on her lip, her nerves stretching thin, a chill passing over her skin. Shame filled her and sent a wave of fire to her face. She shouldn't have blurted it out like that, but there was nothing she could do about it now. His stillness, and the silence that seemed to extend, had her clearing her throat. She could tell he was shocked. Women were not to speak of such things, but he had been on top of her kissing her like there was no tomorrow. So if he was embarrassed by her outburst, it was his own fault.

She couldn't figure out his reaction as he continued to stare at her. Jamie would have understood if he pitied her, or left her in disgust, but the laughter was the last thing she expected. And not a snicker or chuckle, but a full-bodied cackle. As he continued to hoot, mortification quickly vanished and was replaced by anger.

"I'd appreciate it if you'd leave." Her tone was as cold as a blue norther sweeping across the plains.

He calmed himself enough to offer her an indulgent smile. "You're going to have to come up with a better reason because I'm not buying that."

Needing some protection from him, she crossed her arms over her chest. It didn't help much, but she figured unless she was in full armor, she would still feel vulnerable. "It's the truth."

He tilted his head to the side as he watched her. "As told to you by Sid McEwan?"

Not able to say anything, she nodded. He rounded the bed. As he slowly walked toward her, he never broke eye contact. Heat flared and danced along her nerve endings.

He took her hand, his fingers sliding over her skin. "I have a feeling your husband, God rest his soul, was a jackass."

For a moment she goggled then chuckled. No one ever said anything critical of Sid McEwan. Even years after his death people were afraid to utter a word against him. To hear him called a jackass was not only funny, but too true.

"That may be, but Sid wasn't the virgin in the marriage. He had more than enough experience."

Even as she said it, humiliation crawled through her again. It was really stupid to get embarrassed considering the situation. Sid never hesitated to let her know what a failure she was at pleasing him, but if she would've said anything about their failed attempts at lovemaking, he'd have been appalled.

Seth had no such problems, since he still held her hand in his, caressing the back of it with his fingers. She shuddered as goose bumps appeared in a path down her arm. Deciding they had talked long enough, she tried to tug her hand free. But, being the stubborn man he was, he didn't loosen his grip.

She stopped her struggles and said, in her most matronly tone, "*Seth.*"

His smile deepened, warmed, as he used her hand to draw her closer to him. "Why don't we just try this and see where it goes?"

She shook her head to deny him, but more to fight the need growing within her. It bubbled just below the surface, her control slowly slipping bit by bit out of her grasp. As he stepped behind her, she felt the warmth of his body. The muscles in her stomach tightened when he splayed his hand over them. He gently urged her back against him.

She tried to hold herself rigid and straightened her spine. It didn't help. His body heat seeped through her nightwear. When she drew in a deep breath, the strong masculine scent of him made her head spin. It was a combination of man, leather and night air. Longing like she had never felt, bigger than the whole damn state of Texas, swelled and expanded inside of her.

How would it feel to just let go? To lean back, enjoy the tenderness of the embrace, forget the world for just a few minutes? It tempted her more than anything else in the world ever had. She had been strong for so long, ignoring her desires. She'd thought they had dissolved with her first night with Sid. Seth had proved that misconception wrong. Now, her body clamored for his touch, her thoughts of denying him slowly dissolving.

What would it hurt to dive headlong into lust, bend a little and take what Seth was offering?

Because nothing would come of it, nothing could. She knew she would end up with regrets. Enough of those haunted her on a daily basis, she didn't need more. She tried to straighten away from him, away from the wonderfully delicious comfort of his arms, but he held her steady.

"Seth, this can't go anywhere. I already told you—"

All of her thoughts halted and her hormones danced when he nuzzled the side of her neck just below her ear. "I heard ya." He nipped at her lobe. "I just decided to ignore ya."

She huffed in annoyance and he chuckled. His chest vibrated against her back. Her nerves jumped before a burst of energy slipped over her skin, causing her to shiver. As he kept one hand splayed across her stomach, he skimmed his other up to her breast. She should pull away from him and order him from her room. Seth would go if she were serious, if she really wanted him to leave. That was the problem. Propriety insisted that he leave, but she couldn't seem to get the words out through her lips. Not with his teeth grazing her earlobe, his hand caressing her breast.

"Ahh," he whispered as his thumb grazed her nipple. It tightened under his attention. "Now, I would say that was more than a good sign." With one last little nip, he pulled away, the action so fast she almost lost her balance. She bit back the irritated sigh that rose in her throat.

He turned her to face him, then backed her up against the post of the canopy bed. When Jamie looked up at him, she drew in a quick, loud breath. She had known him for years and had probably seen just about every human emotion from him except this one. Desire etched his facial features. The arrested look in his eyes deepened their color as he drew her near. Slipping one hand around her waist, he stepped closer. Gently, almost reverently, he brushed the backs of his fingers over her cheek, then allowed his fingers to play along her jaw.

"Seth." Her tone no longer held the stern reprimand it had earlier. Even she could hear the change in her pitch and the way her voice caught on his name.

But he said nothing. He trailed his hand down to cup her untouched breast. Her breathing hitched when he rubbed his fingers over her nipple. Everything seemed to slip away. As he held her gaze, it was as if they were the only two people in the world.

Jamie wanted to close her eyes, wanted to slip into a blissful daze. But he would not allow it. Instead, he leaned in and brushed his mouth over hers. The sweetness of the gesture, the simple touch, had her mind whirling. Jamie sighed, shutting her eyes and losing herself in the pleasure of it. He groaned in reaction, wrapping both his arms around her waist. She lifted her hands to his shoulders as he pressed his lips against hers. This was no longer the gentle caress but a kiss full of desire and passion. His tongue thrust into her mouth and she welcomed it with a moan. The taste of him was beyond anything she had ever experienced. Before she was ready to stop, he pulled away. Their harsh breathing was the only sound in the dark room.

"Tell me now."

He was talking. She saw his mouth move but she didn't work through what he said. Her brain was melting, and he wanted to have a conversation?

"Wh—what are you talking about?"

When he spoke, his voice was harsh and abrupt. "Tell me now you don't want me. If you don't stop this now, there will be no going back."

She should tell him to go. Doing this, taking him as her lover even if for one night, would not be a good idea. The ghost of her marriage would never disappear. It wouldn't solve her problems. But none of those things truly mattered to her at the moment. What did matter was the heat blazing through her blood, the way her body responded to his every touch, and she never wanted that feeling to go away. It would in the morning because this would never be anything but a one-night affair, but she needed this. She craved to experience one little taste of heaven.

"Jamie?"

"God help me, I know I shouldn't want it, or even think about doing it." She took a deep breath, gathering her courage. "But I can't seem to refuse you."

He rested his forehead against hers and released a sigh of relief. She thought she heard him say, "About time."

After he gave her a kiss, Seth tugged her away from the bedpost and pushed her back on the bed. With a laugh, she bounced on the mattress. Before she could adjust to her new position, he was slipping his body over hers and stealing her breath again. This time there was no sweet interlude, no wooing.

Possessively, Seth settled his mouth on hers. Spearing her fingers through his thick hair, she held him closer, wanting nothing more than for this feeling to continue. He pushed himself up to his hands and looked down at her. The smile he gave her made her curl her toes into the bed linens.

"I knew you had passion in you, Jameson." He gave her a quick, forceful kiss. "And I intend on enjoying it."

A rough edge deepened his voice, the tone, a strange mixture of tenderness wrapped with lust. He pressed his groin against hers, his hardened cock rubbing against her sex. Tension curled in her belly, tightening further.

He bent his head and nipped at her chin. He moved on, lowering himself to cover her body and kissing his way down her neck. She felt the scrape of teeth, the raspy lick of his tongue against the hollow of her throat. She moaned, closing her eyes. He lifted himself away to untie the bow at the top of her nightdress. The soft fabric slid away, the night air cooling her flesh. She opened her eyes and watched as he lowered his head to her nipple, first licking it and then drawing it into his mouth.

She bowed up, her hands clenching the sheets beneath her. As he continued to torture first one then the other nipple, her mind blanked of anything but him. He drew away. With rough movements, he tugged on the sash of her wrapper, then eased it from her shoulders and down her arms. He pulled her nightgown up and over her head, leaving her breathless, not to mention frightened.

He settled between her thighs, pushing them apart to accommodate his body.

"Seth." At once, she was horribly embarrassed and wonderfully excited.

He didn't look up, just laid his hand against her curls. Excitement pulsed from that point outward through her body. He drew in a deep breath.

"Beautiful." That one word, and the deep, throaty sound of his voice, had her forgetting her embarrassment and surrendering to the pleasure he was offering with his hands and his mouth. He moved against her and slipped a finger between her slick folds. The tension that had centered in her belly shifted down to her groin. With each stroke, the pressure grew. She placed both of her feet on the mattress and joined in his rhythm. Mindless now to everything but achieving the goal her body craved, she followed his lead, not even flinching when she felt his mouth touch her core. His tongue replacing his finger, she raced to the edge. As he ravaged her, his finger slipped up and over her pressure point. Once, twice...

The unfamiliar tension wrapped around her emotions. Panic and confusion surfaced first, then she exploded, her body convulsing with her orgasm as he continued to move his lips over her sex. Before she had fully recovered, he was tearing at his dungarees and joining her on the bed. She looked up at him as he stared down at her. It struck her that this was the position they had been in when he'd awakened her earlier. He'd left his shirt buttoned, but she wanted to touch his skin. Lifting her hands, she swiftly slipped the buttons free, then brushed the fabric aside. She skimmed her hands over his chest. Delight stole through when he shuddered at her touch. He bent to give her a quick kiss and she tasted herself on his lips. He took her hips in his hands, positioning her, and entered her with one swift stroke.

Holding himself still, he said, "Oh, baby, you feel good."

When he pulled out of her, then thrust back in, he closed his eyes and groaned. The sound of it ripped through her, spurring another rush of excitement. This time, though, it was more visceral than before. She lifted her hips, joining in the mating ritual, and he moved his hands to change his position. Liquid fire poured through her, her body no longer under her control but possessed by the need to reach the pinnacle again.

Seth opened his eyes. His gaze locked on hers as he bent for a kiss. She was racing closer to the end, her body bowing as another orgasm ripped through her.

"*Seth.*"

"Jameson, that's it, honey. Come for me."

He continued to move deeper, more forcefully, pushing her over the edge a third time before he followed her into bliss.

Collapsing on top of her, he sighed. Their bodies were damp from their exertion, both of them breathing heavily. A few moments later, he pushed away, rid himself of his clothes and crawled back into bed with her. When he got them both settled, he wrapped his arms around her waist as she rested her head on his shoulder.

Jamie waited for regrets, waited for her self doubts to resurface. Nothing but sheer contentment filled her. With the musky scent of their lovemaking surrounding them and her body satisfied physically, she couldn't—wouldn't—worry about the consequences until the morning.

Seth brushed his lips against her hair. He murmured something she could not make out as he drifted deeper into sleep. Thinking that a fine idea, she followed his lead and joined him in slumber.

Chapter Five

Jamie stirred some time later, rolling to her side. She froze the moment she came into contact with a solid wall of skin. Opening her eyes, she sighed when she saw Seth sleeping peacefully beside her. The night's events slipped over her. Delight and satisfaction settled within her chest.

Seth shifted and reached for her, his arms sliding around her waist and rolling her on top of him. She found herself straddled over his hips. Seth looked up at her through half-lidded eyes. He stretched his arms then folded them behind head. She knew he was attractive, but laying there beneath her, he was the picture of perfectly satisfied male.

When she realized she was sitting there staring at him, Jamie cleared her throat. "I'm sorry I woke you."

He smiled. "You can wake me anytime you want, Jamie."

His voice deepened when he said her name. She blushed in response to the sensuality she heard there. It was odd that she would blush, even odder still that she was sitting on top of her brother's best friend. If anyone had told her that during this trip she'd be perched on top of him while neither of them wore a thread of clothing, she would've told that person they had to be crazy.

"I can hear the wheels turning in that pretty head of yours."

She frowned down at him. "What do you mean?"

He brushed his fingers over her nipple, which hardened before she had a chance to bat his hand away.

"What I mean is you're trying to figure out just what the hell you're doing here with me."

Her face grew hotter. "I was not thinking that."

One eyebrow rose. "Really?"

Thinking it best to change the subject, she skimmed her hands over his chest and asked, "So, how long have you been planning this?"

His lips twitched. "This in particular or getting you in bed in general?"

She loved the way the crisp, dark blond chest hair crinkled against her fingers. "Either." When he didn't answer her, she looked up to find him staring intently at her. Her stomach muscles clenched. "What?"

"You have no idea what that simple touch does to me."

She moved her hands away, but he stopped her, placing his hand on top of hers and urging her to touch him again. "No. Don't ever be ashamed to touch me, or afraid of what we have."

Shame wasn't what came to mind, but rather fear. It lanced through her body, a chill following quickly in its path. The sincerity in his voice scared the hell out of her. It made her want something she couldn't have. Even as the rational side of her brain told her it could never happen, the irrational side, the one that had yearned for a true marriage based on love, was starting to take over. She didn't want just one night of this, one night to touch, to taste, to feel.

Seth wasn't looking at the long term. His past relationships had been short. He'd ignored his mother's attempts to marry him off. Jamie knew it would happen one day. Seth was too good a son not to do as his mother bid. Coveting having him in her life this way, then not attaining it, would be painful. She'd lived through one man humiliating her and she refused to have regrets. But, they had the rest of the night.

Wanting to share her feelings with him through actions, she slipped her hand over one of his nipples and bent to kiss his chest. His skin was warm beneath her lips. Seth sucked in a breath when she swiped her tongue over his other nipple.

She kissed her way up his chest to his throat. Seth took her by her hips and scooted her down his body. He situated her over his cock. The long, hard length of him rested against her sex. A shiver of anticipation passed through her.

When she closed her eyes and pressed her mouth on his, he cupped her face and brushed his calloused thumbs over her cheeks. He relinquished control of the kiss to her. It allowed her to explore the feelings welling up inside of her. She grew bold and slipped her tongue past his lips and into the warm, wet crevice of his mouth. Jamie had never tasted something so sweet and so hot at the same time. Before she knew what was happening, though, Seth was taking control. His mouth hungrily feasted on hers. It was as if he hadn't eaten in a month of Sundays and she was a five-course meal. She greedily returned the kiss, reveling in the passion she stirred within him.

Seth shifted from her mouth to feast on her earlobe. Taking her by the hips, he moved beneath her. Jamie gasped when his hardened cock pressed harder against her slit. With every twist of her hips, the head of his shaft rubbed her clitoris.

"Take me inside you, honey."

His gruff whisper heated the sensitive skin below her ear. She opened her eyes but hesitated, unsure of herself. She'd never been on top to make love. Her experience in the bedroom had been neglected, at least until tonight. A look of understanding lit Seth's eyes. Gently, he eased her back into a sitting position then urged her onto her knees. She took hold of his cock and, with a little maneuvering, situated herself above the head. Slowly, she sank down on him.

Like before, he filled her to almost bursting. She rose to her knees again before dropping back down. Although she had not been steady in her movements, Seth groaned in appreciation. That was all the assurance she needed as she started to move with more confidence. He joined in her deliberate tempo, keeping up with her, but not pushing her to go any faster. Sitting up, he took a nipple into his mouth, his tongue swirling around then his teeth grazing the tip.

She rode him unhurriedly, enjoying the slow slide down his cock, the feel of pulling off him. She knew she was driving him crazy because as he focused on her other breast, his own actions became more frantic, more out of control. Still she moved, her excitement growing, her body heating. Jamie wanted to rush, to push herself and Seth to the pinnacle, but she kept her pace the same, wanting to enjoy the joining of their bodies.

Seth flexed his hips, trying to increase the speed, but she refused to heed his direction. Soon, though, her body was clamoring for release. He'd moved his hands from her hips and used his fingers to stroke over the hidden bud within her folds. With each brush against the small bundle of nerves, she shuddered. Before she knew what was happening, Seth grabbed her hips and rolled on top of her.

Her head was still spinning from the reverse in positions when, with a quick, hard thrust, he entered her. Jamie rose to meet his measured thrusts, but instead of increasing their pace, he kept it slow, intense and devastating. Wanting—needing—to push him faster, she placed her feet on the bed. That small gesture seemed to shove him over the edge.

Rising to his knees, Seth arranged her so that he could move deeper. The force of his thrusts shook the bed, slamming it against the wall. Each time he plunged within her, her body clamored for release. She arched up. He pulled out, then pushed back in one last time before she shattered. She was still trembling, her heart pounding, when he groaned her name and poured himself into her.

CR

The first rays of the morning sun peeked through curtains, dappling Jamie's golden skin. Seth traced his fingers over her bare back, enjoying the silken feel of her flesh. It was all he could do not to take her again. He really didn't have time if he wanted to ensure he didn't get caught by the staff. But his body was paying no attention to his good sense. Even after having her twice the night before, he could feel his cock hardening at the thought of slipping into her pussy, feeling those little muscles grip him like a vise.

Jesus, he was driving himself crazy. He threw himself back onto the pillows and turned his head to look at her. She snuggled deeper under the covers, then moved closer to him, seeking his warmth. Seth brushed a stray strand of her ebony hair from her face. There was no doubt the woman was beautiful. The bastard McEwan had married her for more than the debt. She'd been barely a woman, and Sid hadn't been blind to her potential. High slashing cheekbones, the delightful full mouth—usually curved in a welcoming smile—not to mention the gorgeous golden eyes framed by the blacker-than-night eyelashes. Those things were only part of her beauty.

Sid had seen the potential, but he hadn't gotten to see the woman she'd become. Jamie's true loveliness lay beneath the polished exterior. Not many young women would take up running the ranch and do it so well. The dedication to her men, to her family and to that ranch was astounding. There was a strength in her Sid McEwan would have squashed under his boot like a bug, if he had lived. Not for the first time, Seth thanked McEwan's bad heart and propensity for whores. Now Seth knew he was the only man to have tasted the passion lurking inside of her.

His shaft twitched again. Reaching down, he gave it one long stroke and silently berated himself. It was useless, because when it came to Jamie, he was always a hairsbreadth away from losing control. It didn't matter how long Seth lived, he would never forget what it was like to watch her as she gave herself in to the desire, or how it felt to slip between her thighs.

He brushed the back of his fingers lightly over her cheek. Jamie might not realize it, but this was not a one-night-only thing. She probably assumed he was just out for kicks. Seth intended to make sure she understood it was much more than that. He needed to stamp the memory of this night on her brain. Every time she thought of San Antonio, every time she lay in bed, he wanted her thinking of him and what they shared.

She moved closer to him, cuddling her face against his palm. A moment later, she opened her eyes. The satiated look within their depths made his chest grow tight. He would never get tired of watching her wake up in his bed.

"Hmm." She kissed his hand. "I can't think of a better way of waking up."

Sleep clouded her voice. She pulled herself up onto the pillows. The sheets didn't quite cover her breasts. One nipple peeked above the edge of the cloth. Seth brushed his fingers over it. He had expected her to play coy or be embarrassed. She surprised him with a chuckle.

He glanced up. The smile she offered him stole the rest of his good sense—not that he had much to begin with. "I was wrong about that. *This* is the best way to wake up."

She leaned forward and brushed her mouth over his. The simple touch had what little blood left in his brain heading south. He had told himself to keep the love play light but he couldn't. Not when the sweetness of the kiss squeezed his heart.

He cupped the back of her head, deepening the kiss, opening his mouth and invading hers. When her tongue slipped against his, it was his turn to groan. Quickly, the kiss turned openly carnal. The control he'd always bragged about slid out of his grasp as he kissed down the column of her throat.

She was driving him crazy with her little moans and mewls. He pulled away, and she complained with an incoherent mutter, which brought about a small smile.

Jamie opened her eyes. The desire shimmering in them made him shake, but he wanted to take it slow, show her how much fun she could have in bed.

He eased back off the mattress, searching for a stocking, a sash, just anything.

"Seth?" Jamie's voice was filled with a strange mixture of irritation and worry.

When he spied her wrapper, he grabbed it, freeing the sash from the loops. He turned to find her sitting up, the bed linens pooled around her waist. Damn, but he was lucky. For a second, okay, two, he stared at her. He wasn't able to move as he wondered just how the hell he'd gotten so lucky. The weak morning sun gave him enough light to see her breasts. Not overly large, just big enough for his palms, they were bottom heavy, with the most succulent coral nipples he'd ever seen. He remembered the taste of them, the way Jamie moaned when he scraped his teeth across the tip...

"Seth."

He returned to the bed with a chuckle. "I need you to lay back and put your hands above your head, baby."

She glanced down at the sash he held in his hands, then back up to his face. He fought a laugh at the dubious look she afforded him. But he wanted her to understand, wanted her to experience the freedom of losing control to pleasure.

With a scowl, she obeyed. He kneeled beside her. Avoiding making eye contact, he tied her hands to the headboard, then finally looked at her. The frown she gave him didn't speak of anger or irritation, but of confusion.

"I want you to enjoy."

She opened her mouth but he wouldn't let her speak.

He placed a finger on her lips. "No. Don't speak and try not to move. Let yourself just feel."

Not waiting to see her reaction, he settled on top of her. With a light touch, he skimmed his hands over her flesh, enjoying the way she reacted. When she moaned, he stopped.

"I said no talking *and* no moving."

A huff of irritation was the only sound in the room, and he had to bite back the laugh that threatened. Even as he ached with need, he held back. He moved his mouth over her, tasting her nipples. When he reached her belly, he slipped his tongue over her bellybutton, then inside. Her indrawn breath delighted him, the sound shooting straight to his heart. Knowing he was the one to introduce her to desire wasn't only damned sexy, but it touched him beyond that. It brushed against his soul.

The scent of her desire called to him, and he set his mouth against her pussy. Sweet, tangy, she tasted of heaven. His balls tightened, and a drop of precome escaped. He pulled back and ordered himself to settle down. He'd embarrass himself if he didn't watch it. That would definitely wreak havoc in his show of control.

When he pressed his mouth against her sex, she moaned again. He stopped. She huffed, but said nothing. He smiled since he knew she couldn't see him.

Gliding his tongue between her folds, he sighed with contentment. Over and over, he tasted her. Her legs moved beside him restlessly, and he heard her mews, but he was too caught up in the wonder of her essence. He skimmed his tongue over the tight bundle of nerves. Three swipes and she came apart, shivering with her orgasm.

He untied her hands and flipped her over, pulling one of the pillows from the top of the bed and sliding it beneath her hips. He drew her to her knees and placed his hand between her legs. Slipping his finger over her slit, he smiled when she moaned his name.

When she tried to push herself up, Seth raised his hand and brought it down on her rounded ass. She paused, and he waited. He worried he'd gone too far. Then she shivered, as if delighted by the feel of his hand slapping hard against her flesh. He positioned her where he wanted her and pushed into her in one thrust. The heat of her cunt surrounded his cock and he held himself still, enjoying the pleasure of being deep inside Jamie. Slowly, he pulled himself out then slid back in.

Her moans grew each time he drove himself into her. Soon, she had gained his rhythm, moving in tandem with him. The force of their mating had the bed shaking.

With one last scream of his name, she came apart. Even as she shivered from her first orgasm, he pushed her harder, further, driving her up and over into another one, as he shouted her name and followed her into pleasure.

Chapter Six

Jamie watched Seth button his trousers and sighed. He looked up at the sound and smiled, and not for the first time, her heart tightened. It was a shame their night had to come to an end, but she knew it had to. Seth had to leave before any of the staff saw him. Any kind of detection could ruin her reputation and that of the ranch. She cared nothing of the former but would give her life to protect the latter.

Still, she yearned to drag him back to bed, slowly strip him out of his clothes and devour him in one huge bite. As he slid his belt through the loops, she thought of those quick, capable hands on her body and shivered.

"What time did you want me to meet you downstairs?"

His question brought her back to the present and she blushed. She'd never been particularly lustful before but it seemed Seth brought out the harlot in her.

"I wanted to get to the mercantile right after breakfast. Then I have a meeting with Johnson about that three hundred head he was looking to get rid of."

"I still can't believe he's pulling up stakes and moving back east." Seth shook his head, and Jamie could understand his confusion. The idea of leaving Texas was as foreign to her as lying in bed naked while talking to her first paramour. If she were honest with herself, he was going to be her only lover. Ever. There was a good chance no one would be able to compete, Sid sure couldn't have. But also, she had to worry about getting caught. Widows were allowed some discreet affairs, but a woman in her position couldn't afford any hint of tawdriness.

The Seduction of Widow McEwan

"I guess if we head out of here by noon we should be able to make it back to your ranch before sundown," Seth said. She nodded and smiled when he slid onto the bed beside her. "We'll have to wait until tomorrow to talk to Jack."

The first tremors of worry curled into her stomach. "Talk to Jack?" Oh Lord, her voice sounded high and strained. She ordered herself to relax. There was no reason for her to jump to conclusions. "Why would we need to talk to Jack?"

He picked up her hand and played with her fingers. "We need to tell him about us."

He leaned forward to kiss her but she stopped him by raising her hand to his chest. Even through his clothing, the warmth of his skin heated her palm. The memory of feeling his naked flesh under her hands tripped through her mind before she could stop it. She pushed the recollection aside.

"Why would we tell him about us? Jack doesn't tell me about his *women* and I definitely don't tell him about my lovers."

"I've been your only lover since your marriage—will be your only lover from here on out."

His propriety tone didn't sit well with her. "The first part is true. I'm not sure about the second part." She felt a twinge of guilt, but ignored it. She knew very well there would be no one after him, but she didn't want to bolster his out-of-control ego. "I definitely won't be discussing any of that with my brother."

His smile faded. "You mean to deny me?"

Deny him? She worried that if he requested she live in sin with him, she'd do it. She'd throw caution to the wind. "It isn't as if I would tell him about this."

"Why is that?"

"Seth, this is one night. I don't want to ruin your friendship or partnership with my brother. Telling him we shared a bed isn't smart. You know he'd get upset."

He stared at her for moment but didn't say a word. Something close to panic darkened his eyes, but it disappeared so fast she was sure she'd been mistaken.

"You have to marry me."

Her worry exploded into full-blown alarm at his tone. It turned her voice cold when she spoke. "And why is that?"

"You're ruined."

"Ruined? After one night?" She shook her head. "Why is it that one night in bed with a man ruins me, but my husband could spend the better part of our marriage in whorehouses and no one cared. Besides, I am a widow."

She tugged her hand free, which was difficult because for a second he tightened his hold. When he finally let go, she slipped from bed and donned her wrapper. Once she was clothed, she felt more confident to face him. He was now sitting up with a frown darkening his usually light features. The urge to rub her fingers over his brow to rid him of the scowl was so strong, she curled her fingers into her palm.

"I don't know why you think we should marry. You're much younger—"

"I'm not that much younger than you. And another thing. If you think I'm giving you up after one night, you're crazy."

Even as fear churned in her gut, hope sprang to life in the depths of her soul. *He still wants me.* She shouldn't yearn for that, even think of anything beyond this night they'd shared. But the temptation was there, the desire to explore more of what she'd discovered with him. Propriety didn't allow for that, not outside the bounds of marriage, but the lure enticed her. It was a gamble, playing with the very reputation that she'd built, but the idea he still craved this as much as she did was too much to dismiss. "What are you saying?"

"Marriage is the only option."

"No, it isn't. If you still want me—"

He snorted.

"—then I propose an affair."

He crossed his arms over his chest. "An affair?"

"I see no reason why we couldn't be discreet."

"I don't want an affair."

"You just said you still wanted me. That one night—"

He waved that away. "No, I do still want you. But only after you wear my name. After you're mine by law."

Anger surged ahead, dissolving her fear. "I think I made it perfectly clear my views on marriage. I will not get married again."

"Your reputation would suffer if people find out about us. You have no choice."

"No choice? I do have a choice and I choose an affair."

He captured her gaze as he rose from the bed and walked slowly toward her. "I don't want an affair. I want marriage. It's the only reasonable thing to do. It's the right thing to do."

She shook her head and resisted the urge to take a step back. If she did, he would know how he was affecting her and would press his advantage. "I know you aren't thinking straight. Consider what your parents will say. How it will look that you married—not only a widow—but someone much older than you."

"I have never given a damn about appearances and you know that."

"Do you think your parents would accept me?"

He grunted. "Mamma likes you and she would be happy that I was getting married."

"Liking someone and having her for a daughter-in-law are two different things."

"You can't be serious about having an affair."

She hadn't really planned on throwing that option out to him, but it was hard to refuse. Resisting just one more chance at the pleasures he offered was too much for her.

"I don't see that there is anything wrong with what I proposed."

His nostrils flared. "It isn't proper."

She laughed, thinking he was joking. Seth had never worried about other people's opinions, something she knew bothered his mother. When he didn't join in, just stood there and stared at her with a stone face, she tried to stifle it. "You? You don't think it's proper?"

He nodded.

"Again, I have to remind you of a rather busty soiled dove and the money I had to pay to get you out of jail." Anger added a flush to his skin that she found appealing, almost arousing.

She would have never felt like this with Sid since his temper had scared the hell out of her.

"First of all, it was your brother's fault." He bit out each word from behind clenched teeth. "Secondly, it's a bit different for a woman with your stature in the community."

Irritated with the situation and the role she had to play, Jamie had to fight the urge to scream in frustration. Especially since she still wanted him in her bed even now when she was angry with him. "You make it sound like I'm a pillar of the community."

"You are. It wouldn't be right to carry on this way."

"You didn't seem to have a problem with *carrying on* last night."

"That's why we have to get married. It's the right thing to do."

The anger that had been heating her blood now chilled, icing over any of her emotions. Jamie had spent her life doing what was right. She married once out of family loyalty, thinking there was a chance for love to grow for a man she respected. The reward was a barren existence with a husband who never loved her. Not like she deserved. That had almost broken her and she had made a decision the day she'd laid him in the ground. She would never marry again unless it was for love. And she knew without a doubt there was only passion between her and Seth.

"There is no reason to marry just because of last night."

"You're comfortable with walking away, forgetting everything?"

Anger deepened his voice, irritation vibrated beneath the calm façade. His male pride had been bruised. Seth was used to getting whatever he wanted, but marriage was too serious a matter to allow him to force her into it. Not only would she lose her way of life, but she would lose a man she considered a good friend.

"Seth, I know you feel you have to do this. You feel obligated." She held up her hand when he started to object. "No. I know you do. You're too young to understand and I don't want to ruin the rest of your life just because we spent one night in bed. All that we can have is passion. That fades. I've watched it happen all around me. My own parents were said to have married because of some grand passion. By the time she died my folks were barely speaking to each other. And they aren't the only ones. There is no reason to make a lifetime commitment and ruin our lives."

He grabbed her hand and jerked her forward. Before she could think, he crushed his mouth down on hers. The kiss was hot, possessive. What little thought she had drained as he slanted his lips over hers again and again. He released her hand, sliding his arms around her. His hands moved to her bottom, urging her closer. The long, hard length of him pressed against her sex. Heat flared, her bones melted, her blood surged through her like molten steel.

As abruptly as the kiss started it stopped, with him pushing her away. Both of them were breathing deeply, almost gasping for breath.

"*That* will not fade in time."

He said nothing else before opening the door. With one last heated look, he slipped out the door and closed it quietly behind him. The action was so at odds with the emotions he'd evoked, her head was whirling. Slowly, she made her way over to the bed and collapsed on it. Her body was still shaking with a need so powerful, she thought she might faint from it.

She lifted her hand to her swollen lips, rubbing her fingers over them. Fear and lust twisted through her and she couldn't stop the sob that escaped or the tears that followed. All these years she had been strong. She had not cried once after she realized the only reason Sid married her was for money and to have a young wife on his arm. Even when people laughed at her behind her back, mocked her because her husband spent more time in whores' bedrooms than their marriage bed, she didn't crack. The news of his death was fitting, one final embarrassment she couldn't help thinking Sid would have found fitting.

She'd seized her tattered pride, held her head high, ignored the insult to her and forged ahead.

But now, the pride she'd coveted was no longer as important. Here in the silence of her room, she could admit, if just to herself, that she'd been tempted. Tempted to accept that proposal, to pretend they had more than the passion they'd shared in this bed. It would have led to disaster because the truth was staring her in the face.

For the love of God, she had gone and fallen for Seth. A tiny part of her had been in love with him all along. Each time he'd stood behind her decisions, she'd felt something warm grow within her. No other man had supported her the way he did. Good Lord, how long had she been falling in love with him?

She sighed and wiped her face dry with her hands. Time didn't allow for self-pity. At least she had one night of memories, ones that would keep her warm until the day she died.

CR

Jamie's booted footfalls sounded on the walkway in front of the mercantile as Seth watched her approach. Just seeing her hurt. Deep in his gut, in his heart, the pain twisted. He'd avoided her since their confrontation this morning. He knew he'd messed up. Shit, there was no way around the fact he had assumed she'd just go along with his plan. But this morning, all warm from his loving, as she talked of having a blasted affair, he'd realized he'd made a huge mistake in assuming her compliance.

Damn, the woman was beautiful. She always dressed for work. A dark blue split skirt with an ivory shirt and her black hat wasn't what anyone would call stylish. It didn't matter because he didn't care what she wore. Either way, he wanted her. She didn't need fancy clothes or sparkling baubles to be attractive.

Her dark curls swayed against her shirt, bringing the memory of how they felt sliding over his skin, how they looked tangled and lying on the pillows...

His body reacted, just as always. But this time it was worse. Now that he knew what it was like to have her, to wake up next to her, feel her muscles grip his cock as she came apart beneath him, his anticipation intensified. Sweat popped out on his forehead as he ordered his body to settle down. She stepped next to the wagon, giving one of the horses a pat as she walked by.

The Seduction of Widow McEwan

He cleared his throat. "How'd it go with Johnson?"

She squinted against the sun and studied him for a moment before answering him.

"Good. Had to do a little haggling with him on the price, but in the end it was a good deal. It'll make up for the loss we've had the last few weeks."

She stopped short just a few feet from him. The uncomfortable silence stretched, but he refused to make it easy for her. It might make him a jackass, but he wasn't going to play nice.

Sighing, she said, "Seth—"

"Mrs. McEwan!"

The shout drew their attention and cut off whatever she'd planned on saying. Both of them turned in the direction of the voice and Seth inwardly cursed when he saw the owner. Tucker Portman came striding down the boardwalk.

Portman wasn't an attractive man. He never had been. The years of drinking and whoring had left him with soft jowls and a nasty reputation for a predilection of violence in the bedroom. Not to mention the rumors about the death of his two wives.

The sigh from Jamie, along with an irritated mutter he couldn't make out, told Seth him she wasn't any happier about Portman showing up than Seth was.

By the time the older man reached them, he was clearly out of breath. His face was flushed from exertion and sweat beaded on his bald head. "I heard you were in town."

Jamie paused, then said, "Mr. Portman. You know my brother's business partner, Seth Conner? Seth, I'm sure you remember Tucker Portman."

Seth played along and nodded. "Of course."

Jamie shot him a look of warning for the cool tone of his voice but it didn't matter. Portman didn't even acknowledge Seth.

"I wanted to talk to you about the matter we discussed several days ago."

Jamie's back stiffened. "I gave you my answer." She looked at Seth again. "I'm not going to change my mind."

Portman stepped closer, crowding Jamie. She didn't budge an inch. Seth had to bite back the growl and the urge to push the man away from Jamie.

"I don't think you understand what it could mean for our ranches."

"I understand. Still, the answer is no."

"You're a woman, so you don't understand—"

Jamie took matters into her own hands. "I know you think combining them would be good, and it would be, for you. Amazing that my ranch, run by a woman who doesn't understand anything, is making more money, isn't it? I don't think it would be financially beneficial for me to combine them."

"I know Hank has been running things since Sid died. You would have an easier life if you allowed me to take care of everything."

"Is that what you told your wives?"

The color drained out of Portman's fleshy face then flushed back in anger.

Jamie shook her head. "I don't want to know. What I want is for you to leave me alone. I will not marry you. End of story." She bit off each word.

He didn't say anything else, but with slumped shoulders turned to walk in the direction of the saloon. Seth moved closer to Jamie, who watched Portman leave.

"What was that about?"

"I told him I wouldn't marry him the day he asked. Does everyone think I'm an idiot? He's so bad even Sid said to avoid being alone with him."

"Why did you tell Jack you were considering it?"

She closed her eyes and pinched the bridge of her nose. "Because he didn't give me a chance. Just started telling me what to do. He's worse than Pa sometimes."

"You were never considering it?"

She dropped her hand, opened her eyes and looked back over her shoulder. "No."

Seth stared at her, thinking of everything she set in motion by being stubborn. That one little lie to her brother had led to things that could never be undone and would change the rest of her life. The fact she had done it just to needle Jack was damn funny. The amusement of the situation bubbled up and he couldn't stop the bark of laughter. Even with how horrible the day had started out, he allowed the humor to take hold.

"What's so funny?"

He wanted to tell her, but he wasn't ready. Seth was sure she would get a kick out of it someday but today wasn't the day. He shook his head. "Nothing. Nothing a'tall."

Chapter Seven

The ride back from San Antonio was uneventful and tense. Granted, Jamie had tried to talk to him. It hadn't been about anything important, just casual conversation. But Seth had refused to cooperate. He wouldn't pretend that nothing happened. The ache in his chest expanded and twisted.

When he left her at her ranch, Jamie had tossed him a mean look over her shoulder and headed into the barn without another word. He'd had to fight the urge to jump down off Comet and storm after her. But deep down he'd known he didn't have the right. That had made him angrier.

Damn her for worrying about what was proper. The way she'd responded the night before, Seth had never thought she'd deny what they had together. She'd been so free with her affection, but apparently that was just for behind closed doors. Marriage was the only option, but she acted as if it wasn't even worth considering.

As the Double C came into view, Seth waited for the familiar surge of completeness that usually filled him whenever he returned home. It didn't come. Emptiness ate into his gut. Every day since they had opened their horse ranch, Seth had felt the rightness of being there, that he finally belonged to something. He'd always been the odd man out in his family. His brothers thrived in the life his parents had in Austin, loved the political world in which they moved. Seth hadn't. He couldn't give his parents a reason, but the idea of being a politician made his skin crawl. He'd been on the verge of giving into their demands to work in the government when Jack came up with the idea of their ranch. Now the one thing he'd found no longer filled the void. He needed something else.

He needed Jamie.

After settling Comet in, he headed into the house.

As soon as he entered, Jack called out to him. "Hey, Seth, how'd it go?"

Knowing it would be impossible to avoid his best friend, and even though Seth wasn't in the mood for company, he turned in the direction of Jack's voice. He was sitting at the kitchen table, a book in front of him and a coffee cup in his hand.

"How's everything going?"

Jack smiled, his eyes lit with humor. "The ranch didn't fall apart because you were gone for two days."

Seth grunted and headed to the stove for coffee.

"I hired a new man. Boy, really."

Seth poured his coffee, then took the chair opposite Jack. "Where'd ya find him?"

"Hewitt came over to talk about Comet covering that mare of his. Brought along JP and introduced us. Hewitt just doesn't need him right now, mainly because harvest is over. Word was out we needed a new hand. Hewitt said the boy was eager to work, pulls his weight, so I figured we ought to hire him."

Seth nodded and took a sip of coffee.

"So, how was my sister?"

Seth choked, dropping the cup down on the table with a thump. Liquid spilled over the edge, but he ignored it as his eyes started to water and he continued to cough.

When he made eye contact with his friend, he noticed Jack had cocked his head to the side and was studying him. Seth cleared his throat.

"Your sister is doing just fine. Better than fine. The whole idea of her accepting Portman's proposal was horseshit."

"Really?" For some reason, Jack didn't sound so surprised.

Seth paused for a moment before answering, trying to figure out just what the hell was up. "Yes. We ran into him in San Antonio. Seems she already told him no."

Jack smiled. "I'll be damned. Ain't it just like her to pull something like that? The woman has always been headstrong. She's gotten worse since Sid died."

"I didn't think she had much choice in the matter. If she wanted to keep that ranch going, she had to take a lot."

"Pa wanted to take it over. He would have done it too if you hadn't talked him out of it."

Anger swift and brilliant roared to life within Seth. "Your father had no right to that ranch. He wasn't the one who paid for it with his body."

The look of amusement faded from Jack's face. "Just what the hell do you mean by that?"

Mentally, Seth kicked himself in the ass, then sighed, knowing Jack wouldn't let the comment go. "Do you really think your sister wanted to marry an old man, one who couldn't stay faithful for a month after their marriage? Jesus, Jack, get your head out of your ass."

"She wouldn't have done it if she didn't want to."

Seth recognized the stubborn set of Jack's jaw. He'd seen it more than once during their friendship and it was the exact same look Jamie gave him when they argued.

"Wake up. Your father owed Sid money."

All expression drained from Jack's face. "What the hell do you mean?"

Seth hated to do it, but it was about time Jack faced the facts and grew up. He'd been sheltered long enough.

"Your father lost a lot of money to him in a card game. Not to mention the amount of money he'd borrowed from him. Your father was already in debt up to his eyeballs, and the one thing he could use to get out of it was your sister. Did you really think she married Sid because she loved him?"

"That isn't the truth."

Seth knew from his friend's tone he was coming to the realization that it was. "Your father might have been a good father to you, but he wasn't to Jamie. She's not dumb. She understood she was being bought thanks to your father's debts, but she vowed to make the most of it."

"She seemed like she wanted to."

"You were too young at the time to know better."

Now he frowned. "Why the hell didn't she say anything if that's true?"

"You were twelve, why would she tell you? And knowing your father, he didn't tell her to begin with. They probably let her believe it was a legitimate courtship." For a while.

"Why did she tell you?" The accusation in his friend's tone didn't sit well with Seth but he let it slide. His best friend was a smart man, knew the ins and outs of the horse business, but when it came to women in general, he didn't know a damned thing. He was especially dense when it came to his sister.

"She didn't tell me. People talk." One in particular had been Jerry Olbermeister, a hand at the Circle M Ranch. Seth had busted his nose and split the jackass' lip to let him know he didn't appreciate talk about Jamie. "They'll say things in front of me that they may not say in front of her brother."

"I can't believe she didn't say anything." Jack shook his head. "There was a time when we shared everything."

"No woman wants to admit to her brother that her marriage isn't working."

Jack slumped back in his chair. His brow furrowed and his mouth turned down in a mean frown. "You must think I'm stupid for not noticing." Jack sighed, tilted his head back and closed his eyes. "Hell, I knew it was bad. The bastard was at the whorehouse more than we were. Dying there was just icing on the cake, I suppose."

"There wasn't anything you could do. Once the deed was done, there was no undoing it. Besides, I have a feeling Jamie would've been appalled if you tried to help. Her pride wouldn't have allowed it."

"You understand her better than anyone." When Seth didn't respond, Jack raised his head and his gaze zeroed in on Seth. The sharp look his friend gave him should've warned him. "And I might be an idiot about things of that nature, but I'm not completely blind. It's one of the reasons I sent you with her to San Antonio."

Heat crept up Seth's neck and he fought the urge to tug at his collar. "What do you mean?" His attempt to sound nonchalant failed miserably.

"I figured since you've been in love with her for years, this would give you the opening you needed."

For a second, he couldn't speak. His brain seemed to have frozen over. He'd been so careful all these years, never revealing the depth of his feelings. He opened his mouth but Jack stopped him with a laugh.

"Don't even try to lie to me. You never could lie worth a damn."

"Really?" Oh great. Now he sounded like an outraged virgin whose honor had been besmirched.

Jack let loose with a belly laugh. "I think that's the reason you couldn't get into politics. Everyone in your family is good at telling those little white lies. Now, you can bluff with the best of them, but having to say a lie, you turn all red like a little girl caught stealing candy from the store."

Seth opened his mouth again but no sound came out. The knowing look on his friend's face had Seth snapping his mouth shut.

"I thought so. Did you think I hadn't noticed that when you have a choice, the whores you buy resemble Jamie?"

"They do not."

Jack's snort was not only loud, but annoying. "Hmm, so the whore you got in Austin last time we were there didn't have long black hair and light brown eyes? Then there was the one last time we were in Hell's Acre in Fort Worth. That one not only looked like her, but had the same imperious *I am the queen of the manor* voice my sister has."

Christ Almighty. Is that what he had been doing all along? As Seth tried to remember the women he'd paid for over the years, nothing really came to mind but their long black hair...

Seth's face grew hotter by the second as he shifted his attention away from Jack's shrewd study. It wasn't that he'd knowingly chosen them, and even though he could admit it to himself now, he didn't want to discuss it with her brother. Granted, it'd be impossible to go back to pretending now that he'd experienced the real thing.

"I don't want to discuss—"

"Don't tell me you didn't succeed. I mean, you had a room, no pesky relatives in the way."

Seth looked at his friend, trying to decide if he should be amused or horrified. "How can you talk about your sister that way?"

"I'm the only family she has left, and while I didn't know my father paid for his debts with her marriage, I did know she wasn't happy. She needs someone and that someone is you." Jack leaned forward, placing his forearms on the table. "So, tell me, do I need to get the shotgun?"

A hint of humor colored his tone but the underlying threat was still there and real. Seth truly didn't want to admit what happened to Jack but he didn't see a way out of it.

"She refused."

"What?"

Seth cleared his throat. "I asked. She refused."

"Just what the hell did you do wrong?"

Tired, irritated and feeling more than a little harassed, Seth clenched his teeth together. "I didn't do anything wrong. Leave it up to your pigheaded sister. She can never do a damn thing like any other woman." He shot up out of his chair and started pacing. "Truth is, I rushed it this morning when I proposed. I planned on waiting awhile, but she started talking about it was a one-time thing, and I just lost it. She is more stubborn than a mule, seriously. Just what the hell did you and your father do to her to make her that way?"

"She isn't always that way. Just with me and you. Well, and about the ranch."

Seth didn't want to listen to any kind of rational comments. "She tells me that I don't know what I'm doing. That I'm too *young* to know. Christ, I'm older than she was when she married. And, get this. She says she's trying to save me from making a mistake because of my good honor."

"Seth." Jack's shout finally stopped Seth's tirade. "Are you even listening to what you are saying?"

"Hell, no. Your sister has me wound up tighter than a sixty-year-old spinster."

"Seth." Jack's calm, steady voice caught his attention. "There are only three things Jamie has ever truly been stubborn about. The ranch, me and you."

"Yeah, and she mentioned that too. How she didn't need a man to help her who would come in and tell her what to do. Did I say I wanted to tell her what to do? Lord knows I have enough to keep me busy around here—"

"Will you shut up? Lord, you are as bad as Jamie when she gets on a roll." With a huff, Jack sat back in his chair. "Tell me how you proposed."

"I...ah...well this morning."

Jack crossed his arms over his chest. "I already know what went on. Not in detail, thank God, but I know you. Tell me."

"I did it this morning. In bed."

"Seth, what did you say?"

"I panicked, okay?" He shoved his hand through his hair as the unfamiliar nervous energy gripped him, and he resumed pacing again. "She started going on about one night. So I told her that her we had to get married to save her reputation. She said no, but she did offer the benefit of an affair."

Silence greeted his confession, lying heavily in the air between them. Seth stopped once more and glanced over at Jack.

He pursed his lips, then asked, "You told her you loved her, right?"

"Yes. No... Wait." He thought back to his proposal, of the blank look that passed over her features. "Shit, no, I didn't."

Jack was pursing his lips again. "Let me get this straight."

"Jack—"

Jack held up his hand. "No, give me a moment to take this in. I've known you for over ten years now. I've watched you talk your way out of just about anything. You started early when all you were trying to do was get us free sweets from the mercantile. Then, you moved onto girls for a kiss or two. Lord knows you're a favorite at Miss Bessie's—"

"Now, just wait a minute—"

But Jack kept on talking like Seth hadn't said a word. "But this woman, the one I know you love, have loved since you met her ten years ago even though she was already taken, is in your bed, and you tell her you have to get married because of her reputation."

"This isn't funny."

"No, son, it isn't funny. What you did was get her back up. I know my sister, and one thing she could care less about is her reputation, unless it would hurt the ranch. Granted, she'd be mortified if someone questioned her word as a rancher. She got a lot of flack from some of the women around here when she refused to relinquish it to my father. So you know that isn't important to her. I'm sure by now she's dug in her heels and it's going to take some fancy footwork to get her to change her mind."

"Tell me something I don't know." Seth dropped down in the chair, his shoulders slumped. "It'll take me forever to get her back in that particular position again."

"Please, I said I didn't want to know about that."

"I'm being serious here."

"All right, settle down. You don't have to wait. That was always your problem. You sit around, thinking a problem to death."

"Yeah, like the last time we were in San Antonio. Remember me saying, 'Hey, Jack, let's not start a fight with that big mean son of a bitch just because his whore stole my money. We'll end up in jail or laid up in bed.' Remember that? Well, your sister did, and she reminded me on the trip. Twice."

Jack waved that away. "Are you going to accept my help or keep making smart aleck comments?"

"I'll take your help."

"In my mind, the worst thing you can do is wait. She's not immune to you and if you hadn't messed up the proposal, you might be here with her to tell me of your upcoming wedding."

"What do you mean?"

"We have JP, the new hand. I can handle things."

"What?"

"Go with my plan. If you're in her face every day, there's no way she can keep ignoring you. I figure one way or another, you'll get her to admit she loves you."

When he didn't respond, Jack cocked his head to one side. "You do know she loves you, don't you? Hell, she wouldn't fight with you the way she does if she didn't love ya, and she definitely wouldn't have given herself to you."

Seth's brain refused to function. But slowly, everything Jack was saying slid into place, like a bright light flickering on. "She loves me."

"Of course she does."

Hope sluiced through him, breaking some of the fear that had held him by the balls. "You sure?" He looked at his best friend, who was smiling at him.

"Now, what are you going to do about it?"

Chapter Eight

Jamie slowly made her way downstairs just before dawn the next morning. She'd given up on sleep a couple of hours earlier, but couldn't face the day until now. Scenes from the last two days played through her mind, teasing her with the memories. Until the day she died she would never forget how it felt to have Seth's hands on her skin. She could still remember the warmth of his body next to hers, and how hard it had been to turn down his offer of marriage.

She stopped her descent and closed her eyes. It would have been weak to accept it. Marriage based on lust would prove disastrous. Passion didn't last. It would fade in time. Before long, Seth would wander to another woman. That was something she couldn't accept. With Sid, she'd ignored it because she'd rather he went to a whore than bother her. But with Seth...

She opened her eyes and started walking down the stairs again. On top of everything else, the ranch had lost some more cattle and one of the line cabins had been set on fire. Hank didn't understand it, especially since they seemed to be the only ranch with missing cattle. They'd had a few problems in the past, but nothing that went on for several weeks. When they'd had rustling, so had everyone else in the area. Hank was positive they'd been targeted. Jamie thought it a ridiculous notion, mainly because she had no enemies, and most of the ranchers in the area had voiced true concern. All of that was enough to cause her to lose sleep. Pile on the dilemma of Seth Conner, and she ended up with bags under her eyes and a pounding head.

She wished he had taken her up on her offer. Granted, it wasn't proper and there was always a chance they'd be discovered. She had more freedom as a widow, but she didn't want to think of how people would act if she carried on like that. If Jack found out, he'd demand Seth do the right thing and there was a good chance it would ruin their friendship. No matter how much she wanted to have Seth in her bed, Jamie refused to come between the two men.

When she stepped off the bottom stair, she rubbed her eyes. She'd not had a good sleep since before leaving for San Antonio. It would take a month of Sundays to catch up on her rest. The aroma of coffee reached her and got her moving again. It wouldn't be as good as a day spent sleeping, but it would hit the spot, that was for sure. It was odd that Marlene would be here this early. She usually showed up right about dawn and started cooking. Not that Jamie was thinking of complaining. Truthfully, she'd give her soul for a decent cup of coffee this morning.

When she turned the corner and walked into the kitchen, she stopped cold at the sight before her. Seth sat in one of her chairs, his booted feet resting on her kitchen table. He was sipping coffee, looking again like he owned the place.

He was paying attention to something outside the window and hadn't noticed her yet, so she felt free to study him. The shadows cast by the lamp on the table caressed his face, highlighting his strong jaw and proud, crooked nose. It still stunned her that he had been her lover.

She must have made some kind of sound because he turned his attention toward her.

The moment their gazes met, he smiled. Her body warmed and her pulse raced. It took a monumental amount of control not to lick her lips. His smile deepened the longer they stared at each other, and—damn him—he knew how he was affecting her.

She wasn't ready for this. One night of little sleep and a yearning that wouldn't fade didn't allow her to be prepared. No, she wasn't ready. Not now, and Jamie doubted she ever would be.

"Good morning, Jamie." His voice was like aged whiskey, smooth and wicked and not helpful to her self-control.

The Seduction of Widow McEwan

She needed space. She needed him to go away and not ever come back. But as soon as that thought came into mind, she pushed it away. As much as it hurt to be in the same room as him, it would kill her never to see him again.

Her stomach knotted. She didn't want to deal with this, or the multitude of emotions he was bringing to the surface. To protect herself, she straightened her spine and frowned at him.

"What the hell are you doing here?"

Seth had to admit he'd had his doubts about Jack's advice. More than once last night, and on the ride over this morning, Seth had worried he was going to make a jackass out of himself. Being that he'd already done that in front of her, he didn't want to repeat it. If he were truthful with himself, he didn't know if he could handle her rejection again.

"Are you going to answer me?"

"What am I doing here?" he asked.

She nodded, her irritation easy to see. Her nerves were jumping just below the surface. Seth could sense them and felt a spurt of satisfaction. It was nice to know he wasn't the only one out of his depth. "I decided to take you up on your offer."

Her expression blanked and Seth had to fight a smile.

"My offer?"

"Yeah, I offered marriage—"

"Which I refused."

He kept his expression passive. Seth had a feeling that if Jamie knew what his plan was, she'd become even more stubborn on the subject.

"You're right. And if memory serves…you made an alternative offer."

She lifted her chin slightly. "I did. If I remember correctly, you said you wouldn't lower yourself to play my paramour."

Oh, she didn't like that. He could tell by the barely restrained anger in her tone.

"I've had time to think about it."

She didn't say anything, but raised one eyebrow and crossed her arms over her breasts. Knowing he had to keep her unbalanced, he stood and slowly walked over to her. The superior look in her eyes faded to confusion then to panic. Seth stopped several inches from her and drew in a deep breath. Lord, he'd remember the exquisite scent of her until the day he died. She didn't perfume herself like most women. Her bouquet was natural, something completely unique to Jamie.

"Jack said you were short a hand, and since he just hired a new man, he sent me over to fill in for a couple of days. I figured that would allow us to ease into our…arrangement."

She pursed her lips as if she'd just sucked a lemon. "I'm confused. Yesterday—" She stopped talking when he brushed a lock of hair over her shoulder. Her eyes narrowed and he smiled as innocently as he could. "As I was saying, you refused."

"That I did. But after thinking about what you said, I decided you might be right."

He cupped her face with one hand. Leaning closer, he took pleasure in the catch of breath he heard. Without closing his eyes, he brushed his lips over hers. He meant to keep the kiss light, but the moment she closed her eyes and moaned, he forgot that plan and jumped in.

He pulled her closer, closing his own eyes and falling into the kiss. Nothing had ever been as beautiful and tempting as a kiss from Jamie. As she opened her mouth, he slipped inside, allowing the sweet sassy taste of her to sink into him. He would have taken her right there up against the wall, but the sound of the front door opening stopped him.

Both of them stared at each other for a moment, then he shifted away before Marlene came bursting into the kitchen. She didn't even give them a look or acknowledge that Seth was there.

"Sorry, I'm late. Overslept. I'll get to work on breakfast right away."

As she started to putter around the kitchen, he said, "I'll talk to Hank about getting a bed in the bunkhouse."

She shook her head. "You know I have plenty of room here."

He smiled. "Now, that wouldn't be proper."

With that he nodded to her, then to Marlene, and left feeling decidedly better. He might have made a muck of things, but there was no denying her response to him. That was a damn fine start.

○※

Three weeks later, Jamie stepped out onto the porch and sighed. The heat of the sun was already powerful by midmorning and summer was definitely looking to be a hot one. The idea that she was going after Seth to seduce him in the barn was stupid in this heat but she couldn't refuse. Not him, or the chance to be alone with him.

Almost every night he visited her. Each time was more intense, more threatening to her peace of mind. She was falling further in love with him, but was helpless to resist. No matter how much time they spent loving each other, the tension didn't ease. All they had to do was be in the same room and her skin started to feel itchy, her clothing restricting, and she had to fight the urge to jump him.

He'd turned her into some kind of sex maniac.

She headed across the yard. Hank had sent more hands out to patrol today. They hadn't had any more cows disappear, but he was worried about it. That left her with time alone for Seth, and for once she was going to ignore her duties and take time for her pleasure.

As she approached the barn, an odd voice sounded from one of the outer work sheds. She paused, listening, trying to decide what was making the sound. When it stopped, she stepped in the direction of the barn once more, but she heard it again. Looking at the open barn doors, she sighed and started on the path that led to the shed. Turning the corner, she gasped. One of her cows lay on its side.

Jamie rushed forward, then stopped when she saw the blood. Someone had gutted the cow, its entrails strewn over the ground. She lifted her hand to her mouth and nose, trying to fight off the scent of fresh blood. Knowing the culprit had to be close, she spun around to run back toward the house. A sharp blow to the back of her head had her losing her balance and stumbling forward. Her hands took the brunt of the fall, but her cheek hit the ground hard. She tried to lift her head, but her vision blurred then faded to black.

※

Seth was brushing down a frisky little mare that Hank preferred to ride as he talked to the older man. He was trying his best to keep up his part of the conversation, but his mind was on Jamie. Hell, what was new? It was always on Jamie.

Something simmered within her, deep below the calm exterior she showed everyone. He felt it each night he laid with her. Whenever she gave herself to him, she allowed him to take control and never held back. But during the day…that was a different matter. Playing friend to her, not being able to touch her as should be his right, was driving him out of his ever-loving mind.

He shook his head at his weakness that seemed to be growing by the minute and tried to focus on the conversation.

"So nothing was missing today, but I still think there's someone targeting the ranch."

"Jamie and Jack said something about that. Neither of them seemed very worried over it."

Hank shrugged. "No one else is having problems. Usually something like this, a few cows here and there, we all get hit. Takes longer for us to find what's missing. But with it just being us, it's not like they're doing it for money, if you get my meanin'?"

Seth paused. "You told Jamie all of this?"

Hank nodded. "Told her and she waved it off. She didn't think she had any enemies, and I would agree. Still, it's really strange."

The thought of Portman's face when she turned him down in San Antonio floated through Seth's mind. "Tucker Portman might."

"Portman? What kind of complaint would he have with Jamie?"

"He asked her to marry him." When Hank pokered up, Seth held out his hands. "She turned him down, but he showed up in San Antonio and pressed the point. She wasn't gentle with him."

"I can't believe that bastard tried to get her to marry him."

"I heard she said yes," said Gerald Jefferson, one of the hands, as he led his horse into her stall.

Seth set down the brush and walked around the mare and over to Gerald.

"I was there when she said no. Where did you hear she said yes?"

Gerald shrugged. "I heard Portman bragging last night at the poker game. Some of his hands run a game on Monday nights. He said Mrs. McEwan agreed and they were getting married in a few weeks."

"That's hogwash." Hank offered up that comment.

"I have to agree." Seth's voice was cool, but he felt anything but. Anger bubbled beneath his skin, but he forced it back. He would wait until he got a hold of Portman.

"Has anyone seen Jamie?" Marlene broke into his thoughts with that question.

"No, isn't she in the house?" Seth asked.

"No. When was the last time you saw her?"

"Right after breakfast."

Her brow furrowed. "She never came in for lunch, and I assumed she rode out to check on the patrols."

Worry niggled at the base of his spine. Before he could tell Marlene that Sadie was in her stall and Jamie hadn't taken her out, a shout sounded from outside the barn. Seth dropped his brushes and hurried outside, all of the others right behind him. They ran into Frederick, another of the hands. His face was pale, his eyes filled with terror.

Seth reached him first. "What the hell's wrong?"

He shook his head, as if trying to clear his mind, and closed his eyes. "A heifer, gutted."

Hank was already moving to check on it, and Seth was hard on his heels. The moment they broke free of the yard, they both smelled it. The stench was unmistakable. The closer they got to the shed, the stronger it became.

"Holy Mother of God," Hank's horrified whisper reached him right before Seth saw the cow. The blood had soaked the ground and was now dried. The stench was so strong, Seth had to swallow to keep from gagging. How the hell had everyone missed this?

His next thought was simple.

Jamie.

Cold, sick dread settled in his belly as he turned and ran back to the barn. His only thought was finding her, making sure she was all right.

"Everyone spread out and look for Jamie. She's missing."

They turned to do his bidding, but Gerald approached him. "Mr. Conner. I hate to say this but...well, I saw Mr. Portman riding over by the ridge today. He had something big laying across his lap. I didn't think anything about it, but it was odd."

"Son of a bitch." Nerves already stretched to the limit pulled tighter. He looked at Gerald and Hank. "Take a few men and have a look around the grounds, just in case."

He waited for their nods, then, without another word, strode into the barn. The sound of a horse riding hell bent for leather into the yard gave him hope, but it was dashed when he saw Jack. His best friend jumped off the horse before it came to a complete stop.

"I thought you said Jamie turned down Portman."

Not wanting to waste time, Seth started to saddle Comet. "She did. I saw it with my own eyes."

"Apparently he called on the preacher in Smythville. Portman's booked the church for next Saturday."

Seth looked at Jack, trying his best to fight the panic crawling through him. "I think he has Jamie."

Chapter Nine

Jamie winced as she touched the back of her head where her hair was matted with dried blood. Sharp, nauseating pain spiked through her and her senses swam. The blow Portman had given her still had her mind mixed up.

"I hope you feel okay. Being out in the sun like that isn't good for a woman. Too delicate."

When Jamie turned in the direction of her abductor's voice, an explosion of stars had her closing her eyes. She swallowed the bile rising in her throat with sheer will.

Opening her eyes, she licked her lips and forced herself to look at Portman. The ass had dressed in formal wear for dinner. She was still in her bloodied and dirty clothes, but he acted as if she were dressed for the ball. It wasn't a formal dinner party, but there were candles lit, and the best china graced the table. She wished he had held to true fashion and seated her at the opposite end of the long dining table.

She wasn't sure how many hours it had been since he'd hit her, but light still filtered into the room, telling her the sun hadn't set. He studied her with his bulging eyes, reminding her of a dog that had gone crazy with rabies. He wasn't a likable man, but she'd had no idea just how insane he was. Understanding that, she realized there was a good chance she'd never see Seth again. A man as insane as Portman wasn't going to let her go. Just the idea of what he did to that cow was enough to make her retch. She accepted that she might not get away. The only thing she regretted was failing to tell Seth she loved him.

"Jameson!"

She blinked when Portman yelled and brought her back to his comment about her delicacy.

"It wasn't the sun."

He chuckled, picked up a decanter of wine and poured it into her glass. "I know women think they can handle things men can, but you just don't have the stamina." After filling her glass to the very top, he set the decanter down and looked at her. "I thought we might discuss our wedding."

"We aren't marrying. I told you no."

Without warning, his hand lashed out, striking her across the face. The force of the slap toppled her chair. Her head hit the floor, causing another jolt of pain to shoot through her. Before she could gather her wits, Portman reached down and grabbed her by the arm. With a jerk, he pulled her eye level with him. Her head was throbbing and her face smarting from the slap he had given her.

"I told Sid you were too smart mouthed. He'd just laugh at me, told me I was jealous. I was right, too. Look at you thinking you know how to run a ranch." With each word Portman uttered, the scent of onions drifted over her. Again her stomach roiled and her head spun. "It's about time a man teaches you how to behave like a proper lady."

With a shove, he sent her flying. She slammed against the wall and slid to the ground. She was sure every bone in her body was bruised. Jamie knew she should get up and run, do anything to get away from the man. But she couldn't get her mind to work, and her vision was blurred.

"Women these days don't understand that they have to obey. Sid could have cared less about you, which made him an ass."

He squatted in front of her and leaned down in her face. His rancid breath wafted toward her and it was all she could do to keep herself from throwing up. He brushed the back of his fingers over her cheek.

"If you're denying me because of Conner, think twice."

The pain he'd caused faded as alarm flashed through her. He must have recognized it because he smiled.

"I see you understand." He rose and walked back to the table and poured himself a shot of whiskey. "I was surprised to say the least that you were carrying on with a man, let alone someone so much younger. Can you imagine how that would look to others? How it looked to me?"

He glanced at her out of the corner of his eye. "My first wife was a slut. Thought she could marry me and keep a man on the side." The grin he offered her held no warmth, only cold, cruel satisfaction. "She came to regret that decision.

"Her lover, he regretted it even more. I can tell you he didn't go quietly. I'm sure since you've been around a ranch, you're familiar with castration." He paused and licked his lips. "You've never heard true agony until you listen to a man cry as he pleads to be killed. Is that something you want for Conner? I can't imagine him begging me, but it would be a joy to take the bastard down a few pegs, especially with you as an audience."

Jamie couldn't wrap her mind around the horrific picture he painted. It wasn't the idea of his actions, but the pleasure he took in the act. She could see the memory was fond just by the delight shining in his eyes.

As Portman approached her, he began unbuckling his belt, which sent a fresh wave of panic through her. She could survive a beating, but the thought of the man touching her, forcing her, had her gagging. She tried to scramble away, and he laughed.

He pulled the belt free of its loops, but instead of moving on to his pants, he folded the belt in half and swung it in her direction. The lash of it bit into the skin of her arm. Tears sprung from her eyes.

As he pulled back to give her another lash, the door to the dining room crashed open.

Seth filled the doorway. Angry, solemn and holding a pistol in his hand, he stepped into the room.

"What the hell are you doing here?" Portman yelled.

"I've come for Jamie."

Portman dropped the belt and moved to the table. Fresh fear slammed through her when she saw the gun lying next to his plate. "Why? She's mine."

"The hell she is." Seth cocked his gun. "I'd think twice about that, Portman."

Portman paused, but then quickly reached for the pistol. Seth didn't hesitate. The moment Portman had the gun in hand, Seth fired. The bullet hit Portman in the chest. He dropped his own gun as blood blossomed over his white linen shirt. He stumbled back, falling to the floor.

Jack drew closer to keep his own gun on him as Seth made his way over to her. He kneeled beside her.

"Oh, baby." It wasn't until he said those words that she noticed how cold she was. He gathered her in his arms, holding her close. Every part of her body ached, but she didn't care. Being held in Seth's arms, knowing everything was all right, made the pain of his embrace worthwhile. His body heat wrapped around her, but the reassurance he offered was lost among the chills vibrating through her. Memories of Portman's threats colored her mind. She knew in that instant that losing Seth would have cost her sanity, her very will to live. That's something she couldn't—wouldn't—accept. As her teeth started to chatter, she broke down.

She didn't even fight the sob that escaped. Needing his warmth and comfort, she slipped her arms up and clung to Seth. He tightened his arms around her, but it didn't seem to be enough. She tried to burrow herself into his chest. The emotions she'd held at bay seemed to gush out of her. All the fear, the horror of what she'd been through bubbled up. The physical pain didn't compare to the anguish coursing through her veins, piercing her heart.

Seth cussed under his breath. Even in her state of mind, she heard the tremble in his voice when he spoke. "I should have beaten him before I shot him."

"You'll have to be satisfied with the shot," Jack said, his voice raw with anguish and anger. "Right through the heart, he's gone."

Jamie tried to look, wanting to see if the bastard really was dead. But Seth stood and gathered her back into his arms. Her will to see Portman faded as she gave into the need to be anywhere but in that room. "I want to go home."

Seth stepped out of the dining room and walked through the parlor and out onto the porch. "I know, baby. So do I."

His lips brushed her temple. The gesture comforted her. Knowing she was safe, that nothing could hurt her now, she allowed herself to drift away from the pain and into oblivion.

The Seduction of Widow McEwan

○℞

Seth climbed the steps to Jamie's room with determination. It had been a long few weeks while Jamie made her recovery. When the swelling and bruising had been in full force, she'd been confined to bed. Marlene had tried to get him to leave, but for the first two days, he'd refused, sleeping in the chair beside her as she fought through the terror in her dreams. When Jamie became more coherent, she'd tried to get him to leave, but again, he refused.

It was apparent to anyone with half a brain there was something between them, and except for Jamie, everyone else had left him alone. Jamie, though, was a different story. After ranting and raving at him to leave, she closed in on herself, barely speaking to anyone, even Jack. She had horrible memories. More than once he had rushed to her room after hearing her screams of fear. And even though she clung to him while she sobbed, she said little to him about it. She wouldn't discuss anything. Not Portman, not her abduction, not even their relationship.

It was as if the Jamie he loved was wasting away to nothing and he was damn tired of it.

He opened the door without knocking. It was rude, but he didn't care. Jamie was standing by the window, dressed in her wrapper. Most of the bruising was gone. The split in her lip had healed as had the gash in the back of her head. Still, the memory of seeing her laying there battered by that bastard made Seth want to go kill Portman all over again.

"What are you doing here?" Her voice held no emotion. She didn't look at him when she asked the question, just kept staring out the window as if he didn't matter.

He fought the usual panic that came when he heard her speak. Instead of calming his fears, it fed them. The lack of feeling in her tone scared the hell out of him.

"I've come to talk to you."

She didn't say anything.

Irritated, he calmed himself with a deep breath and plowed ahead. "Don't you want to know what I want to talk to you about?"

She shrugged. That action was starting to get on his nerves. Every time someone tried to get her to talk, to ask her if she needed anything, she just lifted her shoulders. She wouldn't even choose what to eat or wear.

"I want to talk to you about us."

"There's no us." Her voice was devoid of any emotion, so flat, so distant that it scared the hell out of him.

He walked over to her, stepping behind her. The panic was now growing into full-blown terror. It took every amount of control he had not to grab her and shake her, then beg her to take him back. "I think you're wrong, Jamie."

She shivered, the first reaction she'd had to him in weeks. A tiny spark of hope warmed his heart, but he had to be careful. Seth knew she wasn't willing to accept him, but it was about time she changed her mind.

"I don't want to discuss it."

She turned away from the window and stepped around him.

Irritated with her dismissal, he seized her arm. "What the hell is going on?"

Looking down at his hand then up at him, she said, "It's nothing. The sooner you learn that, the better." She pulled away and walked to her bed. "If that's all, I would prefer to go to bed now."

He couldn't lose her, refused to lose her. Three weeks of worry, fear and guilt exploded. With purpose, he strode over to stand behind her. He took a deep breath and admitted the truth that had been scaring him almost to death. "I can't lose you."

"You never had me."

That one comment had his anger surging, mixing with the shock of her actions. "Yes, I did. I had you more than once, but that isn't exactly what I'm talking about." When she still said nothing, he grabbed her arm again and spun her around to face him. "Do you know how long I waited? How many years I tried to ignore the feelings I have for you?"

The Seduction of Widow McEwan

She still didn't say anything, just stared through him as if he weren't even there. He thought loving her from afar, never having her, had been hell. That was nothing compared to the fear slicing through his gut...his heart.

"I've loved you for years. Good Lord it was embarrassing to be that infatuated with a married woman. I thought I was just in lust, but when it didn't fade, when this powerful feeling I had for you grew, I knew I loved you."

"It doesn't matter because I never loved you."

The words pierced his heart. He could've handled her rage, even her pain. If she had done that, if she had showed him some temper or cried like the night Portman had taken her, he'd know she was fighting her feelings. But the indifference she showed, he realized she had never loved him. He'd been nothing but a diversion, a way to pass the time.

He swallowed the hurt and the anger and met her gaze. "And just like that, you decide you want me gone. You want to live your life in this lonely, empty house, then die alone. Never knowing love, never having children."

She nodded and turned away. If he hadn't seen the sheen of tears glittering in her eyes, he would've believed her.

"To hell with that." He pulled her around to face him and crushed his mouth down on hers. At first, she did nothing, just stood there like a doll. The pain that had cut through his heart tore at his soul, ripping his hope to shreds. He was ready to move away, admit defeat. No man should put himself through something like this, not even for love. But then Jamie shuddered and opened her mouth. He slipped his hands around her waist. It wasn't until he heard her sob that he realized she was still crying.

"Oh, baby, I'm sorry." He tilted her head back and looked down into her eyes. "I didn't want to bring back any bad memories."

She shook her head, and another sob escaped. "No. There was..." She closed her eyes. "There was nothing like that. He didn't touch me that way."

Relief filled him. Jamie had refused to talk about what had happened, even with Marlene. It wouldn't have changed the way he thought about her, but he didn't want to even to contemplate her suffering that. He pulled her close.

"I was worried."

"It wasn't that. It was...you could have been hurt. Portman knew about us and planned to kill you. He was completely crazy."

He rubbed his chin over the top of her head. "I wouldn't have let him kill me. Not after everything we shared."

"How do you know that?"

"I just do."

She tried to pull free of him, but he wouldn't allow it. After a few moments of struggling, she stopped and looked up at him with fire lighting her eyes.

"You don't. You don't have any idea just how evil that man was. He took joy in pain, in making others suffer."

"And you couldn't allow me to be hurt." He smiled at her, joy filling him. "I knew you loved me."

Jamie placed her hands on his chest and shoved. Caught off guard, he stumbled back, releasing her.

"I don't love you. I don't want that."

Her appalled whisper shouldn't have made him so happy but it did. He might have to fight her, but he knew without a doubt she loved him now.

"Yes, you do." Seth couldn't keep the satisfaction from coloring his voice.

"Do you think I want to love, to risk that. If something were to happen to you..."

His breath tangled in his throat as he waited for her to continue. When she didn't, he stepped closer. "What?"

"Nothing."

"No, it's not nothing." She looked away from him, but he grabbed her by the arm and forced her to meet his gaze. "What?"

"If Portman would've gotten a hold of you, he would have made you suffer. I couldn't take that."

"Because you love me."

"Stop saying that." She shot him a glare before trying to turn away again. He tightened his hold.

"I don't want to love you. When you love, you get hurt. I don't want to take that chance." Her shoulders slumped and she bowed her head, but he didn't let it discourage him. Instead, he tugged her back into his arms.

"That's what happens, honey. You fall in love, you risk your heart." He settled his cheek on top of her head and drew in the clean, unique scent of her. "I know what you're talking about. Riding to Portman's, I aged a thousand years thinking about what you might be going through. Even if we hadn't gotten there in time, if we hadn't saved you from the bastard, I wouldn't have changed a thing about our time together. No matter what the cost to my sanity—to my soul—I'd do it all the same."

She drew back but didn't move out of his arms. That fact pleased him to no end.

"Why?"

He raised one hand to gently wipe away the tears dampening her cheeks. "I'd risk everything just to have what we had, even if for just one moment in time."

"Oh, Seth." Another wave of tears flooded her eyes and she pulled her bottom lip between her teeth. She swallowed and took a deep breath as they stared at each other. "What did you mean about loving me all those years?"

"Well, I..." He took a deep breath and met her gaze head on. "I've loved you since the moment I saw you."

"You were only sixteen. And I was married to Sid."

He nodded. "Okay, so it was lust to begin with, but it didn't fade. I thought you would never take me seriously, so I kept my distance. When Jack told me about you and Portman, I figured I couldn't wait."

She stepped away from him, out of his arms. "Let me get this straight. You decided to seduce me to try and force me into marriage."

He couldn't read her expression. "No. What I had planned was seducing you so that you would marry me."

Cocking her head, she said, "That sounds like the same thing."

"What I meant was that I would convince you because you couldn't..."

"What? That I would be so lustful for your body, you would lure me into marriage?"

He frowned. "No, not really." He sighed. "Okay, sort of."

"And during that whole thing of telling me it was for the best that we get married to save my reputation you never once told me you loved me."

"I messed up. I admit it. It wasn't like you said anything other than no. Oh, and you would prefer an affair with me than marriage. And another thing—"

"Seth."

The amusement in her voice caught his attention. He stopped his rant and looked at her. Warmth and love filled her expression. It struck him dumb. She smiled, the joy in it capturing his heart.

"I love you."

The moment she said it, a whoosh of air he didn't know he'd been holding escaped. He'd hoped, dreamed that she loved him, but he'd been so worried he'd lost her. The need to pull her into his arms, to hold her close to him, overwhelmed him. He stepped forward, anticipation humming in his blood. Something of what he felt must have showed in his expression because she held up her hand.

"No. Let me speak." She licked her lips and drew in a shaky breath. "After the way I've been acting the last few weeks, I really don't deserve you, but I do want you. I never dreamed I'd have a man in my life again. Sid, well, that was a big mistake. I didn't trust myself, didn't believe in myself. You changed that."

He knew he should hold onto his anger for making him wait for so long, for almost ruining everything they had. The woman had him wrapped around her finger, and she knew it.

"I love you, Jamie."

She opened her arms, and he went to her. He kissed her slow, sweet, staring into her eyes. Passion and love melded together, heating his body and warming his soul.

By the time he pulled back from the kiss, they were both breathing heavily.

"I do insist on marriage."

She smiled again. "Only if you promise to always love me."

"That, I can promise without a doubt."

With a laugh, he tumbled them both back onto the bed and went about proving his promise true.

About the Author

Born to an Air Force family at an Army hospital Melissa has always been a little bit screwy. She was further warped by her years of watching Monty Python and her strange family. Her love of romance novels developed after accidentally picking up a Linda Howard book. After becoming hooked, she read close to 300 novels in one year, deciding that romance was her true calling instead of the literary short stories and suspense she had been writing. After many attempts, she realized that romantic comedy, or at least romance with a comic edge was where she was destined to be. Influences in her writing come from Nora Roberts, Jenny Crusie, Susan Andersen, Amanda Quick, Jayne Anne Krentz, Julia Quinn, Christina Dodd, and Lori Foster. Since her first release in 2004, Melissa has had close to 20 short stories, novellas and novels released with six different publishers in a variety of genres and time periods.

She has always believed that romance and humor go hand in hand. Love can conquer all and as Mark Twain said, "Against the assault of laughter, nothing can stand." Combining the two, she hopes she gives her readers a thrilling love story, filled with chuckles along the way, and a happily ever after finish.

She can be reached at her website, www.melissaschroeder.net, her myspace page, www.myspace.com/melissaschroeder, and you can keep up with her activities at her yahoo groups: groups.yahoo.com/group/melissaschroederchat, groups.yahoo.com/group/melissaschroedernews.

Look for these titles by
Melissa Schroeder

Now Available:

Grace under Pressure

The Harmless Series
A Little Harmless Sex
A Little Harmless Pleasure

Once Upon an Accident Series
The Accidental Countess
Lessons in Seduction

Coming Soon:

The Harmless Series
A Little Harmless Addiction

The Last Detail

GREAT CHEAP FUN

Discover eBooks!

THE FASTEST WAY TO GET THE HOTTEST NAMES

Get your favorite authors on your favorite reader, long before they're out in print! Ebooks from Samhain go wherever you go, and work with whatever you carry—Palm, PDF, Mobi, and more.

Samhain Publishing Ltd

WWW.SAMHAINPUBLISHING.COM